THE GIRL AND THE LAST SLEEPOVER

A.J. RIVERS

The Girl and the Last Sleepover
Copyright © 2022 by A.J. Rivers

PROLOGUE

WINTER WAS LETTING GO.

It wasn't quite spring yet, but it was coming. The edge of it was there, just under the lingering cold and chilling dampness. In the woods, tiny pinpricks of fragile green were showing up on long, bare tree branches like someone had gathered a palmful of finely ground sea glass and blown it into the wind.

Somehow the changing of the seasons seemed to soften the silence. Those pale hints of green and the beginning of give underfoot, where the final freeze of the season had thawed, faded the edges of the emptiness among the trees. If it had been just weeks before, perhaps even days, the ice still in the air would have made the silence sharp and harsh.

The cold heightened anticipation. Waiting for the next sound became painful. A breath could create a rush of fear, a pounding heart, a shiver along the back of the neck.

The promise of spring, even tenuous, offered soothing.

Without it, the sound of the footsteps might have been more startling. It might have been easier to know how many heavy feet were crushing down the fallen leaves and snapping tiny branches that had come down under the weight of winter.

But the hope and reassurance that came with the thread of warmth also gave anonymity. The sound of footsteps could be animals emerging after the long winter. Moving leaves and pushed aside branches could be the wind, droplets of water released from the trees and hitting the ground.

The softening helped keep secrets.

But somebody knew.

"Is this far enough?"

"Farther."

"I can't keep going much longer. You need to pick a place."

"Ask him."

There was no response. The man ahead of them kept walking. One set of footsteps followed by two more. Another behind.

He didn't expect a response. The man ahead didn't want to be there. He didn't want to be doing this. Not that this was something any of them truly wanted to do. It was a necessity. But only he was there by force.

At least, he was the only one who knew.

They weren't following a path. They'd left it shortly after coming into the woods. But their steps had purpose and direction. The man ahead knew where they were going.

Finally, they stopped. He looked around, orienting himself even without the plan of ever coming back here. Behind him, leaves shifted. Something was dropped onto the warming ground.

"Is this it?" he asked.

The man ahead nodded. He hadn't spoken a word since they'd walked into the trees. The words were there. They just hadn't been said. It left the question hanging over them.

If the man opened his mouth, which would come out: ice or new green leaves?

"Let's get this done."

There was the sound of something swiping against the ground, brushing aside leaves, and the smell of the air changed. He turned from it. It wasn't the first time he smelled it and he knew it wouldn't be the last, but that didn't make him want to breathe it in.

As the others worked, he scanned the trees around them. Everything was still. The paths would wake up in a few weeks when people started to venture out of their homes more, craving air they hadn't breathed a thousand times already. When the promise of drops of sunlight sliding over their skin was enough to entice them from the depths where every degree the temperature outside dropped sank them deeper into their homes.

His grandmother used to tell him she could feel the presence of others even when she didn't see them. She knew when someone was coming around the corner of the house from her garden. She could sense a restless grandchild stirring in the tiny guest bedroom where they slept on their visits from the other side of the house. Sometimes when she spoke of feeling others, it settled into his bones that she was talking about people no one else could see. People who weren't alive.

He wondered about them now. He felt what his grandmother had described: the slow feeling of fingertips passing just above his arms. Not touching, just passing heat and energy to the tips of the hairs and the surface of his skin. It was breath on the back of his neck that came from nothing, words whispered in his ear that he couldn't hear but hung in the air and brushed the side of his face when he turned his head to look.

It was what he felt as he stood there among the trees. It made him push the others faster. He wanted to get away from there.

The feeling followed him as they left. It faded the further they got, like he was leaving it behind. Maybe it would still be there, waiting for him. He never intended to find out.

Getting back into the car at the far edge of the woods was a relief. It wasn't fear that held tight to his stomach. Not guilt or regret. But there was something there. One day he would know. It wasn't until the door was closed beside him and the roar of the engine filled the silence that he realized the feeling wasn't really gone.

It was tucked into the back of his mind, crouching as if in anticipation. He wanted to claw at his skin, brush away the fingers. Instead, he pressed his foot to the ground to force the pavement beneath the tires behind the car.

They drove along the gradually darkening road. Evening was coming. It had followed them into the woods; he hadn't realized how long they'd been there. It was the only thing he wanted to bring home with him. The rest would stay behind. Each second that separated him from the trees and the trails and the leaf-strewn ground brought them closer to being no more than memories. Then he would wait for it to dissolve away, to seep back into his mind and become a collection of moments no longer linked together, seeds to grow into stories and lies.

As the car came around a curve in the road, a flash of something to the side caught the vision at the corner of his eye. He turned a sharp look toward the trees beside the car and saw it again. A light flickering in small doses, dim now in the lingering sunlight. It would take only a few minutes for it to glow bright and strong, cutting through the darkness that would settle in.

It was leading someone. He knew the feeling now. It wasn't someone who couldn't be seen. It was someone he hadn't seen. But they were there. The trees weren't empty. The paths weren't abandoned. Someone had been there with them.

The curve of the narrow road kept the car from traveling as fast as he wanted it to. That and the light moved along at nearly the same pace.

"What is that?" the passenger beside him asked.

"A light," he told him. "Someone in the woods."

"Did they see?"

"I don't know."

The light disappeared behind a thicker stand of trees where the curve of the road didn't correspond to the direction of the path. But as the car came out of the turn and onto the straighter path, he saw it again. It was at the mouth of the trail, where it had cut through the trees and brought it out to the road faster than the car could get there.

It wasn't just a light now. There was a figure. Shadowy and indistinct at first. It moved in a smooth, inhuman way, and just before he could see it clearly, he realized what he was seeing. A man riding a bicycle. The figure came out at the trailhead as his foot pressed harder on the gas. The white signs at the side of the road didn't stop him.

They tried. They warned him. It wasn't enough.

A horrible accident. The car went out of control. Too much speed. Too little light. A curve taken too sharply.

His heart raced in his chest as the car sped up. The bicyclist was coming out of the woods, ready to cross the street. There was an instant of eye contact through the windshield before the sound of metal crushing metal. The windshield cracked, splintering into a spider web but not shattering.

Sugar glass. No shards to slice or puncture. The bicyclist's face came to rest just above his, open eyes watching glass sprinkling down onto his lap, sparkling like Christmas cookies.

He lurched forward. The tires bounced over the bicycle in the path. Screaming tires and twisting metal. The light was gone now. A hard brake and pulling back away from the trail made the face slide away. He was back on the road, gone before he could look at the ground. Driving through the spider web before he noticed another light. Blinking like a firefly in the tangled undergrowth. Nearby, a tiny figure, mouth sweet with the last of a lollipop, fingertips reaching to touch one filled with sugar glass.

Ten years later...

The neon lights outside were like walking through a pinball machine.

Temporary buildings, dressed-up trucks and trailers, and shadowy corners made spots to bounce off of. Lights and jingles and flashes and bright-colored signs all for one goal: collecting points.

Ten points for buying a heart-shaped funnel cake.

Twenty for riding the spinning teacups.

Fifty for the Ferris Wheel.

One hundred for getting to third base behind the Tunnel of Love, an extra fifty for inside.

Game over for riding alone.

Maya had been bouncing around since before the lights first turned on. Now they saturated everything around her with liquid color and dizzying motion.

There was still oil on her fingertips from the deep-fried concoctions that had replaced a decent dinner that night. The slightly queasy feeling in her belly was like freedom. In a few months, she would be eighteen. For now, her mother could still fill her plate with perfectly portioned segments of the food guide pyramid and tell her they were vital to her growth.

Maya had told her more times than she could count that the pyramid wasn't a thing anymore. That wasn't what the schools taught children to help them learn about nutrition and how not to make their dinner out of fried dough, powdered sugar, and melted cheese. That most of your diet shouldn't be bread and cereal. But her mother didn't listen. Build the pyramid every day. Fill the plate with colors.

But for tonight the only colors were the glowing lights and the reflections off glittery eye makeup and gaudy jewelry gifted on teddy bears and around plastic-wrapped roses. Most had been handed out in the halls of the high school, giddy transactions with a strange black-market feel. She'd watched them happen the same way she had every year since the first time she didn't have a little cardboard box sitting on her desk to be stuffed with teacher-mandated cards and sticky lollipops. The classroom parties when everyone hesitated to include red-wrapped chocolates with their little white flags because they didn't want to have even the appearance of offering a classmate a kiss.

The end of those parties and the beginning of the showy exchanges in the hallway were a blunt transition. Maya wasn't the kind to end her day with hands full of chocolates and bears and wilting plastic-wrapped roses. From that first day, she'd watched the holiday ritual like she was looking through bakery glass. She'd never experienced any of the treats. She didn't know what they tasted like or even if she would enjoy them, but she couldn't help but want to dip her fingers into the decadent glazes and fillings and sample them.

At the same time she felt that tug, there was also the knowledge in the back of her mind that nothing beyond that glass was good for her. Too sugary sweet. Too elaborate and rich. But always one-sided. Always the beautiful girls with the shimmering hair and the glistening eyes accepting the tokens from eager puppies in sweatshirts for college football teams and sweaters made expensive by the dozen stitches it took to add in a label.

It made Maya wonder about the other side of the transaction.

She was still wondering about it when she got to the carnival. It wasn't summer. Not that it didn't look like it. The glowing lights and spinning rides, the fried oil smell, and sugar-fueled groping better belonged with the backdrop of summer heat and threatening rainstorms. It felt out of place against the stark tail end of winter and the cold chill that still had a few weeks to hang on before spring came.

And yet, there it was. Every year. A carnival filled with garish hearts and lights in every shade of red and pink. Games with titles clumsily altered to make them seem like they fit for a Valentine's Day celebration. It had been going on for years, the kind of local event that happened in small towns and fed into stories still told by older generations while trickling down to the younger ones. People went because they had always gone. They brought their children because their parents brought them.

But it was really designed for teenagers. The options for Valentine's Day dates were slim; the rural community was scattered and the small main town had barely changed since those older generations were the young ones themselves. To keep the young couples out of basements and steamy cars out on the old logging trails, the town hosted the carnival. While there were still plenty of teenagers who preferred the basements and steamy cars, the carnival was the traditional date for both established couples and fledgling pairings.

It was the scene for first kisses and nervous, sweaty palms. Wandering hands and pushing boundaries. And every year at least one screaming match that ended up the dramatic highlight of the night. The question was always if that couple would find their way back together before spring break brought the next round of town-sanctioned entertainment.

None of that was why Maya was there. If she really let herself think too much about it, she realized she didn't know why she was there. She hadn't been to the carnival since she was a little child. Her father had brought her. The thought still made her throat feel tight. It hurt to swallow and hurt even more not to.

The last time she'd come, her father had won her a pink bear holding a velveteen rose in one hand by throwing darts at a wall of balloons. It was still sitting in the corner of her room, the petals of the flower worn down to dull patches from how often she touched it. Rubbing them between her fingertips comforted her when she was scared or sad. For a long time that was nearly always.

She hadn't been back since. She hadn't been asked. Well, a couple of times, years ago, a neighbor was planning to bring her own children and called Maya's mother to ask if she wanted to go with them. Maya used to watch the neighbor boy out in his yard. He liked to wear brightly colored shorts and stand in the sprinkler during the summer. Not play in it. Just stand there. In the winter he rolled dozens of snowballs and lined them up along the edge of the lawn like an arsenal. She never saw him throw them, but the threat was always there. Somehow, that made them more frightening.

Maya knew he didn't want her to go to the carnival with him. He didn't want to be seen with her. Not Maya. Not *that* girl. But she wanted to go with him. She hoped that he didn't know that. She hoped he didn't know she was dying for him to talk to her. That he wouldn't pretend she hadn't lived next door to him for their entire lives or that he hadn't ever spoken to her.

Of course, he wouldn't say that to his mother. He wouldn't look at her and say he didn't want to have anything to do with her, that he didn't want his friends to see him with her. He would never call Maya *that girl* out loud.

And Maya would never tell her mother the way he looked at her, or that he didn't want to be near her because of who she was. Because of the empty part of their house and her heart. Because of the teddy bear sitting in the corner of the room.

It would make his mother angry. It would make hers cry.

There were things mothers didn't need to know. They didn't understand them.

That might have been why her mother's eyes widened the way they did when Maya told her she'd been invited to go that night. She tried

7

not to show it. She tried to seem casual and dismissive the way mothers did when they wanted their children to see a friend and not a parent, when they wanted their children to open up to them and tell them all the things there was no way they would actually tell them.

Maya told her mother more than most. But there were still things she kept to herself. She was sure her mother hoped it was one of those things that was actually behind why Maya suddenly wanted to spend her Valentine's Day going to the carnival.

"Genevieve McGuire?"

Her mother asked it in the same way the voice in the back of Maya's mind had when the girl invited her.

"It's not just me. She invited Melanie, too."

"I didn't know the three of you were friends."

Neither did Maya.

"We're in Biology together. We were lab partners a couple of times."

It sounded worse coming out of her mouth. It didn't make sense. But she wasn't going to say it. She wouldn't argue. Genevieve McGuire hadn't so much as looked at her since they were little and were forced to pose next to each other in their kindergarten picture. It wasn't that she was mean. She could have been. She was exactly the girl who should have been mean. She was beautiful and popular, at the top of everything she ever wanted to do. She could have been horrible.

Instead, she was just there. Decorative. Like the girls in stock photo ads you never actually believed were doing the things they were shown doing in the pictures. The ones who laughed about everything.

Maya wasn't a target to her like she was to many of the others who existed somewhere near her plane. Genevieve didn't make fun of her or send her nasty looks. She didn't laugh at her or toss her backpack at Maya's feet in the hall to try to make her fall. To her, it was like Maya didn't ever exist at all.

Until she suddenly did.

It started with a smile. Not one of those secret ones that were supposed to be just for her. A real smile. Tossed casually across the hall. It could have been meant for everyone, but Maya felt it land on her. It took too long for her to smile back. She was too taken aback by the gesture and too busy processing it, trying to figure it out, to actually return it. By the time a smile found her lips, Genevieve was at the back of the crowd shuffling down the hallway. Maya felt too ridiculous to hang onto it and send it when they saw each other in class later.

The next day, there was a look across the lunchroom. The girl sitting across from Genevieve, one of three Emilys who enjoyed walking through the halls together like they were part of a bad movie, was having a very animated conversation and hadn't yet seemed to realize there was no one on the other end of it. Her gestures were wild and overwrought, nearly knocking over various components of the lunches spread on the table in front of her.

At one point, she threw her head backward and dug her fingers into her glossy blonde curls as if she was so devastated about something she didn't know how to cope, only to carefully withdraw them seconds later to avoid ruining the style she undoubtedly took far too long to achieve.

That was when Genevieve looked over at Maya again. Emily was too wrapped up in her own performance she didn't notice the confidante who was supposed to be listening to her turn to the quiet, unnoticed girl sitting against the brick wall to the side of the room. She didn't notice the slight tilt of Genevieve's head or the roll of her eyes. But Maya noticed them, and then the playful curve of her glossy pink lips that followed.

During their next class, Genevieve talked to her like they'd always been friends. The conversation felt like it didn't have a beginning, like she was trying to pick up something that hadn't ever actually started. Maya listened until she found the frayed end of the chat and latched on, not always knowing exactly what was happening, but trying to keep up.

By the end of the class, she'd invited her to the carnival and to her house to sleep over for the night. She quickly mentioned Melanie had already agreed, like she was using Maya's best friend as a bargaining chip. They weren't truly friends, either. Not according to the rest of the school. But being in the same after-school activities meant they interacted more.

Maya didn't know how to react when she invited her. She wanted to. She tried to not care and not to overthink it, but she couldn't stop herself. Genevieve saw it, but she didn't seem to know why Maya was hesitating. Rather than realizing the strange dynamic of the conversation, that she was in essence going through an invisible social wall to talk with her, she hurried to fill the awkward space with her appeal.

She and her boyfriend had just broken up. It was her first Valentine's Day without a boyfriend and she didn't want to spend it alone.

Her friends had sided with him. They were all dating or angling to date his friends, so he had his claim. But she was alright with that. She'd been thinking a lot about the people she surrounded herself with and decided they weren't the right kind. They weren't helping her be the best person she could be or guiding her toward the kind of life she should have. She was on a path toward being a trophy wife who was only defined by the man she was attached to, and that wasn't what she wanted. She wanted to be someone. To be something. Like Maya was going to be.

Maya didn't know if she should feel like she was being used or manipulated. She searched for the slimy film that always settled over words when one person was trying to mold the other person and do something only to get something out of it. But that wasn't what this felt like. Strangely, it felt genuine. Like after all these years, Genevieve suddenly saw her.

Even with that revelation, it still felt odd to be getting ready for a Valentine's Day celebration with her. Most of the time her mother would never dream of allowing her daughter to go out on a school night, much less sleep over at someone else's house. But the holiday was an exception. There was the unspoken expectation that most kids wouldn't be at school the day after Valentine's Day and a suspicious number of the adults around town would have come down with the sniffles or have a spontaneous need for a paid personal day.

So Grace let her go. She stood at the door to wave goodbye as her daughter, duffel bag slung over her shoulder, walked out to the car where Genevieve McGuire waited.

Maya could see the emotion in her mother's eyes but didn't know what to call it. The surprise that was there when she had first told her about the invitation wasn't there anymore, but there was something else. Hesitation. Excitement. Sadness. Uncertainty. Relief. They were all there. They came together to make something distinct, but Maya didn't know what it was. The word for it and the ability to understand it were just out of reach for her. Even then she knew there were things her seventeen-year-old eyes couldn't fully see. They were on the other side of her birthday, in the expanse of adulthood. When she got there, she would understand.

She felt so close to that edge when she walked out of the house to join Melanie and Genevieve in the car. The space between childhood and adulthood seemed so narrow. It was like she could almost see it through the windshield in front of them as they drove along the main roads of town to cross to the other side where Genevieve lived. She couldn't get to it right now. No matter how fast they went or how hard she tried, they wouldn't be able to catch up to it. Not yet. But she could see it. It was there.

That was gone now.

She felt like a child again as everything around her seemed to close in. Outside, the neon lights were glowing brightly. The sounds were clear in the thin, chilly air. The pinball machine bounced the crowd from one attraction to the next.

In here, she was alone.

She hadn't come in alone. It was Melanie who'd first noticed the sign for the Fun House and said they needed to go through it. Genevieve had hesitated. Wasn't it for little kids? A bunch of badly painted murals ripping off fairy tales and rows of mirrors meant to distort you into funny shapes but really just fostered body image issues? Maybe an inflatable slide at the end?

No inflatable slide, Melanie had pointed out. Nothing at the end but a fireman's pole coming from a spinning tunnel. That didn't seem like it was for little kids. They wouldn't be able to hold on. And it required either five of the little pink and white tickets sold at the booths scattered around the edges of the carnival grounds or for the person wanting to go through to have the unlimited wristband. Little kids didn't usually get those. They were too expensive for the handful of baby rides. The Fun House had to be meant for older people.

It was carnival logic. The kind of twisting and interpreting that made sense out of the nonsensical. Those kinds of justifications that took a person afraid of heights and hesitant about the integrity of elevators and inspired them to climb the rickety metal steps to a tight car sitting on a roller coaster track built up from nothing in a matter of hours. That kind of logic was like taking thoughts and holding them up in front of one of those mirrors and watching them melt and change and bend until they were something completely different and yet the same.

Whatever the reasoning, the three girls, clutching each other by the elbows, scurried across the path toward the Fun House, narrowly avoiding a couple laden with stuffed animal prizes and towering cotton candy they were attempting to share. The man sitting at the entrance to the attraction looked at them with hollow eyes. Everywhere else, the lights reflected in the eyes of the people at the carnival. They sparkled on the excitement and adrenaline, making the laughter in them visible.

For this man, the lights seemed to disappear into a void. There was nothing there for them to reflect off of. Nothing for them to translate to shine. The stare stopped Maya and for a second, she felt trapped. His eyes were trying to drag her in to where the light had disappeared.

It was a feeling she knew. She'd felt it before. Only once, but it had never left her.

The tug on her arm felt like Melanie was pulling her out of the abyss. Her best friend didn't know she was rescuing her, but Maya came out of the hold of the darkness like deep water and sucked in deep breaths of the red and pink lights.

The girls held up their arms as they rushed past the man, showing him the unlimited wristbands that made the carnival their playground. They could bypass the regular line and didn't have to hand over individual tickets. It meant they could do whatever they wanted and never run out. Maya had never had that before. The first time they'd walked past a line of people clutching their tickets and were given a wide smile by the attendant who ushered them onto the attraction, a fevered thought had gone through her mind: was this what life was like for Genevieve all the time?

Maya went through her days with a handful of tickets, carefully doling them out for admittance to moments in time. For many of them, she didn't have enough. But everything opened for Genevieve. She could go anywhere. Do anything.

Maya wasn't proud of the satisfaction she got from hearing the insecurity in the beautiful girl's voice when she talked about trying to better herself. She knew there had been a few rough moments, and as impressive as she was with other aspects of her life, her academics didn't match up. It wasn't that she got bad grades or that she struggled through her classes. Genevieve just didn't stand out when it came to that aspect of school. She was a good student. But good didn't buy a future outside of Cold Valley.

That was one thing Maya had. When she felt like there was nowhere else to go in her life, she'd lost herself in school. It was easier to dig herself deep into her studies than to wander around in reality, not knowing what to do next. It meant she was always at the top of her class. Always had the best grades. Her term papers were the ones that were shown to the rest of the students to be used as an example. The one chosen to answer the impossible to answer questions. Trotted out for fun when another teacher stopped in to visit or the principal perched on the stool beside the desk at the front of the room.

There was a reality somewhere that would have lauded her for that, where she would have been the one who was appreciated and honored and held up to esteem among the students and faculty alike. Her intelligence and drive for success would be seen as admirable qualities that should be sought after.

But in her reality, the reality of a basic high school in a small town smack in the middle of a rural no man's land, intelligence wasn't often at the top of the priority list. And when it came along with a plain face wearing no makeup, hair that had far more personality that Maya often felt like she did, and whatever conglomeration of clothes she could find at the end-of-season sales and thrift markets her mother could afford, it was even more of a hindrance.

If her brain could be transferred into Genevieve's body and it was Genevieve's plush lips and clear eyes that presented speeches and answered questions, or her perfectly painted nails and smooth hands that filled in the answer balloons of test papers with exact precision, Maya knew for certain the words that were hurled at her would never be uttered in the halls of the school.

Maya had honestly believed high school would be different. She wouldn't be made fun of and bullied for things like her looks or how hard she studied. That wasn't what happened anymore. Not now in a world of acceptance, tolerance, and resistance against the status quo and the predictable structure of society from the generations before.

Maybe it was wishful thinking. Maybe it was watching too many uplifting teen movies where the ugly outcast turned out to be the most beautiful of them all. Maybe it was the surge in the concept of fandom and identifying as a nerd suddenly being socially desirable. At least, in theory.

As it turned out, rallying cries and splashy phrases on clothes and bumper stickers didn't always equate to being treated well. She didn't walk through the doors of the high school into the open arms of a new generation, a new reality for the little people who had been tossed aside and forgotten.

It was all the same shit, just in different packaging.

And now Genevieve was the one who wanted something about her. Not from her. But *about* her. It was a distinction that might not sound important, but meant everything.

She only wished that boost it gave her was enough to carry her through the Fun House once they were inside. Her feet hit the studded metal floor heavily, shaking the structure around her and clanging far too loudly in the small space. She grabbed onto the handrails on either side of her. The metal was cold on her palms, the paint slick.

"You okay?" Melanie's voice called.

That was when she first noticed the dimness of the space. She'd squeezed her eyes closed as soon as she walked in and barely realized she'd opened them. It was hard to see in the narrow tunnel they were walking through. She was the last of the three to enter, and though she could hear the footsteps on the metal ahead of her, she couldn't see either of the other girls.

"I'm fine," she called ahead, waiting for her voice to echo back or for her to respond.

She didn't hear anything but more footsteps, so she followed them deeper into the building. Her eyes adjusted to the darkness and she could see pinpricks of light beside her. They were moving, spiraling around her slowly as the tunnel spun like she was in a cement mixer. The points of light shimmered against the black background and Maya realized they were supposed to be stars. She was moving through the universe. Or through time. Something.

It didn't convince her of anything. She was still walking across a metal bridge through a spinning tunnel in a rickety carnival Fun House. But she kept walking. The fun had to start at some point. And she wouldn't turn back. She thought of the eyes of the man at the front entrance. She wouldn't turn back. Melanie and Genevieve were ahead. They were in there somewhere, and as long as they were, she would be, too.

"Melanie?"

"We're up here."

It was Genevieve's voice. She kept following it. The end of the bridge slipped beneath her feet and she stumbled going down two steps to another platform. Thankfully, she caught herself before she fell; the instant her legs were straight beneath her again she wondered if there were cameras watching everything she was doing. It would make sense if there were. Dark corners, sightless hallways, and subtle dangers didn't fit well with lack of supervision. A strange compulsion rose up inside her. Something about the dulled sound and the containment made her feel not like herself.

Turning slowly, wondering where the camera might be, she stopped and threw her arms up in the air like a gymnast finishing her floor performance. She felt ridiculous and exhilarated at the same time. There was something oddly freeing about doing something so nonsensical, even if no one could see her—or even if they could. As if she was making a statement. She didn't know what it was, but it felt like something.

She continued on, ending up at the bottom of another staircase. Gripping hard to the rails, she climbed to the top and found herself facing what looked like massive punching bags hanging from the ceiling. Somewhere in front of her, she heard laughter.

"Wait for me," she called ahead. "I'm coming through the punching bags."

"We can't stop," Melanie replied. "They won't let us."

"They?"

Maya got only silence back. The thrill began to drain out of her. Lights recessed in the tops of the walls gave enough illumination to see the bags hanging in front of her, but not enough to penetrate the shadows behind the first row or to even show what was beneath them.

She wanted to turn back. She couldn't. She didn't know who Melanie was talking about, but for her, they meant the man's eyes.

Her feet found the edge of the metal floor. There was nothing beneath her toes. She reached for the first bag, hoping to wrap her arms around it and move to the next. Something moved in the silence behind her. The sound of something hard against the metal. Not a footstep, more an impact.

Maya tried to tell herself her heart wasn't pounding. She hated the way that felt in her chest. She hated the feeling of being startled, of fear crawling up her legs and clawing her veins until they shredded and pooled at the bottom of her feet and were replaced by cold water. She hated when her chest swelled until it felt cavernous and rattled when her heart pounded hard against her ribs. The feeling trembled through her insides until they shook and her stomach felt sick.

Every time it happened, it lured out memories from the edges of her mind, forcing her back to the first time she'd felt it. She never wanted to go back to that moment.

The sound behind her happened again and she clutched onto the hanging bag. It swung slightly, but her hands slipped and she dropped. Her body braced for the fall, but it was over almost instantly. Her feet hit a surface that bowed and she rebounded as something hit her on either side. Maya looked down and saw she was surrounded by chunks of foam. A step affirmed that she was walking on what felt like a trampoline. The buoyancy made it difficult to fight her way across to the other side. She pushed the bags away and felt them hit her on the back and sides almost as soon as she moved past them, but at least she didn't have to swing across.

She was scrambling up onto the other side of the pit when she heard voices ahead of her. She hoped it was Genevieve and Melanie. It sounded like laughter; she focused on it, rather than the neon splashes of paint that created disorienting images and garish faces on the black walls as she ran down the hallway.

The voices didn't seem to get any closer and the paint faded until she was in a solely black passage again. Red lights up at the top of the walls seemed intended to mimic the lights outside, but these were ominous. Almost threatening.

Maya heard the sounds behind her again. They echoed until they seemed to come at her from all sides, drowning out the sound of the laughter. She wanted to call out for the other girls, but she couldn't bring her voice out of her throat. She hated the silence but was also afraid to shatter it. She didn't want the attention. She wanted to stay unnoticed.

That was what her father should have done. He never should have noticed. And maybe *they* wouldn't have, either.

She swallowed the thoughts and pressed her lips closed. She reminded herself she was here. Not there. She wasn't a little girl. This was supposed to be fun. It was designed to be a little disorienting, to make you question and wonder and feel off balance. She wasn't in danger.

Ahead of her, the laughter continued. She kept chasing it, hoping it would get louder or that she would be able to tell which direction it was coming from. But no matter how far she went, no matter how many turns she took through the darkness with her hands running along the painted walls, it never sounded like she was getting any closer.

A pale rectangle appeared at the end of the hall and Maya let out a breath of relief, but it was short-lived. The doorway didn't offer her the deliverance from the Fun House she'd hoped it would. Instead, it was her own pale cheeks and wide, darting eyes that confronted her as the hallway fed her into a maze of mirrors. She hated them. She hated her reflections and the way she couldn't believe the tricks of her eyes. She hated being able to see behind herself, to see her own eyes focused away from her and staring into the distance like she was outside of her body watching.

Movement in the corner of her eye caught her attention. Maya whipped around to look. Something dark moved across the front of one of the mirrors like someone was slipping around a corner, but the angling of the reflective surfaces made it so she couldn't tell where they really were.

The shuffling of something brushing across the floor turned her around again, but it was only her own frightened expression behind her. She could hear the laughter again, but as she ran through the maze, turning around on herself, trapping herself in corners and dead ends, the sound began to twist. Rather than laughter, it twisted to screams.

There was someone behind her coming through the mirrors. She caught brief flashes of their reflection in the mirrors around her. She heard their footsteps and their breaths. The screams reverberating off the walls around her sounded familiar. She knew the voice. She had to get to it, to stop it.

The mirrors were endless. She couldn't find her way out. No matter how many times she turned or how many different decisions she made when she came to the end of a hall, she kept finding herself in the same spot. There were no dark walls, no metal frame. It was only the mirrors. She was in the heart of the maze, surrounded by herself. There was nothing but her own eyes, her own mouth open, gasping for breath, her own hands, clawing for a grasp on anything.

But something was getting closer. Someone.

She didn't know who.

Light brightened overhead and glowed brighter against the glass. Maya focused on the dark edge of the floor at the bottom to guide her along. She watched as it turned and moved in different directions to show her where to go. She watched for the Something to appear above it and hoped it wouldn't.

Finally, the stretch of mirrors broke. There was a gap. A span without reflection. Maya stretched her hands toward it and ran. She hit a metal bar going across it and it moved. A door. She didn't know where it led. She didn't really care. What mattered was it would bring her out of the mirrors and away from the Something.

She tumbled through the door, slammed it closed behind her, and ran forward without paying attention to where she was. It wasn't until she nearly fell from the edge that she realized she was on the loading platform of a ride. Thrashing her arms kept her balanced until she was able to recover her stability and look around.

Nothing on the outside of the Fun House had mentioned there was a ride inside. There were no attendants nearby. No one to take a ticket or check restraints. Maya turned back to the door. She couldn't remember if there was an emergency exit sign above it or anything on it to say where it went. She hadn't been paying enough attention to notice. All she'd cared about was getting through the door and away from the mirrors.

Now she wondered where she was and how she ended up there. She didn't know where to go, if she should turn back and go through the door again, or if she should continue on, trying to find another. The small ride vehicle in front of her looked like it was waiting, but there was no one around to start a ride and nothing to tell Maya even what was waiting down the track.

Part of her wanted to stay where she was. Here, there were no screams. The Something didn't feel so close.

But complacency could too easily feel like safety.

She went back to the door, trying not to focus on the trembling of her heart and the way her head was spinning. The handle felt stiff when she grabbed it. She tried to press it down but it would only shift a tiny bit. It was locked. She wasn't going to be able to go back through to the mirror maze. She was filled with relief. And despair.

Pressing her hand to the wall again like she did when she was going down the hallway, she walked the perimeter of the loading dock, hoping for something. The sound of her own voice was still silent in her mouth. She couldn't call out to anyone. She couldn't ask for help.

Her fingertips found nothing along the walls that might lead her out. There was no other door. No other gap. Nothing.

The small ride car sat, still waiting. Maya shook as she walked toward it. Somewhere in the back of her mind, she thought she heard the screaming again, but she didn't know if she actually heard it or if it was the memory of it replaying against the silence.

She stepped down into the car. It felt surreal. This shouldn't be happening. It didn't make sense. She wanted to force herself back into reality, to tell herself this wasn't happening. It couldn't be happening. Things like this didn't exist in life. They belonged in one of those creepy books she used to read when she was younger, the ones with preteen kids running around seemingly unsupervised making bad decisions without any care for things like the laws of nature, social rules, or logic. The ones where things like ancient mummies being accidentally delivered to archaeologists at home and kept in the basement, or burned-out houses in the suburbs being left standing for a year, or children trick-or-treating for endless hours into the night by themselves, were not only completely reasonable but were so commonplace no one batted an eye.

But this wasn't one of those books. She wasn't curled in the corner of her bed with her blankets wrapped around her and her back pressed into the corner of the wall as she read them, telling herself they weren't scary, reminding herself she would never do the kinds of things those kids did. She would never make those decisions if she did find herself in one of those situations.

A decision like climbing into an empty ride vehicle while trapped in the Fun House at a carnival.

It wasn't even Halloween. It was Valentine's Day. She should have been suffocating on the smell of cheap perfume and trying not to be on the receiving end of unintentional indecent exposure when she came around corners on the midway, not letting terror seep in and control her.

But it didn't matter how much she tried to talk herself out of it, or how many times she repeated the stale, recycled words from years before that were meant to make her feel in control but never really had that effect. She could tell herself this wasn't happening, but it didn't change it.

As she sat down, a sudden thought went through her mind and she lifted her hips just enough to stuff her hand into her pocket and fish out her phone. The rectangle of light from the screen made the dimness around her seem deeper, but it was a relief to bend over it and pretend it was surrounding her. There were no missed calls. No messages. Nothing that indicated the other girls were even concerned about losing track of her inside the structure.

Maya wanted to find that comforting. They didn't think anything was really wrong. They were probably just outside waiting for her and would eventually figure out she hadn't emerged. At the same time, it left her feeling even more alone. She remembered the screams, and the tendrils of fear crept up the back of her neck again, like the Something had gotten inside and was running sharp, pointed fingers along her spine. Maybe they hadn't reached out to her because they couldn't.

Beside her, a loud bang against the door made her jump, a gasp breaking her silence. She couldn't move. She waited for the door to open, for what had been following her to finally come through, done with taunting her and ready for the confrontation. But it didn't move.

She didn't realize her hands were so tightly clenched around the metal lap bar of the ride car until she felt it shift and come down over her thighs. Maya shook it, trying to pull it back up, but it wouldn't budge. It was firmly locked in place, and somewhere, she heard a rumbling.

She'd been thinking about the red lights outside the Fun House and how she should be out in them, and now it seemed they'd come for her. Bright round lights swelled in the dark ahead of her, creating what looked like a tunnel. She shook her head. This didn't make sense. It couldn't be real. It couldn't be what she thought she was seeing.

They came into a modified shipping container attached to a trailer. That was all it was. She couldn't be here now. Squeezing her eyes closed, Maya tried to remember what she saw when she'd run toward the entrance to the Fun House with Genevieve and Melanie. But she couldn't see anything but the marquee lights outlining the name and the man sitting at the bottom of the steps.

His hollow eyes still haunted her. They'd caught her when she was going up the steps. She'd fallen into them and maybe Melanie hadn't actually pulled her out.

The rumble got louder and Maya's eyes snapped open as the car lurched and shot forward. It probably wasn't going very fast, but it felt like she was rocketing into nothing. Sudden movement always felt faster than planned.

She wouldn't let herself close her eyes. As much as she didn't want to see what was ahead, it felt like the only option she had. She didn't want to be even more out of control. Whatever was in front of her, she needed to see it coming. It was the only way she could possibly have a chance.

The track was kept dark with only the red lights to give any indication of where she was. She couldn't see how far it went ahead or how it would shift and change. Every twist and drop were unexpected, making the center of her chest ache and her stomach drop low. It felt like she would never stop, that this would go on forever.

Just as soon as that thought went through her head, the car stopped. Maya lurched forward with the sudden stillness, the metal bar crushing against the bottom of her ribcage and forcing out a gush of air. The car stopping made a harsh metallic noise that seemed to swell and echo in the quiet tunnel, fading at the same time as the red lights. It descended her into total darkness. The only sound was her breath shaking around her.

The Something was behind her. She could feel it coming closer, stalking down the track toward her. She couldn't move. The bar had her wedged, pressing down on her thighs so she couldn't slide out. The pressure fed the panic in the pit of her belly. Heat started rising around her. It thickened the air first, then started to sting on her skin. Tears came to her eyes as she struggled to get out from the hold of the bar.

When she closed her eyes she could smell wet dirt and rubber, so Maya kept them open.

The heat intensified and she realized she wasn't in darkness anymore. Light rushed toward her along the track; it took a few moments for her to realize this was not the red lights from before. This was a roaring flame. Fire glowed under the track, hissing as it slipped under the car and rose up on the sides. Maya gasped and pulled her arms in close, trying to get farther away from the side of the car so the flames couldn't touch her.

Finally, she screamed.

She grabbed hold of the bar again and shook it with every bit of her strength, pushing against it to try to lift it just enough to squeeze out. The flames crawled up the walls and started to move across the ceiling. They made her eyes sting and turned everything yellow and orange. She reached for her phone again and tried to call Melanie, but there was no reception. Nothing would go through. Her ribcage felt like it was going to crack with the force of her sobs. She couldn't move. She couldn't get away from the fire. She was helpless.

She curled down against the bar, covered her head with her hands, and closed her eyes. At least if she had to feel the metal pinning her down and the heat moving across her skin, at least if there was nothing she could do, she could close her eyes and see his face one more time.

CHAPTER ONE

January

"I CAN DO IT, EMMA."

Xavier carefully turns the marshmallow in his hot cocoa over so it can absorb on the other side. There are no miniature marshmallows for this man. When he wants cocoa—which can under no circumstances come from a packet, can, tin, or anything else with the word "instant" on it—he requires a single jumbo marshmallow positioned right in the middle of the full mug. It nearly takes up the entire thing, like one of those fancy cookie mug toppers that became extremely popular with party planners and ambitious housewives for approximately ten seconds before everyone caught onto the sheer bullshit that is a cookie too big to dunk into the beverage.

The marshmallow sits in Xavier's mug soaking up the cocoa for a few moments before he flips it over to get maximum saturation. He then fishes it out with a spoon, puts it on a plate, and cuts it into pieces. There's always a moment of disappointment when he gets to the center of the marshmallow and it's still white. I believe it is one of his life's ambitions to have full absorption so the marshmallow turns into some kind of chocolate fluff Jell-O combination.

"I know you can," I tell him, wrapping my hands around my own mug to warm them up and give them something to do. I'm not great at knowing what to do with my hands in moments when my mind is racing and I feel not totally in control of the situation. "It's just that…"

"Emma," Xavier says carefully. "I can do it."

He's looking at me in that way that means he's speaking not to me but to the person in my head who keeps thoughts, memories, and ideas precisely organized in tiny filing cabinets and rolodexes. He told me once it's how he makes sure I fully understand him. If he talks to that little person and has what he says recorded for me, I can go back through it later.

I don't question why he envisions a tiny secretary with woefully outdated record-keeping technology keeping my thoughts under control for me. He never told me if he has one, too. But from my experience with Xavier, I can comfortably say the chances of just one tiny secretary being able to hold down the fort in that mind are very slim. Unless it happens to be one of those no-nonsense ones from the private investigator movies who rarely speaks, seems to know the complex policies and inner workings of all organizations, and types like the wind.

So either Xavier has an entire corporate building maze of cubicles and sputtering coffee machines in his head, or one bare lightbulb and a middle-aged badass in a tweed skirt and jacket.

"I just got off the phone with the warden," my father announces, coming into the room and sliding his phone onto the coffee table before sitting down in his favorite of the chairs in my living room. "They're going to be ready to take you in next Wednesday."

"Do I get to be arrested?" Xavier asks.

"I don't think that would be necessary," I say.

"Maybe they could meet me on a street somewhere and rough me up a little. Someone will be around with a cell phone camera. It will go viral and then the others will have already heard about me by the time I get in there."

"No one is going to rough you up," Sam says. "They'll cuff you, but I don't think a street fight is needed."

"That's disappointing."

"This isn't County, remember," Dean says. "The people there didn't just get plucked up off the street."

"That's right," I add. "This is federal prison." I lean toward him, my elbows on my thighs so I can meet his eyes. "Prison, Xavier."

He nods, the emotion on his face not changing. "I'm familiar."

"Then you remember you were brought in after sentencing, not before. You were wearing a suit, I'm assuming," Sam says.

His voice slides up in an unsure curve at the end of the statement. Over the last few years, he's learned not to assume anything when it comes to Xavier, but sometimes the sentiment still comes out and he catches himself partway through. This time I can see he's wishing he'd had this conversation with Xavier before talking to the police in Breyer. Not because he thought he'd be able to change anything. Just because at least then he would have been able to better prepare the officers.

"Jumpsuit," Xavier tells him. "Sandals. White socks. Shackles on my ankles and a chain around my waist. It was a nice shade of pink, though."

I bristle, looking over at Sam. His face has gone slightly pale. He hadn't thought what he was saying all the way through. He forgot what Xavier had gone through. In his mind, Xavier's sentencing was like any of the ones he attended as Sheriff of Sherwood. He would be given a time and place for his sentencing hearing and allowed to go back home and return for the appointed hearing. And if they had remanded him after trial, Sam figured he would have at least been afforded the opportunity to change into court clothes.

He doesn't like to think about the details of Xavier's actual experience. None of us do. But I choose not to push it out of my mind. I can't hide it away in the back corners of my thoughts because I figure if I do that, they could get lost or wander away. At any second, they could burst out, and then I'd have to deal with them. I'd much rather keep those memories close enough to my thoughts that they are easily accessible and under my control, but veiled so I didn't have to replay them constantly.

When I do, I can still hear Xavier's voice as he first described that horrific time in his life. There's no emotion when he talks about it. Xavier describes finding the body of his closest friend in his garage, getting arrested, and being convicted of the murder as if he's talking about someone else's life. There's a smooth, precise tone in his voice when he talks about it, recounting those moments like he's not reliving them, but showing a slideshow projecting directly out of his brain.

As much as I try to, I know none of us can really understand what Xavier went through after that. From the moment he found Andrew dead, he was alone and disconnected from the world around him. Andrew's death took away his source of connection and interpretation.

Situations like being arrested, questioned, jailed, and tried are confusing and terrifying for anyone. For someone like Xavier, each step was torture. In the midst of processing the death of the one person he trusted and who could make the world seem like a safe and bearable space for him, Xavier was immersed in situations he had never experienced without anything to help him hold onto. So he spiraled. His confusion, anxiety, and fear were interpreted as instability and risk. He never had a chance.

Xavier wasn't afforded the luxury of going home after trial. He didn't get a chance to find a suit. He spent long stretches in separate housing, under suicide watch, in the infirmary. Anywhere they could try to keep him out of the way because they didn't understand him. None of them cared to realize he couldn't understand them, either.

"I'm sorry," Sam says.

Xavier fishes out his marshmallow onto the plate already waiting beside him.

"Sorry for what? You weren't involved."

Sam starts to say something else but thinks better of it. Dean slides in the way he tends to do. We don't talk about Dean as a replacement for Andrew, even though that is more or less what the courts would say. Xavier was an unexpected addition to my life. I wasn't investigating his case or Andrew's death. I met him just to gather information in my missing persons case. I walked into the room in the facility where he was being held awaiting a retrial hearing, thinking I was going to get a few insights and hopefully a direction to go. I walked out completely changed.

From that moment, Xavier became as integral a part of my family as I've ever known. The court decided to release him pending a new trial, but they were very aware they were releasing him into a world indescribably changed from the one he'd left more than eight years before. For someone who already struggled with day-to-day activities, didn't drive, and had a considerable amount of wealth awaiting him, it could get dangerous quickly.

The solution came in the form of my cousin, Dean Steele. A private investigator with a murky past he sought to find meaning in by turning to the military special forces, he came out the other side severely injured, hardened, and distrustful. I was only just getting to really know him when we found each other, and I could see the harm his life had done to him. We understood each other in a way no one would ever want to be able to understand us.

But something about Xavier got through that. And something about Dean felt safe to Xavier. The court determined it would be Dean's responsibility to help Xavier, to watch out for him and help him assimilate with the world, and ensure he participated in his new trial and everything else he was supposed to do. To those on the outside looking in, Dean is Xavier's handler, the same role Andrew fulfilled. But to our family, he's a friend, a confidante, a guiding light, and someone who has found a true, deep connection to Xavier. I feel privileged to know Andrew will never be replaced and Dean is far more than a replacement.

"For this to work, it needs to look authentic," Dean says. "Remember, the warden is the only person inside that facility who is going to know what's really going on. As far as the other administrators, the guards, the inmates, the visitors, and the vendors know, you are a prisoner just like the rest of them. You are coming in to serve your sentence, which means you have already been to jail, through trial, and have been sentenced."

"That's right," I say. "You'll go in as a self-surrender rather than being transported from the courthouse."

"Why?" Xavier asks. "Shouldn't I go through a sentencing hearing and have officers bring me in from the courtroom? For authenticity?"

"The court system is funny about using resources for fraudulent cases to trick law enforcement and Department of Corrections officers," I tell him.

Xavier stares for a second, then bobs his head a couple of times. "I can see that."

"The warden is putting you into the system so you'll show up just like any self-surrender inmate and be processed in. As Emma said, he's not informing any other members of his staff, so the entire process will be exactly the same from the moment he's dropped off," Dad chimes in.

"Did you thank him for me?" I ask. "I know this is a huge favor."

I probably could have used my FBI sway to encourage the warden to allow Xavier's experience, but this is a situation when it seems a personal friendship is more influential than a demand and a badge. My father and the warden aren't the kinds of close friends who go out to the bar and throw darts around, but they give firm handshakes and genuine smiles when they see each other and have deep professional respect for one another.

And I just had him pull the mother of all strings for me.

"I did," Dad says. "He did ask me several times if you are sure about this. Both of you."

"I am," Xavier nods without hesitation.

Dad looks at me. "Emma?"

CHAPTER TWO

I DON'T KNOW HOW TO RESPOND.

This isn't a new conversation. It isn't like Xavier showed up at my house this morning declaring he wants to put himself back into the prison system because he just had such a fabulous time the first go-around and he feels like this time he could really have fun with it. This is a conversation that came up weeks ago, before the Christmas tree was in the corner of the living room. Before the army of Gingerbread People of the World was baked. Before Xavier rolled plums in coarse sanding sugar and decided that was close enough.

It's been more than a year since Jonah escaped from the prison that was supposed to be holding him for the rest of his life and then some. And in that time, no one has been able to figure out how he got out. We know he had help. A woman named Serena, who was pretending to be a missing woman named Miley Stanford, died trying to follow the plan they'd crafted to get him out.

I know that much. I also know him well enough to know she wouldn't be the only person he had planned to help him. He's too savvy for that. Too untrusting. Even behind bars, Jonah was a powerful force. His followers were—are—devoted to a degree of obsession. It would be the highest honor to be asked to help him, even if it meant to die for him in the process. But Jonah also knows he's hated. He's being hunted at every moment. And people turn. In a second someone can go from worshipping at your feet to handing you over to the slaughter, and there isn't always an explanation why.

So he plans. He makes sure he has strings on all his fingers and makes the people on the ends dance. Most of the time, they don't know about each other. Thinking they are the only one who has been granted favor in the eyes of their revered leader, their Lotan, deepened their devotion.

But that isn't how he always approaches it. Sometimes he let them know. He pitted them against each other. For those followers, the competition was a threat. It meant the special attention they were getting and the favor being shown to them was tenuous. They were teetering on an edge that drove them nearly to madness. They feared the tiniest mistake or oversight that would cause them to tumble off and give the other person an advantage.

However he played the people he lined up to help him escape, I still haven't figured out who it was or how he accomplished it. Searches of the prison, interrogations of the few inmates known to interact with Jonah, and deep dives into every form of surveillance the prison had offered up nothing but some concerns about the reliability of the technology in the prison. I haven't been able to identify who helped him, what they did for him, or how he got out.

And it's been driving me to the edge of my sanity.

He won't tell me how he did it or where he is, claiming it isn't his truth to tell. I don't care. He's betrayed everyone who has ever crossed his path. Now is not the time for him to start worrying about his honor and discretion.

My thoughts drift back to Serena. She was different. I don't know everything that happened between the two of them. The fact that he used her as a weapon against Salvador Marini, better known as the Emperor, tells me he was nowhere near above taking advantage of her, but something about her was set apart. Jonah rescued her. He saved her from a world I don't want to think about. But that is where my admiration of his actions and compassion for whatever feelings he had for her ends.

Instead of rescuing her and making sure she was brought out of a life of horror and into a life of protection and safety, Jonah made her a member of Leviathan. When I was first discovering the depths of my uncle's depravity and learning the layers of his organization, I thought there weren't any women. Now I know there might not be many, but the ones who do exist are fierce and cunning, able to use not only the same intellect, strength, and connections as many of the other members, but also what Jonah calls their 'feminine wiles.' The description makes me sick. And yet seems appropriate.

Serena's tattoo on her back, the mermaid that was at once beautiful and terrifying, marked her as belonging to him. It was the only thing that enabled us to trace her away from the identity she assumed. That mark on her back proved her devotion to him, sealed in ink underneath her skin, heated and cemented by the way he took her from her abusers and ensured they would never hurt her or anyone else ever again. It proved she was willing to do anything for him. Including stalking and preying on other women for the Emperor to use for his own pleasure while she also fed information about him back to Jonah.

"Emma?"

I look up, realizing I've been staring at a patch of carpet on my living room floor. My elbows are still perched on my thighs and I'm slowly twirling my wedding band around. The other faces in the room stare back at me and I wonder how long I've been wading around in those thoughts while they were trying to talk to me.

"Hmm?" I ask.

"Where did you go?" Dean asks. "You looked like you were a thousand miles away from here."

"No," I reply, shaking my head. "Not a thousand miles. Right here. Right on that front porch."

"What do you mean?" my father asks.

"He came here on Christmas Eve. Right up onto my front porch, and I didn't even know he was there. I've been driving myself to the very edge for over a year trying to hunt him down and haven't been able to. Then he walks up to my house in the middle of the night when we are all here and none of us notice. The longer he's out, the more dangerous he's going to be," I explain.

"Which is why we need to end this," Dean says. "He won't tell you how he got out or what he's been doing. You've tried to get him to. I know you have. But until we can figure out what got him out of that prison and where he's gone, you're not going to be able to get him back in and know he'll stay there."

I look at Xavier. He looks back at me with peace and calm in his eyes. There's no fear. There's no hesitation. He told me weeks ago he could do this. The same words he's been repeating over and over this morning. *I can do it, Emma.* Deep inside me, I know he can. He understands the prison system and can move through it. He can also see things other people can't and recognize the most subtle changes and shifts that could direct him to find Jonah's path out.

But I can't stop the worry. I know he survived years inside and it won't be anything close to that long this time, but there are still dangers. And without the guards and other inmates knowing he's undercover, he could be put into situations that threaten his safety and even his life.

This wasn't my idea. It is still not my idea. I know it's our best shot. I understand that. We've tried everything else. I've even offered Jonah the one thing I know matters the most to him -- a relationship with me. He's given me a lot of information, but what he won't give me is the details I need. He knows what I'm after and he's not going to give it to me. Which means I'm out of ideas. I can keep trying to hunt him with my observation skills and what I know about him, hoping to trap him in one of the buildings Leviathan was known to use, or track him down with one of his followers, or even hear or sense something when I'm talking to him that will narrow down the search.

But something tells me I'll have to simply use the resources available. I was a Girl Scout for a very short time when I was younger. I was terrible at selling cookies, I ate the bag of marshmallows before s'mores could get made, and we moved on before I had much of a chance to earn the badges, but I took the Law to heart. Maybe that was a glimpse into my future. Or maybe I just really appreciated the sentiment of making the world a better place with a clear plan for how to do it. Either way, the idea of using my resources wisely stuck with me.

And right now, Xavier is my resource. I might not like the idea, but I can't stop it. Or at least, I won't. I want to protect him. I always do. I also have to remind myself he isn't a child. He isn't a helpless little boy I have to keep tucked under my wing to keep him safe from the world.

He's unlike anyone I've ever known. There are times when it seems like he can't handle things, but the truth is Xavier is strong. He's resilient and forceful in a way that is hard to understand, but impossible to ignore. The fact that he struggles doesn't show weakness.

He's alive. Intensely, sharply alive. And that simple reality, that he thrives in his own vibrant way in a world not designed for him and in some ways specifically designed against him, shows his strength.

He could give up. He could have given up a long time ago. He could have left this Earth, allowed someone else to take him out of it, or even just stashed himself away somewhere dark and quiet where he didn't have to face anything and could exist alone for as long as he could hold out. But he fights. He might do it with tears in his eyes and his hands shaking. He might do it in a state of utter confusion with no idea of where he is or what he is supposed to do next. He might do it without the ability to explain himself or communicate what he's going through.

But Xavier fights.

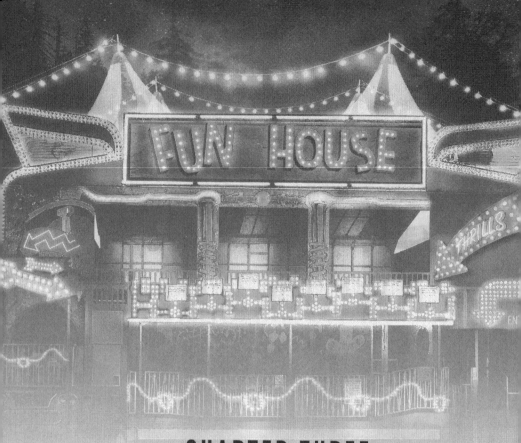

CHAPTER THREE

"**D**O YOU THINK IT SHOULD BE ME?"

I'm in the kitchen washing dishes and listening with one ear to the conversation between my father and Xavier in the other room. They're back in the depths of planning what I've come to understand is some sort of game, but I'm not totally sure what it entails. Their talks over the rules can get very heated, and yet I still haven't been able to catch on to what they're talking about or get an idea of how the game would be played. But they are very passionate about it.

Glancing over my shoulder at him, I finish the plate I'm rinsing and shake it a couple of times before setting it in the drainer.

"Do I think what should be you?" I ask.

I grab the last plate in the sink and start washing it.

"Going to prison," Dean says. "Instead of Xavier. Do you think it should be me? That I should be the one to go into the prison undercover rather than Xavier? I've been down. I know…"

The words come fast and his voice climbs higher as the emotion tightens around them. I can see them in his eyes. I'm surprised to see it. He's been encouraging of this idea ever since Xavier latched onto it and it turned from a half-cocked throwaway statement into an actual plan. He's been the one telling everyone Xavier can handle this, that he will get us the information we've all been trying to find. Now he looks on the verge of losing his grasp on something he's been holding onto with all his strength.

"Dean," I sigh, wiping my hands on a kitchen towel as I turn around to face him and rest my back against the counter, "stop. No. I don't think you should be the one going. You can't let your thoughts go down that path."

"Why not?" he counters. "Everybody keeps saying Xavier should go because he went to prison. Well, so did I. Doesn't that make me a candidate, too?"

"He went for eight years," I say. "You were in and out of county jails and you spent, what, a year in prison?"

"Fourteen months," he corrects me. There's an almost defensive edge to his voice, like he's offended to have the duration of his stay in the Big House diminished.

His time in prison is one of the things that made Dean the man he is, but that he would rather keep behind him. At least until now. His stint, reduced down from a sentence of two years, came during a tumultuous time in his life. A rough childhood and the brutal loss of his mother only amplified the angry, rebellious streak in him. Those years saw him involved in a wide variety of bad decisions and criminal activities, including a torturous, scarring tangle with a murder investigation that continued to haunt him until just a couple of years ago.

"I'm not saying you don't know what happens in a prison, Dean. Obviously, you do. Spending more than a year in prison isn't easy and no one is ignoring you went through that. No one is pretending you didn't have that experience."

"Then why shouldn't it be me?" he asks. "Why put Xavier through that? You know how it affected him. You know better than any of us because you saw him when he was still in custody."

I do know. I wish I didn't. I don't want to still remember the look on his face the first time I met him. When I walked into the holding facility that day, I had no idea what was coming. I knew I was meeting with Xavier Renton, a man convicted of murder who many believed was innocent, and who had a personal relationship with a missing woman. That didn't prepare me for Xavier Renton, the human being.

He wasn't like I know him now. I didn't know at the time he was being influenced and manipulated by the very staff tasked with taking care of him and keeping him safe. They had a lot of stake in making sure he didn't get a new trial and possibly get exonerated for the murder of his best friend. They decided to reinforce the perception that Xavier was unstable, insane, and dangerous by taking advantage of a heart condition that left him vulnerable to the effects of something so simple and mundane it never occurred to anyone around him: sugar.

But he was willing to speak with me. It was a step. I had trouble following a lot of it and I was still cautious near him, but there was something about him even then that held onto me. It wasn't necessarily purely positive. It unnerved me to encounter someone I didn't understand and couldn't read. That is one of my greatest strengths. Throughout my career, I've walked into situations confident I had the upper hand because of my observation skills and ability to notice things about people that tell stories they don't want told. The slightest movement, the look in their eyes, the way they shift or clear their throat -- it all means something. I'm an expert at collecting those details and pulling out things about them.

Not with Xavier. There was nothing about him that was predictable or that fit in with the expectations and set guidelines about other people. I couldn't look at him and know what he was feeling or thinking. Now after knowing him for this long, I've learned to identify tells of his. I know when he's feeling overwhelmed or when something has sparked in his brain and is churning his gears. But I still don't know what he's thinking, and more often than not, he surprises me.

I've learned to love that about him, but when I first met him, it was frustrating. It left me feeling off-balance and at a disadvantage. I didn't like that. But the longer I spent with him and the more I learned about his perspective, the more I stopped caring about my position and thought more about him. Finding out everything he was going through hurt and infuriated me. I still haven't forgiven the men who tortured him and watched him spiral further and further down into his own personal hell for their own benefit.

Since many of those involved in the Order of Prometheus, the group responsible for all he went through including Andrew's death, are now dead, I don't feel much moral obligation to work toward that forgiveness right now.

I start the coffeemaker and pull mugs out of the cabinet overhead. This is one of those moments I am beyond grateful for the technology of my hybrid machine. It can make a single cup or a whole pot, and when I'm facing a situation like this, the speed is crucial.

"Dean," I start carefully as the machine burbles to life and I fill the cup with fresh grounds. The smell of caramel tells my nose this is an evening cup rather than the inky dark roast that starts my mornings. "How did prison affect you?"

He looks at me strangely. "What do you mean?"

"What did you take out of the experience?"

"That being put in a cage with criminals is a shit way to learn a lesson and if I hadn't made the decision to turn my life around when I did, I'd either be behind those bars for the rest of my life or dead right now. Quite possibly a combination of the two," he tells me.

I nod, filling one of the cups and putting another in place to fill.

"That's a good takeaway," I say. "But what about individual moments? Which of the inmates were the most influential for you? Is there a guard you especially hated, or one who you remember treating you well? Did anything major happen while you were in there?"

"I was in there to do my time and get out, not to make friends. I wasn't holding hands in a spirit circle and making braided bracelets with those guys. And as for the guards, they were there to make sure we didn't rip each other apart and were where we were supposed to be when we were supposed to be there."

"But there aren't any who stand out to you? Just like there aren't any specific moments or events that do?" I ask.

"Emma, what's your point? It was prison. I was there for committing crimes. It wasn't summer camp."

"You've never told me the name of a single inmate who was in with you. You've never told me about your bunk or your job assignment, other than when you spent a couple of months in the furniture shop. If I was to ask you to describe the prison and your daily movements to me, I don't know if you could."

"Because I didn't hang onto them," Dean says, his teeth gritting hard against each other.

I hate to have to do it, but there's no way out of this conversation.

"Because you don't remember," I finally say. He bristles; tension crackles between us, but he knows I'm right.

I wait while he takes a sip of his coffee, the mug covering up the expression on his face. "Look, Dean, I know there is a lot of that whole experience that is still clear for you in your mind, and probably a lot of things you compartmentalized because you don't want to think about them, but if you had to, you could bring them forward. You will be extremely valuable in being able to take what Xavier says and give it context, but the truth is, there are whole sections of your stay you don't remember."

"Just because I didn't cling onto the details…"

"There was a riot," I interject. His face falls and his eyes darken. I hate to see that shift in him. "There was a riot when you'd been there almost a year. Four days. When they finally took back control of the prison, they found you in the law library, reading and taking notes. You seemed completely unfazed by anything that was going on."

"I know," Dean says low in his throat.

"You talked like it was still the day the riot started and you had no idea what happened during that time."

"I know," he repeats, his voice more insistent.

"Other inmates said you helped them and provided protection for hostages. It was part of what got you out early."

"I know," he says angrily. "I've heard it. Don't you think I think about that all the time? That I try to get past the blackout and figure out what happened during that time, or why I can't remember it? Like I can't remember the murders at Arrow Lake or nearly a week in the desert or three weeks after I came home? Or when the Emperor had me captured and thrown into a gladiator ring? Like any of the other fucking times my brain has just stopped and I don't know why?"

"Dean, calm down," I say. "I'm not judging you for your blackouts. No one is."

He takes a breath, sliding down into one of the chairs at the kitchen table. His hands wrap tightly around the mug in front of him and he stares down into it.

"I am," he finally says. "I hate that part of myself, Emma. I hate that I don't have control over my own mind. There's nothing I can do. Every doctor I've talked to about it has said to keep my stress down, don't get too emotional. But that doesn't always work. Sometimes, it just happens and I can't make it stop."

"It isn't your fault," I say. "It isn't something you chose."

"But it means I'm not as reliable for going undercover as Xavier is," he says with resignation making the words sag.

"He remembers everything. With painful detail. Not just about when he was in prison. But every moment. He'll be able to retain it and tell us about it later. We don't know how often we'll be able to communicate with him. It isn't like he can write it to me in a letter or call me every day, and I definitely won't be able to visit him there."

"I can," Dean says. His eyes brighten slightly, like he's finally found something to reassure and comfort him. "I can visit him. A lot of the guards and administration there know you. Hell, a lot of the inmates know you. I'd venture to guess a good portion of them are behind those bars because of you. And the administration knows your father. Some of them know Sam. But they don't know me."

It's true. He didn't come with me when I went to the prison in the early days of investigating Jonah's disappearance. Dean has definitely had greater visibility among the public since we started working together, but his face isn't nearly as well-known as mine. His career as a private investigator necessitates a level of discretion and anonymity. If he was splashed across TV and ended up in interviews or pictures all the time, he wouldn't be able to investigate effectively for his clients. No one wants a private investigator who is immediately recognizable. Kind of ruins the whole "private" angle.

"You can go to visitation with him," I say and Dean nods.

"Xavier may know the prison and how to suss out all its secrets, but I know Xavier. I can understand him. I know what he needs and how to make sure he stays alright in there."

I know he's right. As much as anyone will be able to keep Xavier safe and healthy from the outside, Dean will. And seeing him regularly will also help Dean feel better.

This is going to be hard on all of us. We've created a tight family and having Xavier not only away from all of us, but in a situation as challenging and even dangerous as prison will be difficult. But he's not a child. We might question a lot of the choices he makes and be indescribably unsure of the reasoning behind other ones, but he can make them for himself.

He's in a much stronger, more stable place now than he was the last time he entered a prison. And Ava tells me he has a mean headbutt. I haven't gotten the full details of how she knows that, but I'm not really sure I want them. At least I can feel confident knowing he isn't going back in fully unprepared. It isn't the same facility he was in, but in his way, he is ready to face what he left behind. He's ready to give meaning to what he went through and make a difference.

CHAPTER FOUR

"HAVE YOU HEARD ANYTHING ELSE FROM JONAH?" DEAN ASKS.

I don't want to talk about Jonah. I don't even want to think about Jonah, not that I really have the option. He's always there in the back of my mind. Since I found out about him and learned what he did to my family, I've never been truly able to ignore him. There have been good stretches, long months when I didn't let him actually come into my thoughts or control my movements. When I refused to let him have any influence on me and refused to waste any of my time focusing on him.

Then there were times like this when I had no choice. It was almost as if he knew when he'd managed to wheedle his way into my consciousness and when I was able to push thoughts of him aside, so he did anything he could to make sure he stayed prevalent. It was a way of controlling me, of forcing the bond he would never make. I hated the game. Even more, I hated thinking about what he might do every second, wondering when his next tragedy would strike. He feeds off chaos and upheaval, all the energy and emotion that arise when there is devastation and confusion.

I know the longer he's out of prison, the more likely it is he will slide back into those patterns. The first time I spoke to him after finding out he had escaped from prison, he told me he still has work to be done. He has unfinished business he needs to fulfill and he won't allow anyone to catch up with him and stop him. Least of all me. Those words have stayed with me. They haunt me because I know the type of business he's in. Finding Jonah is not about a vendetta. It's not about proving myself or even seeking revenge on him. It's about justice.

I won't pretend there won't be some degree of satisfaction and personal fulfillment that will come when I have finally hunted him down and put him back in a cage where he belongs. I owe it to my mother, who he raped and murdered. I owe it to Dean's mother, who he manipulated cruelly in a false game of love that ended in her bloody death. To my ex-boyfriend Greg who he brutally tortured just to push it in my own face. I owe it to all the other people he has hurt and tossed aside along the way.

My biggest motivation is trying to protect whoever else may be in his sights. I don't know who else he might be after, or what work he left unfinished when he was captured. I don't know the plans he had in place, but I know there were some. There always are.

Finding him means stopping those plans from coming to fruition and protecting the people who are already marked to be his victims.

"No," I tell Dean. "After I found that note from him on Christmas, I haven't heard anything else from him. I don't like the sound of him saying my Christmas gift was delayed. Coming from Jonah, that could mean anything."

"It could," Dean agrees. "Maybe he's finally going to tell you the truth about Miley Stanford."

"I doubt it. He already told me more about it than I think he wanted to. He's been holding the rest of the details about her and Serena close to his chest. Besides, if that's all he was going to tell me, there would be no reason for him to delay it. It has to be something else." I let out a sigh. "What about you? Have you made any more headway?"

"I talked to Mark Webber a few more times, but he doesn't remember anything else. Nothing that Eric hasn't already told us. And the police aren't talking. A total surprise, I know. It just doesn't make any sense. The timeline of his disappearance is missing pieces, and it seems like there's nowhere to find those pieces. We know he was stopped by police and performed field sobriety tests. Even though he supposedly passed those without a problem, he was at a bar not long before and the bartender himself said he was completely over-served and wouldn't have been able to do those tests reliably."

"And then his car was found somewhere else," I say.

"Exactly. Another traffic stop, apparently. Only no record of what happened during it. Which tells me he was probably abducted by somebody pretending to be an officer. And if that's the case, the question is whether it was a planned abduction specifically aimed at Mark, or if he happened to drive by the wrong place at the wrong time."

He shakes his head as another part of his brain offers up an alternative thought. "But that doesn't make sense. It was late and the road where his car was found wasn't exactly the most heavily traveled. I highly doubt even the most desperate of abductors would just sit around there waiting for someone of the right description to happen by."

"That's true. And we already know Salvador Marini was far from the most desperate of abductors. He had his sex slaves and his gladiators brought right to him. And Serena was exceptional at what she did. No matter what the reasoning behind her willingness to bring those people to him, she did it with skill and finesse. No one ever suspected her or questioned what she was doing," I say.

"But Serena didn't have anything to do with it," Dean points out. "She was long dead by the time Mark was abducted and Eric was tossed in there along with him. She couldn't have been the one to take him off the side of that road."

"There was a woman, though. The 911 call that alerted the police to you sitting up against that sign was made by his accomplice. It had to have been. And when you were found you said something about hearing a woman scream. You couldn't remember much of anything else, but you did remember that. Serena was dead, but that didn't mean he had given up on having the help he felt like he deserved. Remember, this is a man who referred to himself as the Emperor. He believed he was far more important than any of the mere humans who moved around him. He couldn't be bothered with finding his own victims."

"And he was particular about them," Dean picks up from my thread. "He knew exactly what he wanted. Whoever was helping him didn't choose Mark on a whim. Eric offered himself up as bait by using the information we had about the other gladiator victims to draw in the abductor. Each of the men was chosen for their life circumstances and what they could offer to a fight. That means he was being tracked. I only wonder for how long."

He lets the words hang in the air for a second, his eyes staring off into space like they do when his brain is moving too fast for his mouth to keep up. "Did they see him at the bar? Or was it even before that? The police were called a few different times to report Mark's erratic driving and the car by the side of the road. But then he was fine when he was pulled over. How is that? And if the abductor was following him from the time he was in the bar, where were they while all this was happening?"

I shake my head. "I don't know. But if we can find that out, it might help us better understand what happened to you. I still don't understand how you could step outside of the house to make a phone call and then end up being found by the side of the road without any idea what happened. Your blackouts don't even fully explain it. There's no way to know when you're going to have one of those, and the thought that it was just a convenient coincidence, one that should happen right when you're abducted is ridiculous."

"And it wouldn't explain Mark not remembering what happened, or Eric. Unless intermittent blackouts and memory loss are the features that the Emperor was specifically looking for when it came to his victims, and we just weren't aware that Eric has them, which I highly doubt... No, there was definitely something else at play. If either of them had my same symptoms, we'd have known by now," Dean says. "I'd say it was the alcohol because of what the bartender said, but..."

"But not with the way he was acting on the dash cam footage," I complete his thought.

"Right. Which really only leaves one thing," Dean nods.

"You were drugged," I say.

It's what I suggested early on, but Dean didn't want to hear it. He doesn't want to think about himself as being victimized by the Emperor and his grotesque, inflated desire to reign over others and indulge in a life of pure decadence. Now he's willing to come to terms with it, to acknowledge that something happened while he was standing right outside his own home that made it so he not only couldn't defend himself from being taken and forced into fighting for his life, but that he couldn't remember any of it later.

"He chose me because of Jonah," Dean says. "He knows more about him. I know he does."

"I know," I say. "I'm trying to figure it out."

Salvador Marini is dead, but that hasn't provided Dean with the closure he needs. Too much happened to him in just the short time he was held captive, and we know the other men, including Mark, went through so much hell. Eric got through it because we tracked his signal and rescued him from the underground arena during his first fight. But we know nothing about the man Dean fought. He's never been found. We don't know who it was or what happened to him. That thought alone haunts Dean.

Sam comes into the room and leans down to kiss me.

"Coffee smells good," he starts.

The break in the conversation is welcome and I don't hesitate to move on.

"You won't sleep," I tell him as he makes his way toward the coffee machine.

"That's alright. We can catch up on our holiday cards," he shrugs.

"It's almost February," I say.

"That's never stopped you before," he winks. "Pretty sure Thanksgiving and Christmas is a year-round occasion for you."

I chuckle. "Don't let Xavier hear you say that. The specific order of holidays is important."

"Alright. Then we'll do some Valentine's and play Monopoly."

He grins at me and reaches for a mug.

"Don't you have that talk at the elementary school tomorrow?" I ask. "About responsibility and being a good citizen when they grow up?"

I can't help but laugh at the glare my husband throws me over his shoulder. He shuts the cabinet firmly and stomps back toward the living room.

"I can make you some cocoa," I call in to him.

"Chocolate has caffeine, too," he says. I adore the man. He is a master of the grown-ass male pout.

"I can put marshmallows in it," I offer. "They counteract the caffeine."

"Emma, I don't think that's true," Xavier's voice comes from further in the house. The man's ability to somehow follow a conversation from many rooms away never ceases to amaze me. "Did you read that on the internet?"

Dean finally cracks a smile, shaking his head.

"Thank you, Xavier. No, I didn't."

"I'll take the cocoa," Sam says.

"Xavier?"

"Yes, please. I need to enjoy it now. They won't have cocoa in the hoosegow."

I look over at Dean and he shrugs. "I guess commissary doesn't believe in cozy winter evenings."

"He's going to lose all of his marshmallow absorption skill progress," I say as I make my way to the pantry to get the cocoa and marshmallows.

CHAPTER FIVE

S AM IS WORKING PARTICULARLY LONG HOURS THE NEXT DAY SO I'm glad Xavier, Dean, and my father stayed another night. Dad has to head back to his own house later today to get ready for a job that will put him undercover for at least a week, but Dean and Xavier are planning to stay around Sherwood for another couple of days.

It's a change from the last couple of months when I spent more time at their house than I did at my own. Add in the time I spent in Michigan with Sam and it feels like I've barely been home.

But that is what I needed. With everything going on in our lives, I needed to not be at the house by myself for the long stretches that Sam being gone would have left me. So I joined him in Michigan to help him search for his cousin who had been missing for weeks.

His aunt was panicking at not being able to find her only daughter and they were both frustrated and angry with the police department for negligence in recognizing that she truly was missing and not just choosing to stay out of touch with her mother. There was strange evidence left in her apartment that indicated she had gotten wrapped up in drugs, but both Sam and his aunt Rose insisted Marie would have nothing to do with that kind of life.

It wasn't the time for me to point out that people with drug problems are often overlooked by their families as having a problem because they don't seem like the type, or they seem too healthy, or they are too active, or they are just "normal people" and wouldn't do something like that. I didn't need to tell him. He knows. Sherwood is small, but he has seen his fair share of lives destroyed by drugs.

But it's so much harder to be honest with yourself and recognize the potential for those problems when the person is someone you love. He didn't want to think the cousin he was so close to was suffering from addiction and had spiraled so far into the misery of that life that she had chosen to disappear. It was even harder for him to think of the other reasons why she would have gone missing.

I was with him when he had to face the truth. As much as that image is something I wish I didn't have in my mind, I'll always be grateful I was by his side when her body was discovered. Decomposing in an abandoned warehouse, it was obvious she'd been there the entire time she was missing. According to the responding officers, it was also obvious it was just a standard overdose at play. But that wasn't so obvious to us.

Sam isn't in denial anymore. He isn't pushing back against the idea of his cousin being involved in drugs because it hurts him to think she was going through that. He isn't embarrassed to think such a close member of his family was involved in that life when he devoted his own to law enforcement. Instead, he is pushing back because he can't comprehend it. And neither of us trust the way the police investigating have handled this situation.

They were told she was missing. They were told she wasn't responding to anyone and hadn't been seen. And all they could say was that Marie was an adult and had the right to her own life and her own decisions. She didn't have to answer to anyone or tell anyone where she was or what she was doing. Even if that meant being gone from her apartment for weeks at a time or not answering her phone.

They didn't even bother to do a check of her apartment until there was a crime underway. Neighbors reported seeing a man climb her fire escape and go inside. He was there for a short amount of time, moving around in the dark, then left without explanation. It took that for the police to be willing to go inside. It shouldn't have been that way. I've never heard of a police department refusing to do a wellness check, especially when a person goes so far outside of their usual routine and is clearly missing.

There's so much more to unravel and Sam is working himself to the bone to do it. Though he's not an official part of the investigation, he's grinding himself to his very limits to do all the work Sherwood needs from him and also keep digging into the loss of Marie. There've been times over the last month since finding her that I've been really worried about him. The glimpses of his playfulness are reassuring, but there are far too many moments when he is drawn and exhausted, and I can barely get him to stop investigating to sleep or eat.

Not that I really have room to talk when it comes to healthy sleeping habits and keeping a good sleep schedule. For most of our relationship, it's been him trying to coax me into sleep rather than the other way around. It's been a little better recently, but there are still many nights with too much going on in my mind for me to be able to rest solidly. I'll grab a couple of hours of intermittent sleep, but eventually, it's just too frustrating and I give in to the rushing thoughts and constant flurry of questions piling up in the corners of my mind like dry leaves.

That's what has me in my office in the early hours of the morning. The house is still quiet. It won't be long until Sam has to get up to leave for his day at the school and I've been trying to be as quiet as possible so I don't disturb his fragile sleep. The cup of coffee at the corner of the desk is my third since getting out of bed when the sky was still inky dark.

I've had it suggested to me on a couple of occasions that maybe my sleeping issues have to do with the copious amounts of coffee I drink at indiscriminate times of the day. The suggestion is always made with the twist of the mouth and slightly raised eyebrows of a person who thinks they are not only very smart and insightful but also clever and hilarious for making the observation.

I have a different description for those little quips of judgment. Wrong. And obnoxious. But mostly just wrong.

It doesn't matter if I drink coffee or not. If I stop halfway through the morning or go all the way into the night. If I cut it with milk and sugar or leave it black like I prefer. Or even if I switch out my usual high-octane grind for decaf. I will still struggle with sleep. It wakes me up but doesn't keep me up. And that gives me all the permission I need to never settle for weaker options if I have any choice.

I take another sip as I sift through the papers on my desk again. This is my least favorite part of my line of work. As an FBI agent, I thrive on the investigation. I like to be out in the field, tearing back the layers of a crime and digging down until I find the core of truth. I like identifying the person responsible and hunting them down if necessary. My satisfaction comes from knowing a criminal will be held accountable for what they have done, and victims will get perhaps not necessarily peace and closure, but validation.

But it's not all about going undercover, chasing the bad guys, or finding the little clues that untangle the case. Once the excitement is over and the arrest is made comes this part. The most important part—and the most boring. Preparing for trial.

I'm not usually involved in the trial itself. I'll deliver the suspect and all the information I've gathered, and the detectives and prosecution take it from there. But sometimes I'm asked to be a bigger part of it, helping build the case or testifying. That's what's happening with this case. As both an expert witness and a material witness, I'll be right in the thick of the trial from the preparation all the way through to the end.

"Feeling any more ready?"

I glance over my shoulder and see Sam leaning against the doorframe of my office, a groggy smile on his face. His bathrobe tie is haphazardly tied at the front so it hangs mostly open, revealing his flannel pajama pants and white t-shirt. His hair is a mess and when he runs his hand over it, the pieces stand up on end in all directions. Apparently, he is going to be playing his favorite morning game of seeing just how close to the wire he can come when getting ready and heading out of the house.

I'm alright with that. I like my morning hugs when he still smells like warm sleep and bleached cotton. I get up from my desk for one of them now, snaking my arms into his robe so I can curl up as close to his chest as I can.

"I'm ready," I tell him. "I'm just not looking forward to it."

"I know. But you're doing it for Marlowe," he says, kissing me on the top of the head.

Technically I'm doing it because it's part of my job and a legal obligation now that I've been subpoenaed, but I appreciate the sentiment. It's what I remind myself every time a trial drags on me. Getting the suspect in custody is just the first step. The trial ensures the victim is heard, even if it has to be through other people. And I can be that voice. It's especially important for me to be that voice for Marlowe.

I usually hate the phrase "she had her whole life ahead of her," but it's hard not to think it when it comes to her. Barely into her twenties, beautiful, and talented, Marlowe Gray seemed to have a charmed future painted in front of her. But it was a future that wasn't ever to be experienced. Her death in the first hours of New Year's Day put a harsh final punctuation on a life that turned out to be far more complicated and strained than I ever would have thought.

But her life wasn't the only thing that was complicated. Trying to understand what happened leading up to her death brought out more of the difficulty she faced in her relationships and her career, and the more I pulled the threads I found, the tighter the knots caught and the more they overlapped. It took delving into her relationships with each of the people closest to her and understanding what they offered her—and what they took from her—that eventually shined a light on the fateful path to the edge of the balcony in her hotel room.

And eventually proved there was far more to punish than just the circumstances of her death.

"I heard the production company is trying to speed up the editing and post-production of the series so that the premiere coincides with the trial," Sam tells me.

I nod against his chest, then straighten.

"They're hoping the publicity will gain them even more of an audience and maybe get corporate sponsors to buy additional advertising slots and possibly product placement in the series."

"Product placement? All the filming has been done. How are they going to add product placement if a company decides they want it now?" Sam raises an eyebrow.

"The wonder of computer editing knows no bounds," I shrug. "If they can take footage of Tupac and turn him into a hologram that performs for three days at a music festival, they can sure as hell slip a can of soda into a shot of the kitchen or add a store name in the background."

Sam cups his hand behind my neck and pulls me closer to kiss me on the forehead.

"There's my girl using cultural references from ten years ago as evidence of technological capability."

"It wasn't a hologram."

The sound of Xavier's voice makes Sam jump and he nearly takes me with him as he spins around to look at Xavier standing in the hallway with a canister of raisins in his hand.

"What?" Sam asks sharply, not pleased to be startled.

"Emma, how many raisins are too many to put in a pot of oatmeal?"

CHAPTER SIX

A WHOLE CANISTER.

It turns out that is the answer to how many raisins are too many to add to a pot of oatmeal.

They are also mostly contained in a coagulated lump in the middle of the pot, which means it's not actually a whole can, but the vast majority of ones that dried out when I didn't put the lid back on all the way after sprinkling a few over my raisin bran.

Because I'm the type of woman who further raisins my raisin bran.

I stand over the pot, stirring and adding dribbles of cream to encourage the raisins to break apart and plump up. When they look adequately distributed throughout the oatmeal, if a bit dense, I called the guys in. Setting glass bowls on the round table to the side of the kitchen, I carry the pot over and ladle some into each as Dean and Xavier sit down in their places.

"Morning," Dean grunts.

"Good morning. Have you seen Dad yet?" I ask.

He shakes his head. "I don't think he's up."

I nod and fill my own bowl before setting the pot back on the stove and going to the refrigerator for orange juice. Xavier immediately reaches for the juice when I bring it and three glasses to the table. I hand him a glass and he fills it partway. Eyeing the amount of juice he's poured, he looks over at Dean.

"It's been a while, so I'm not totally up on all the news. Is scurvy a problem in prisons these days?" he asks.

Dean opens his mouth to respond, looks at me as if hoping I'll toss some words in, then looks back at Xavier.

"Not that I know of," he says.

"Good," Xavier says, handing the juice over to me in an apparent decision that since he wouldn't be serving his fake sentence in the bowels of a pirate ship, only half a glass of orange juice would suffice for the morning. "During my time there was a bed bug outbreak." He shudders. "They look like apple seeds." Dean and I watch as he takes a sip of his juice and sets the glass down carefully, then takes a bite of his oatmeal. "I no longer enjoy sliced apples."

I take a few bites of my oatmeal, then remember what Xavier said when he came to the door to the office. Setting my spoon down, I get my phone out of my pocket and pull up a video of the Tupac performance at Coachella that caused such an uproar. The shaky quality of the video puts an underscore on the length of time since the show that Sam teased me for. Either that or it just demonstrated the filmographic skills of drunk girls in crochet bikini tops and jeans cut too far up their thighs to even be referred to as shorts.

That's not just an assumption. After an attempt at sharing a clip of an old TV show resulted in Xavier getting Rick Rolled and not recovering for a week, I've added a quick review process to any time I show him a video. That means I get the privilege of seeing the first few moments of the camera swinging around like it's caught in a windstorm, focusing on a gaggle of the aforementioned festival-goers who scream in response, then finally finding the stage.

I watch the performance for a few more seconds just to make sure, scan back to right after the screaming girls, then turn the phone toward Xavier.

"See?" I ask. "This is what I was talking about."

Something tells me Xavier isn't a Tupac fan from way back, so maybe he didn't know what I was talking about. But the man has proven my guesses about him wrong more times than I can count, so I probably shouldn't be surprised even if he burst into song and performed right along with the dead rapper beamed up on stage. Instead, Xavier doesn't hesitate to shake his head.

"That's not Tupac's hologram," he insists.

"No, Xavier, it is. I know it looks really real, but it's a hologram. Look at the caption."

I point under the video where the title clearly reads 'Tupac's Hologram.'

Xavier takes another bite of oatmeal.

"I could find you a video with a caption that says, 'Rare Albino Naked Mole Rat Mutation,' but it would still just be an earthworm squiggling among some chopped fruit."

"Is that an actual video?" Dean asks.

"Are you saying you think Tupac is alive and he went to Coachella to perform but everyone told the festival-goers he was a hologram so they wouldn't be suspicious, and they all just bought it?" I ask. "And then he's disappeared again for the last ten years?"

This is a surreal conversation and I'm starting to wonder if I actually fell asleep next to my toast and I'm still at my desk right now.

"I don't know who that is, but if he's told everyone he's dead, then I'm sure he is. What I mean is that isn't a hologram. It's Pepper's Ghost."

"No, that's Tupac," Dean says, pointing at the screen. "When he was alive. Not Pepper."

I have to be asleep. This can't actually be happening.

"I still don't know who that is. But that's not what I mean. Pepper isn't a person. Well, he was a person at one point. He created the illusion called Pepper's Ghost in the 1800s. That's what they called it because it was used to make the image of ghosts on a stage. It's in the Haunted Mansion."

Xavier says this with absolute conviction, as if the presence of the trick in the Haunted Mansion should automatically display its street cred.

"How does it work?" Dean asks.

I try to follow as Xavier starts down the long stairwell of describing the optical illusion and the mirrors, lighting adjustments, and hidden rooms necessary to create it originally, and how the advancements in the technology of today have made it so the transparent, ghostly images achieved by Pepper back in the day can now be fully solid and look real. But the further he goes into the spiraling explanations of refracting light and angled transparent film replacing glass and basic mirrors, I lose grip and go back to focusing on my oatmeal.

"A hologram is just a bunch of little bits of light shot out of a projector," he says in conclusion.

"Well, there we go," I say.

Dean's phone rings as we finish breakfast and he heads out of the room to take the call. Xavier helps me clear the table, then goes into the living room while I do the dishes and get a tray of cinnamon rolls out of the freezer to warm up on the counter so I can bake them later.

I walk into the living room to find Xavier sitting in the corner of the couch, digging around in a large black tote bag I've noticed him carrying around the last couple of days.

"What are you doing?" I ask.

"I thought about it, and I can't really expect to be searching around the prison and trying to get the other inmates to talk all day long, so I'm probably going to have quite a bit of time on my hands and should pick up a hobby," Xavier explains, continuing to dig around in the bag.

"Well, first, trying to get the other inmates to talk isn't part of the plan. I don't want you getting on anybody's bad side or inadvertently revealing why you're there," I say. "Second, I think they already have your hobbies all set up for you. Things like reading in the law library or playing cards."

"I've already read it all. And I don't like cards in prison, they tend to be sticky," he says. "I'm hoping this prison offers more handicraft opportunities. I've even come up with a blog to accompany my efforts and possibly use as an in to get the other inmates to connect with me. Or possibly use my platform to transmit coded messages they think I can't figure out and that will reveal the secrets of the prison and their covert criminal operations. Both positive outcomes."

"You want to make a craft blog from prison?" This time it's my turn to raise an eyebrow.

"Mmm-hmmm," he says as Dean walks back into the room and sits down. "I'm Knot Crazy."

"What? I didn't—" I notice Dean shaking his head beside me and I look over at him.

"With a 'k,'" he says. "Knot Crazy."

Xavier finally sits up and I see him brandishing a shiny gold hook and a massive ball of yarn. There appears to be a couple of long rows of stitches making up a fiber snake wrapped around the ball.

"Because it's just a bunch of knots," he says with a bright smile. "Get it?"

"You're going to break into the inmate consciousness and gain access to their secrets through the mystical wonders of... crochet?" I ask.

"He made me a pot holder," Dean says.

"For while I'm gone," Xavier adds as if it explains everything.

I suddenly have an image of a medieval woman leaning out of her turret fluttering a handkerchief at her knight riding off into battle, and then Dean at the kitchen window, waving his potholder to get smoke out after burning something.

"At least you have a plan," I say.

Xavier is leaning back against the couch now, his hook moving rapidly as stitches build up along the row.

"And a blog."

CHAPTER SEVEN

D EAN'S PHONE RINGS AGAIN AND HE PICKS IT UP, CHECKS IT, AND gets up for another call. He's back faster this time but looks more on edge.

"What was that all about?" I ask.

"A case I've been working on," he says. "I've gotten exactly nowhere with it and even though it's only been a few days, the family is getting testy about it."

"The agent?" Xavier asks.

"Agent?" I frown. "Like Bureau?"

Dean nods. "Shawn Reichert. He disappeared ten years ago while he was investigating in a town called Cold Valley."

"Cold Valley?" I echo him. "That doesn't sound very welcoming."

Dean shakes his head. "I don't think that's accidental. It doesn't have the most charming history."

"What's the history?"

"Established by moonshiners," he starts.

"That's kind of cute," I say.

"Who massacred the homesteaders already there, weren't discovered for years, and then had a standoff with police that ended with gunshot-riddled bodies littering the ground and others hanging from the trees in the woods."

"Decidedly less cute. How is there still a town after that?"

"Apparently everyone who was directly involved in the original massacre was killed or had already died, so there wasn't really anything the surviving police could do about it. Some distant family of the original homesteaders came and tried to run the people of the town off, but they were steadfast and stayed. They spread out to the surrounding farms and it hasn't really changed a lot since, other than the annual Fourth of July picnic and Valentine's Day carnival."

"Did you get all of that from a brochure?" I ask.

"Chamber of Commerce website," he tells me. "Do you know anything about him?"

I shake my head, trying to go back in my memories to find mention of his name or anything about him. Nothing comes up.

"It doesn't sound familiar. You said he went missing ten years ago?"

"Yeah. Almost exactly."

"I was still new in the Bureau," I say. "Unless he happened to have been at Headquarters at the time, I wouldn't have met him."

"And you didn't hear about an agent going missing?" he asks.

"It isn't exactly a rare occurrence, Dean. Sometimes they are actually missing. Sometimes they are just deep undercover," I point out. "And sometimes, they're dead."

He glances up at me, regret flickering across his eyes as he realizes the kinds of memories he just brought up for me. I have personal experience with people in my life going missing. Far too much personal experience.

"I'm sorry," he says.

"Don't be. Tell me about this guy. What was he investigating?"

"It's his former fiancée who reported him missing originally and who hired me. Nicole Sims. She doesn't know exactly what he was doing there. He couldn't give her the details, but he said it had something to do with a suspected money-laundering operation."

"Was he undercover?" I ask.

"He was when he went," Dean tells me. "But when he didn't come back and she couldn't get in touch with him, Nicole got in touch with the Bureau and they sent other agents to try to find him. They couldn't and an official investigation was launched, which eventually burned his cover."

"And there hasn't been any sign of him since? No movement on his financial accounts or hits on his social security number?" I ask.

"Nothing. Nothing on his real identity and nothing on the one that was created for him when he went undercover. He was staying at a boarding house there and his room had been cleaned out, everything gone."

"So no one has ever been able to review his notes and find out what came of the investigation," I muse.

"He had recorded some notes and emailed them to himself, but there isn't much in them. There wasn't anything that indicated where he was going if he actually did leave, or if he thought there was someone after him."

"Who are you talking about?" Dad asks as he comes into the room on his way to the call of the coffee maker.

"Shawn Reichert," Dean tells him. "He was an agent…"

"Who went missing," Dad says, drawn away from his pursuit of caffeine by the mention of the missing agent. "Several years ago, right?"

"Ten," Dean says. "Did you know him?"

"I did. We weren't close, but he was a good guy. I remember when I heard he went missing."

"Just to be clear, you heard he went missing at a time when you yourself were missing," I point out.

"That would be accurate," he admits with a hint of a smile.

"Good to know you were keeping up with the news," I say. "Both CIA and FBI. You were busy for a presumed-dead man."

"I had a lot to do."

There's still a little part of me that feels like it's distasteful to joke about the decade of my life I spent without him, terrified about what might have happened to him, and also terrified he was doing it all intentionally. But that's outweighed by how good it feels just being able to joke about it. Being able to be in the same room, to actually look at each other, to speak to each other. To know that we aren't being kept apart anymore. I'll take a little bit of distasteful humor over hurting every time I think about my father any day.

"What did you hear about his disappearance?" Dean asks. "Did anyone have any idea what might have happened to her?"

"I was already under. I didn't hear much," he admits. "I know he was investigating something pretty big. It had been in the works for quite a while. From what I heard, there was a major operation happening in Cold Valley that was linked to something that happened years before.

He believed he was going to take down some serious big-time players and when he left for his undercover investigation, he was really positive about the case. Some of the other guys had been trying to get him to share details with them or tell them what he'd figured out, but he was keeping everything close to his chest."

"Like he couldn't trust anyone?" I ask.

"Something like that," Dad nods. "A couple of my buddies who knew him better said he was very withdrawn leading up to the investigation and then standoffish with any contact during it. They said it was like he didn't want to say anything about what he'd found and have it fall on the wrong ears."

"Did he think there was someone from the Bureau involved?" I ask.

He shrugs. "I don't know if it went that deep, but it's possible. It's also possible he was wary of people linked to other agents, or other investigations. No one knows. But it might mean something. Especially if they're looking for him again."

"I don't think it's a matter of looking for him again," Dean says. "Nicole is still broken-hearted over him. She hasn't moved on. She never got married. No children. Nothing. She has been searching for him on her own, trying to work with police and the Bureau, but she hasn't gotten very far. Officially, he is not even considered a missing person in Cold Valley. The stance there is that he came into town, stayed at the boarding house, and left. The news that he was an FBI agent wasn't released to the media and, according to Nicole at least, the Sheriff was asked to keep that information as confidential as possible as to not compromise the investigation and the progress he might have made."

"That means at least someone at the Bureau thinks he's still alive," I chime in.

Dad nods. "If someone thinks he may have just made the decision to extricate himself from the life he was living during that time until it's safe and beneficial to return, they will do what they can to protect the investigation. They don't want the people being investigated to know what's happening because it could have serious consequences."

"Ten years of continued crime seems like a pretty serious consequence to me," I point out.

"Recurrent crime," Dean specifies. "He was investigating a money-laundering operation and it has apparently surfaced again over the last several months. Of course, without his notes and other evidence, we don't really know what's happening or what he found out."

"Why would he do that?" Xavier asks.

He's been so quiet, contentedly stitching away in the corner of the couch, I almost forgot he was even in the room during my conversation with Dad and Dean. Now I notice the yarn snake is in his lap, his hands continuing to move as if they don't need his mind to tell them what to do, as he looks at us.

"Why would who do what?" Dean asks. "Launder money?"

"No. The reasoning behind that is obvious. Money is covered in germs. It's one of the dirtiest objects any of us ever encounter. Tossing it into the washer every now and then seems like a very good decision from an infectious disease control standpoint. Probably with one of those lingerie bag things to keep it from disintegrating. But I can understand why the Federal government might take issue with the washing of their currency. If it goes missing in the Land of Lost Socks, who is going to replace it? And what if someone uses fabric softener and it turns the money all floppy?"

Dean and I stare at Xavier for several seconds, then turn to each other. It's like both of us are hoping the other one has some sort of explanation that would make sense out of that particular canoe trip along Xavier's stream of consciousness.

"Um," Dean starts like he's trying to find the right words and is filling in time before they get there.

"The agent," Xavier says. "Reichert. Why would he disappear and not leave any information about his case? If this is something he'd been working on for so long leading up to when he actually went to the town, it obviously meant something to him to stop the crimes from happening."

"It did," Dad insists. "He was always very dedicated to his job, but he was also restrained and cautious. Some agents like risk. They are far more willing to jump into things and investigate or pursue aggressively and hope to get the right turnout."

"Really?" Dean asks sarcastically, his eyes sliding over toward me. "I can't imagine someone like that."

I stick my tongue out at him and don't feel bad about it for a second. It might be juvenile, but I didn't find Dean until a couple of years ago. I didn't even know I had a cousin when I was a child and that would have been a more socially acceptable gesture. Albeit one that would have earned me staying inside during recess. I have a whole lifetime of pettiness toward Dean to catch up on.

"Well, he wasn't like that," Dad says. "He understood how fragile cases could sometimes be, and the disastrous outcome of pushing a case too hard, too fast. All that hard work could come crashing down and the entire thing could get ruined. I don't know for sure, but it seems like he might have encountered something like that early in his career. But either way, he always wanted to make sure he was completely ready before he went on any of his jobs. He wanted to make sure he knew what he was doing and he wasn't going to find himself in a tangle or not be able to get what he was after because it was too soon. Even with all the prep in the world, though, sometimes a job just doesn't turn out the way an agent expects. You all know that as well as anyone."

He doesn't need to remind me. With all the twists and unforeseen complications that have gotten in the way of my investigations over the years, I can only imagine what could go wrong in a dangerous mission. But the question is: what exactly was so dangerous about his mission?

Money laundering is a major crime, to be sure, but was there violent crime as well? What could possibly necessitate such a risk to Agent Reichert's life that he would fall off the grid for a whole decade?

"But if Shawn recognized a threat to his investigation or his life, he might have gotten out of the area quickly, but also took the time to make it look like he was just leaving after his visit. Then when he got far enough away that he felt he was safe, he could have gone back to his investigation and research."

"Ten years is a long time to do investigation and research on one situation and without anyone knowing about it," Dean points out.

"Yes, it is," I add.

"I need a different color," Xavier announces, looking over his yarn snake, then stuffing it back in the bag. "I'll be right back." He heads out of the room and pauses, looking back at me. "Emma, just so you know, I was just joking about laundering money in the washing machine."

"Good," I say. "Because—"

"I know those fibers are too delicate and would need to be dry cleaned."

With that, he turns and heads upstairs. I watch him for a few seconds before looking sharply at Dean.

"What?"

He shakes his head, struggling. "I don't know."

"Sam should be here," I say. "He's missing his favorite game: Let's Figure Out What's Happening in Xavier's Brain. Comparable only to the sister show Why the Hell Does Xavier Know That?"

CHAPTER EIGHT

Ten years ago…

"OH, GOD, IT'S A KID. SHIT. IT'S A KID."

"What?"

"A little girl. There's a fucking little girl here."

It sounded like the voices were coming at her from somewhere else. Like they weren't really standing there with her. Maybe this was what it was like for the characters in her storybooks, when she was reading the story and talking about the pretty girls and fanciful dresses in the pictures. Maybe they could hear her and knew what she was saying about them, even though she couldn't see them moving.

She didn't feel herself moving. Maybe that was what it felt like, too.

But she didn't remember ever seeing any of those words in her books. They were the kinds of words she wasn't supposed to hear. Her mother gasped when people said them. She usually didn't even hear the end of them, especially the long one, because hands would clap down over her ears and her head would get buried in her mother to protect her from what was being said.

It used to be her stomach, but now that she was getting older, it was getting closer to her mother's chest. She wondered sometimes when she was pressed there in the smell of laundry detergent, cotton, and rose perfume when it would stop. Would it be when she got to the place over her heart, where softness started to turn to bone? Or when she was level with her collarbone with her nose nestled in the dip where her laugh shook? Or when she had her head on her mother's shoulder?

Maybe it would end when she was tall enough to look her mother in the eyes and cover her ears with her own hands.

One time she asked her daddy why she did that. What was wrong with the words? What made them bad? If they were bad, why did they exist at all?

Daddy told her they weren't bad. There were no bad words. Only bad intentions, bad meaning. She didn't tell her mother. Maybe if she told Mama the words weren't bad, she wouldn't think she needed to press her to her chest anymore and she'd forget what laundry detergent, cotton, and rose perfume smelled like. She'd just keep it a secret. Just for her and her daddy.

"Shit. Is she alive?"

"I don't know. Fuck. I didn't know she was there."

"Wait … wait, I think I saw her move."

He saw it. Whoever was attached to the voice saw the flicker of her eyelids. She'd put every bit of energy she could into that, hoping she'd be able to open her eyes and look at them. She wanted to see the kind of person who would say all those words. It sounded like bad meaning. But she didn't know.

She couldn't get them open all the way, but it was enough to see the faces above her just for a second. They made her afraid. She didn't want to see them and let her eyes close again. They wanted to, anyway.

She knew nothing until she was moving. It wasn't her that was moving, really. It was someone moving her. Something was suddenly soft under her and a blanket covered her. She didn't know she was cold until she felt the blanket warm up her skin. But it also hurt her skin. Maybe there was something wrong with the blanket.

It was enough to make her open her eyes the rest of the way. There were more faces around her now, and behind them were trees. Now she remembered the bike ride. It was almost spring. They always started riding their bikes in the spring. The worst part about winter was when she had to put her bike away, alongside Daddy's in the little cedar house he built for them in the backyard.

Every year she tried to drag it out and make the time longer before he would tell her it was their last ride. The best she did was the year before, when they had a ride on Thanksgiving after they ate. But they put the bikes away in the little house at the same time they were taking the Christmas decorations out of the bigger shed.

Putting the bikes away always meant she had to wait. It wasn't so bad getting through December. She had all of Christmas to distract her and didn't think about it all that much. Then came the end of winter and that was always hard. It was so cold and gray and wet outside. After Valentine's Day, she would start sitting by the window, looking out at the backyard and the little house and the tiny window in the little house that she pretended she could see her bike through. She knew she really couldn't. It was too small and too high off the ground. She pretended she could, anyway.

And Daddy would find her sitting there and he'd tell her spring was coming. It would be there soon and they'd take out their bikes and ride.

It was just that morning she'd convinced him that since there were little leaves on the trees and it hadn't snowed in weeks, it meant it was spring. He told her no, it wasn't spring. It was almost spring. Not quite yet. But she said it was. The leaves said it was spring. New leaves didn't grow in the winter. That was what all the poems about weather they had to learn in school said. Winter was when everything was sleeping. Spring woke them up and brought out the little baby leaves. She could see the bits of green on the big trees behind the house and that meant it was spring. They could ride their bikes.

Daddy laughed at her when she said that. He probably didn't believe her, but she didn't care. As long as they could ride their bikes together.

She wondered where he was now. She wasn't supposed to go anywhere with strangers. But she knew one of the faces. It made her feel better. He'd make everything better.

CHAPTER NINE

Now

I'VE PUT OFF TAKING DOWN THE CHRISTMAS DECORATIONS THIS year. It felt like it took so long to actually get into the holiday spirit and feel like it was Christmas that now that it's over, it's like it barely happened. It's like we didn't get enough of it. Taking down the decorations right after would have left too much festivity unused.

For the first couple of weeks it wasn't that big of a deal. Carrying Christmas on into the new year is popular these days. Then that kind of fizzled out and we transitioned into those couple of weeks of the month that are a holiday celebration gray area. It's not exactly socially acceptable to still have all your strands of Christmas lights up on the porch and the inflatable Santa doing his little swaying booty dance in the middle of the yard every night, but it hasn't quite gotten to the point when you've gone full-on trashy with it.

It isn't until this morning during my jog around the neighborhood that I realize we've gotten to a whole new phase.

Jogging in the morning used to be a routine for me. It was something I did at first to keep myself in shape for work so I could be sure I was in good enough physical condition to chase down criminals and hold my own during the inevitable confrontations that were going to happen. Being able to go undercover in a tight dress and towering heels one day and a boxing gym the next didn't hurt, either. But after a while, I figured out that the ritual of the jog was also good for my mental condition. It cleared my mind and gave me time to think things through in a different way than I did when I was just sitting at my desk or pacing the floor. As much as I cringe even thinking this phrase and using it non-ironically, jogging became my "me-time."

My dedication to daily jogs comes in waves. Sometimes I don't even think about the pair of running shoes tossed in the back corner of my closet for long stretches. Sometimes my sports bra has been relegated to the summer days that are so hot even the air conditioner can't keep me from feeling like the time I was making fudge and stirred it with a non-heat resistant spoon. But then I remind myself why I did it in the first place, or I can't think, or I ate too many cinnamon rolls—and I'm back at it.

This morning's inspiration was having far too many thoughts for my brain to hold and process through, and sure enough, that had me pulling on my shoes and heading out onto the sidewalk this morning. For the first couple of blocks, I'm not paying much attention to what's around me. My brain is still whirling with everything: Marie's disappearance and death and everything in that situation that didn't make sense, and Xavier offering himself up to find out what was going on within the prison and try to stop it from happening. On top of this, there are still so many questions about Serena, Miley Stanford, the Emperor, and the victims he left scattered across several states. There's still the mystery of what happened to Dean and what he still doesn't know about his abduction. Which reminds me of his current case about Agent Reichert. And of course, lurking behind it all somewhere in the shadows, Jonah.

I finally turn a corner and look up to realize there aren't any Christmas lights to be seen. All the inflatables are gone. The terrifying manger scene one of my neighbors down the street created out of scarecrow frames that looked like ghosts wearing robes descending on the plastic baby Jesus isn't even in its spot anymore. Then I see it. A white flag with big pink and red hearts posted out beside Julia Delray's perpetually perfect little cottage at the far end of the neighborhood.

It's closer to Valentine's Day than it is to Christmas.

I have officially tipped over from hanging on a bit too long to that space where if you have garlands above your door and a wreath on your mailbox, the neighbors start checking the newspapers at the end of the driveway to make sure you're not dead inside the house.

As I jog back home I think about the couple of times I've walked outside to find Janet standing in her yard smiling at me, or when she dropped by just to say hello. I wonder if those instances really were her just being neighborly and feeling the holiday spirit, or if she'd been appointed by the rest of the neighborhood to check in on me and make sure Sam and I were still alright.

This is great motivation to get me to break down the decorations. I start with the outside and quickly decide I'm leaving the lights for Sam. He's the one who put them up, so he's the one who can crawl around detaching the staples and winding the cords around so they don't end up the tangled mess that seems to be a light strand's destiny.

Once I've put everything back in the convenient green and red plastic totes that fit nicely on the shelves in the upgraded shed Sam put outside, I head inside. What started as a jog in the chill has ended with me dripping with sweat and feeling simultaneously cold and overheated. I feel I can now commiserate with the lasagna Bellamy once served when we were in college that hit the table both boiling hot on top and frozen in the middle.

After a shower and a reviving snack, I set myself to the task of removing Christmas from the inside of the house. Dean and Xavier went home to Harlan yesterday and I'm going tomorrow so I can be with him for one day before bringing him for his self-surrender. I keep wanting to call him. Not for any particular reason, just because I know very soon I'm not going to have the option anymore, so it's almost as if I'm trying to stuff a bunch of calls in ahead of time.

I keep stopping myself. Not just because I don't know what I would say if I did call him other than just chatting with him—which could turn into a very long commitment knowing Xavier—but also because I want to give him his normalcy for a little longer. He needs the time to just be in his home with Dean, doing what they do every day, preparing in whatever way is best for him. He's been steady and strong since we started talking about this plan, but now is not the time for me to test that and end up upsetting him.

The Christmas tree is naked, the ornaments are nestled carefully away in boxes and more color-coordinated totes, and I'm working on the knick-knacks and other smaller decorations set around the house. These are the things I often forget I have from season to season. Christmas decorations are like that sometimes. It's like they populate in attics and storage rooms without any clear origin. You think you know every piece of your collection, and then the next year you stumble on a blown glass ornament of a taco wrapped in multi-used newspaper from years before and have no idea where it came from or why.

Sam calls while I'm rewrapping a couple of these types of decorations and finding corners of boxes for them. I answer and hold the phone between my shoulder and ear so I can keep up with my progress. I love decorating things, but I'm never as enthusiastic about putting them away. What I need is the promise of a new bit of decoration to put out to help me over the hump of getting Christmas officially behind me.

Maybe if Xavier can convince the prison that crocheting is a good life skill and therapeutic outlet rather than a potential opportunity for inmates to craft shiny metal shanks and bespoke nooses, he can use his time in there to make me a throw for the couch.

"I left all the lights on the house," I tell Sam when I explain to him what I'm doing. "And I think there might still be a couple of the little lawn ornament things around. I thought I got them all, but it doesn't seem like all of them are in the box."

"I'll get them when I get home," he says. "It should be an early evening."

"Good. I'll make dinner."

We chat about what he might want to eat, get a couple of shouted suggestions from some of the guys at the Sheriff's office, and then say our goodbyes. I hang up hoping those suggestions don't equate him coming home with a train of extras for dinner. Not that I don't like the other officers, I'm just not in a domestic enough mood today to make meatloaf, a roast chicken, pasta with meatballs, and a pizza on a moment's notice. Right now, I'm feeling like it might be a giant salad and loaded baked potato kind of night.

I finish packing up the decorations and add the boxes to the stack I have staged near the steps leading up to the attic. Finally, it's time to break down the tree and the season will officially be over. Except for the lingering outdoor lights, of course. But now that he has been informed, those are officially Sam's problem. Not mine.

Even without any ornaments or garland on it, the tree looks beautiful with the glimmering lights and for a few seconds, I just let myself enjoy it before unplugging. Now it's just a matter of disconnecting the three parts of the tree and stashing them away in their handy bag. I'm not an especially small woman so breaking down an artificial Christmas tree has never been quite the struggle for me that various commercials and lifestyle home shopping channels would lead you to believe. But it's still nice for the whole process to only take a few seconds.

With all that finished, I head to the kitchen to get dinner started. I'm feeling particularly accomplished for the day by the time Sam comes through the door. He comes into the kitchen and presses a cold kiss to my lips.

"Want some tea to warm you up?" I ask, already making my way toward the pantry to get the tin of his favorite tea bags.

"That would be great. Thanks, babe. Do I have time for a shower before dinner?"

"You should," I say. "Go hop in. I'll bring your tea in to you in just a minute."

"Ah," he says dramatically like he's letting out a big, satisfied sigh. "Nothing says gruff and manly like hot tea drinking in the shower."

I laugh. "Don't think I don't know you use my loofah, too."

He comes up behind me and wraps his arms around my waist, nuzzling his face into my ear.

"And I'm totally going to use that rainforest body wash stuff you have in there."

"That's my man," I say.

He kisses me and starts down the hall toward the bathroom, already stripping out of his uniform as he goes. Like me, he prefers the bathroom down here to the one upstairs closer to our bedroom. The proximity to the kitchen, my office, and the laundry room makes it an appealing choice.

"I got all the lights taken down, by the way," he calls to me. "I went ahead and did it before I came in. And you were right, you did miss one of the lawn ornaments. But I couldn't figure out where it went in the boxes. I didn't even really recognize it."

I laugh, remembering my same thought about the decorations in the living room.

"Where did you end up putting it?" I ask.

"There wasn't any room for it in any of the outdoor decoration totes, so I just brought it inside for you to look at. It's in the living room."

The bathroom door closes and a few moments later, the shower turns on. I use the hot water feature on the coffee machine to get his tea steeping. Scooping up a spoonful of honey from the jar we got at a local farm over the summer, I drop the spoon into the tea and bring it into the bathroom. Sam's proclivity for extremely hot showers has the bathroom steamed up already. I open the curtain enough to hand the teacup to him and let my eyes wander around on him for a bit.

My husband might prematurely remove the wallpaper from the bathroom with his Satan's front stoop shower preferences, but I sure do like looking at him.

CHAPTER TEN

THE DECORATION SITTING ON THE COFFEE TABLE DEFINITELY FALLS into the Christmas UFO category. Unidentified Festive Object.

I stare at it sitting there, trying to place where it even was in the yard. I don't remember putting it in place and I can't even visualize where it would have fit in. It's a great piece. Designed to look like a large version of one of the antique glass ornaments shaped like a hexagon with mirrored sides and a Christmas scene on the inside, its bright metallic red and green colors would be the perfect addition to the rest of the decorations throughout the lawn. It's beautiful and just my style. I would think I would remember that particular decoration and choose a special place for it so it could be seen.

Only, apparently, I didn't. I pick it up and turn it around in my hands a couple of times. The entire thing stretches from my fingertips to the middle of my forearm. Large for something I might have inside the house, but actually fairly small for a decoration that would be outside.

"Do you know where it's supposed to go?" Sam asks, coming into the room in the bathrobe he keeps in that bathroom for when he doesn't grab clothes before his shower.

"No," I shake my head. "I don't even remember putting it out there. Where did you find it?"

"On the ground beside the porch," he says. "It must have been in one of the bushes or hanging from the edge and fell off."

"We don't have any other decorations like this," I point out. "It's weird that there's just one."

An uncomfortable feeling is starting to build in the pit of my stomach. I remember the note I found Christmas morning, the one from Jonah promising my gift would be coming soon. I examine the ornament more closely, running my fingers along the seams between the panels and looking closely at it from every angle.

"What's wrong?" Sam says.

"It isn't our ornament," I say. "We didn't put this out there. It's from Jonah."

"He put it out there with the note?" Sam asks. "Why would he say your gift was delayed if he was putting it out there at the same time?"

"He must have come again," I say. "He wanted me to find it. In his mind he probably thinks it's a cute surprise."

"I was expecting something else," he mutters. "I'm not sure what, but definitely not just a decoration."

"I don't think it is just a decoration," I say.

While Sam goes to the bedroom to get dressed, I continue to turn the piece around in my hands, trying to figure out its purpose. It wouldn't make sense for Jonah to just give me a decoration like this. Especially not to hide it behind the bushes next to my front porch. He obviously has no problem with me knowing he comes close to, or even into, my house.

He wanted to call my attention to the decoration when I found it. Hiding it was his way of showing me it was something other than what it looked like. I've learned over the years that very few of the things Jonah says and does are actually what they initially seem on the surface. It's not the same as with Xavier. With Xavier, it's a matter of everything filtering through his perspective and the way his mind works from moment to moment.

With Jonah, it's just another way to control and manipulate. He knows if he can twist everything into a riddle or a metaphor, if everything can be a little more complicated than it really is, he can keep hold of a person's mind.

As I go over the seams again, I notice slight bumps along two sides. I look closer and realize they are tiny hinges, set into the space between the panels so that they are almost imperceptible. These two panels are doors. There's no knob or handle in place to open the doors, so instead, I use my fingernails at the top of one panel to pry it out of place, then when it lifts, I open the other.

When the two front panels open, the top loosens, lifting out of the way so that the hexagon unfolds and I can look inside. This is the kind of decoration that should have a cheerful scene inside, like children ice skating or a Christmas tree surrounded by presents. Instead, there are pictures.

But they aren't nostalgic images of Christmas or even beautiful wintery scenes. It takes me a few seconds to realize what I'm looking at, and when I do, I'm on my feet rushing into the bedroom to Sam.

"Look at this," I tell him, shoving the ornament toward him.

Sam drops his sweatshirt down over his head and takes the ornament from me.

"It opens," he observes.

"Yeah. And look what's inside."

He stares at the pictures the same way I did, confused at first by what he's seeing, then the realization settles in.

"Is that Salvador Marini?" he asks.

I nod. "And his house. Two pictures of him alive, two pictures of his house, and two pictures of him dead. They look like the ones taken by the responding officers the morning he died."

"Why did he send those to you? Is this his way of commemorating a favorite moment of the year? Other people do those social media slideshows or collages or fill memory boxes. Jonah has a custom-made ornament to mark the death of one of his enemies?" Sam asks.

"He hated Marini, but I would hardly say he was notable enough of an enemy to do something like this. If he was going to commemorate the deaths of everybody he was glad was dead, we wouldn't need to do any decorating for ourselves. There would be enough disturbing ornaments scattered across our yard to warrant being in one of those tacky light shows." I shake my head. "No. This means something else. It isn't just that he's dead. He's trying to tell me something."

"What could he be trying to tell you? He already explained that Serena was working for Marini as a way to siphon off money and power for Leviathan. That the two men were rivals and Dean was abducted for one of the gladiator fights as a way of getting to Jonah."

"I know," I acknowledge. "But he's been cagey about Marini's death since the first day he found out about it. Remember? He was angry about it and he specifically pointed out how strange it was," I say.

"But it really wasn't that strange, Emma," Sam counters. "We've been over this. The man was about to surrender himself after confessing to murdering Serena when she was supposed to be helping Jonah escape from prison, and to the deaths of the sex slaves and the men he pitted against each other. He said in his confession he was burdened by his guilt and just wanted to get it off his chest. That's a lot of stress to carry around. Stress like that is dangerous for the heart. Not to mention a man who referred to himself as the Emperor probably didn't have the healthiest approach to eating or exercise all the time. He was trying to do the right thing as much as anyone can do after murdering more than a dozen people, by telling the truth so no one would have to wonder about it anymore. The universe just caught up with him first."

He sounds like he has it all tied up in his head as he hands the ornament back to me. I shake my head. I'm not convinced.

"No. That's not what this is. I told you the second I saw his autopsy pictures I knew there was something wrong. I don't know what it is, but there's something more to this."

I look at the pictures again. One of him standing in the foyer of his house that looks like it might have been taken for a magazine or to accompany an interview. One of him standing behind a podium at an event, his hands raised up beside his head as he's making some sort of emphatic speech. One of just his foyer. One of the outsides of his house. Two of him lying dead on the foyer floor, taken from different angles.

They don't mean anything to me. They were chosen for a specific reason, but I can't trace it.

"Babe," Sam murmurs, putting his arms around me to try to get me to focus on him instead of the pictures. "Don't get wrapped up in this. He's messing with you. Let's just have dinner and relax. I'll get those boxes up to the attic tomorrow."

I want to keep twisting the pictures around in my head like a Rubik's cube until they click into place, but I nod and let Sam take the ornament from my hands and set it aside.

CHAPTER ELEVEN

THE NEXT DAY I LEAVE BEFORE SUNRISE FOR HARLAN. IT'S A LONG drive, but one I've gotten very accustomed to over the last year. It's one of those drives I can check out during, like my car already knows where it's going so I don't really need to think too much about it. Since many of the roads I travel down to get there are rarely used, the pressure of constantly navigating other drivers and trying not to end up in a crash is greatly reduced. Like jogging, it's another time for me to think.

Today I'm so deep in thinking about the pictures the drive seems to go by in a fraction of the time. I'm tossing the images around in my head, waiting for one of them to spark something or to give me some meaning, attempting to use them as illustrations for everything I remember about Salvador Marini and the things I heard about him. Especially from Jonah.

But nothing comes up and before I know it, I'm pulling up in front of Xavier's house. He's on the porch, bundled up in what looks like several layers of quilts as he slowly moves back and forth in the porch swing.

"Good morning," I call out as I climb the steps. The blankets are wrapped so thoroughly around his head I can only see a small section of the middle of his face. "Please tell me you haven't been out here all night."

"I haven't been out here all night," he says back to me without hesitation.

"Okay. Now, is that true or are you just saying it?" I ask.

"It's true," he says. "I've only been out here for a few hours this morning. Not last night."

I nod. For Xavier, that could very well mean he's been out here since just after midnight.

"Aren't you cold?"

Lumps pop out from his sides as he moves his hands.

"Blankets," he says. "My nose isn't so warm, though."

I smile at him and nod my head sideways toward the door. "Why don't we get it inside and over a hot cup of coffee to warm up?"

He nods and starts the process of getting off the swing. Its movement, combined with the copious layers of fabric around him, makes it a bit of a touch-and-go situation, and I take a couple more steps toward him to act as a spot. He doesn't need to show up to prison already incapacitated because he's broken bones falling off a porch swing.

I finally get Xavier inside and he shuffles through the house molting. Every few steps he sheds another layer of blankets until we've gotten to the back of the house and he only has two draped around his shoulders. Dean has the coffeemaker going and skillets of eggs, bacon, and potatoes are already cooking on the stove. Beside it on a hook is a navy blue crocheted potholder. Seeing it tugs at my heart and I have to look away.

For today, I'm not letting myself be sad. That's the responsibility of tomorrow's Emma. She can deal with the conflicting emotions of sending Xavier undercover and the realization that I don't clearly remember what it was like to have a life before him. Obviously, I know I did. I have memories of being a child and my early career, of first returning to Sherwood and first encountering Dean. I know both of them came into my life late, but there are a lot of times when I look back on memories of my earlier years and there's a part of me wondering what they were doing and where they were, like my mind is trying to insert them into my consciousness. I figure they're there, just in another room or off on an investigation.

But today what matters is I have them. I have both of them and I'm going to spend the day with them and not allow myself to be upset.

It's why I won't ask Xavier why he was out on the porch for hours that morning. I already know the answer and don't need to hear him say it. The prison he's going to doesn't have a yard the inmates are allowed to roam freely. He will get an hour or two outside every week, and even then he'll be confined to a cage. Unless he's being transferred in between buildings, fresh air is not going to be an amenity he'll enjoy during his stay.

The three of us spend the day together and I'm glad they did as much preparing as they have leading up to today. It means we don't have to dwell on the situation and instead can just focus on having a good time and feeling like everything is going to be fine. Xavier already believes that. He's not afraid. He's not anxious. He has no question in his mind that he's doing the right thing and it will all work out without issue. Dean and I aren't getting through it as smoothly.

Our shared concern for Xavier is what has us both up late. I'm sitting in the den staring into a fire roaring in the fireplace when Dean comes in. He hands a cup of tea down to me and I give him a weak smile of thanks as he sits down in the chair diagonal from me.

"What case are you doing your best to think about so you don't have to admit you're worrying about Xavier when he made you promise you wouldn't?" he asks.

I nod, sipping my tea. "The Emperor." I tell him about the ornament and the pictures inside. He listens silently, his face emotionless. "Sam thinks it's basically a morbid scrapbook to commemorate Marini's death."

"But you don't think so," Dean infers.

"I don't. I know he hated Marini, especially after he found out he murdered Serena. But it wasn't nearly as sentimental as people might think. I know he saw her differently than he saw a lot of his followers and he was more attached to her, but this wasn't a warm and fuzzy kind of connection. He rescued her from the family that used her as a pawn and as payment for debts. He killed her brother and took her into Leviathan. But it wasn't because she softened his heart or suddenly showed him the error of his ways. He did it because she was the closest thing he'd ever seen to a female version of himself.

"He told me he could see in her eyes what she was. That she was a calculating, powerful, and inherently dangerous woman who would happily play his little twisted games and tatter lives as they went. He was angry that Serena was gone, and probably sad to the capacity he could be, but it wasn't something that would inspire him to make an art piece about her murderer. He doesn't need to express his emotions interpretively. And after his death, he told me this wasn't over. That I still needed to find out what happened to Miley."

"I thought you said he'd told you everything about her," Dean says.

"Not everything. Everything I think he's willing to tell me. But he doesn't know what happened to her. I know he's said that before about things and was lying, but this time he seemed genuinely pissed that Marini was dead and he didn't have answers about Miley."

"I still don't understand," Dean says. "Jonah put Serena into Miley's life. He helped her steal Miley's identity and use it to stay out of sight from her family. How would he do that if he didn't know what happened to Miley?"

"Remember, Miley's parents are career criminals on the run. They aren't in this country because if they were, they would be in prison. Jonah knows more about them and what they did, but he won't tell me because he promised to tell me his truth and the details about them are theirs."

"That's a hell of a loophole," Dean says.

"Yes, it is. But I know there's more to this. When he was first telling me about Miley and admitting he knew who she was, he said she was lost and that he lost her. He didn't say she was killed or that she ran away or anything like that, but that he *lost* her. In fact, he insisted he didn't kill her. Not only does that mean he had something to do with her going missing, even if it was indirect involvement, he was responsible for it in some way," I say.

"Her parents left Jonah in charge of their daughter when they ran off to Europe to dip the Feds?" Dean raises an eyebrow. "Had they never met him? What the hell kind of parents would choose Jonah to be their child's guardian?"

"The kind who would need someone to be the guardian of their child while they were running from the law," I point out.

"He was her scary godfather."

Both of us jump slightly at the sound of Xavier's voice. He has a fantastic knack for sneaking into a situation without realizing he's sneaking. There are times I'm tempted to believe one of the little gadgets he invents enables him to vaporize and appear in other locations.

Dean looks at him, then back at me, opening his arm sharply to the side to indicate Xavier with an open palm.

"Exactly. He was her scary fucking godfather."

"Miley was a rich girl who had everything handed to her throughout her entire life and was able to do anything she wanted, whenever she wanted. I hardly think that counts her story among the great retellings of Cinderella," I say. "But it brings me right back to wondering what her disappearance has to do with Marini. Jonah was the one who brought her up when I told him that he was dead. He was the one who said this whole thing isn't over because he still doesn't know where Miley is or what happened to her."

"Didn't he think Serena was Miley?" Dean asks.

"Yes," I say. "That's what he called her and he believed Miley's house was Serena's. Which tells me Miley wasn't one of his victims. He wouldn't kill someone and then be convinced another person who had taken that person's identity was that person."

Just saying it is confusing. But Xavier shrugs as he drops down on the floor to sit in front of the fire.

"Not necessarily."

"What do you mean?" I ask. "Miley went missing in March, then Serena took over her identity that summer. You think it's possible he went through so many women he would just forget one of his victim's names and entire life story?"

"Probably not if he knew them to begin with. Who's to say he did?"

CHAPTER TWELVE

H IS WORDS SETTLE OVER ME UNCOMFORTABLY AND I LOOK OVER AT Dean. The expression in his eyes seems to reflect some of what I'm feeling.

"When Serena got the Emperor's victims for him, she changed her identity and personality to appeal to them. She went to them rather than the other way around. He didn't specifically choose the women," I say. "He told Serena what he wanted. He referred to it as praying to his goddess. That was how she chose the names that she used, and how Salvador posed the bodies after they were dead. She was in custody when Miley disappeared, but the gladiator fights didn't start when Serena was around. Salvador had someone after her and obviously had someone before her, too."

"And whoever it was might have used the same method. I have a feeling somebody like him wouldn't want to get too cozy with his victims. They weren't people to him. He wouldn't care about their names or their lives," Dean notes.

"I think that's a fair assumption," I nod. "In fact, I would venture to say that's part of it. He wouldn't want to know anything about them because it wouldn't be important. All that would matter is what they look like and the specific details he was after. He wanted a product, not a person. Which means if he was after a certain type, say a spoiled princess with independence issues, he very well could have ended up with Miley being delivered up to him on a silver platter."

"And when she went missing, Jonah might have suspected the Emperor and put Serena in Miley's place to not only protect Serena…"

"But find out what happened to Miley," I complete the thought. "Holy shit."

"I don't think anyone is getting a happily ever after with this one."

"Depends on what you consider happy," Xavier remarks.

I let out a long breath. "It makes me wonder if that is really what happened. If that had something to do with Salvador wanting to go after you, Dean. He obviously hated Jonah for some pretty valid reasons, at least valid in the world they live in. But he'd already killed Serena for her part in manipulating him for Jonah's benefit. It seems like a lot of effort to go to just to continue tormenting him."

"Unless it wasn't a punishment," Dean says.

"It was a threat," Xavier adds.

"He left you alive," I point out. "And didn't keep you for more fights, which he could have done without a problem. Other men, like Mark, were kept for multiple fights. Most likely until they died or were so badly injured, they wouldn't be able to continue combat of any real entertainment value, then they were brought and killed somewhere. So far, only a couple of survivors have been found, and they are in very bad shape. You were hurt, but not like them. It hadn't made sense to me that he would have you taken and then dump you so shortly after."

"I escaped," he says.

"Maybe," I say. "That's what I thought. It's what we all thought. But we don't know that for sure. All we know is that you were found by the side of the road and you think you remember running. That 911 call was his accomplice. I know it was. Like Xavier pointed out, there was no sound of wind. No sound of other cars. It was a fairly empty stretch of road, but if her car was going by, there would most likely be others. It means she wasn't standing by the road and she wasn't in her car. She knew you were there and she didn't have to call the police. That was all intentional."

"To send a message to Jonah?" Dean asks.

"It makes sense. Serena knew more about Marini than we know. She knew he killed Miley and what happened to her body. Even though she wasn't the one to facilitate it, she could have manipulated the information out of him under Jonah's orders. Marini found out about her connection to Jonah and knew she was going to tell him about Miley's death. It likely wouldn't take much to confirm Miley's identity and the link between Jonah and her parents. He would know she was going to give him the information and likely tip off the police," I say. "Killing Serena wouldn't be enough to cover that."

"And going after Jonah himself would be a suicide mission. He wanted to continue to indulge all his sick Emperor fantasies and needed to stay alive and out of prison to do that," Dean adds.

"So he thought he'd threaten Jonah into submission by showing him what he could do to you. Serena was already dead and we don't have all of the evidence she likely gathered about him. Holding your life over his head was what he had left," I say.

"But he confessed," Dean counters. "He confessed to all those murders."

"And then ended up dead on his foyer floor," I point out.

"I thought he died of a heart attack," Xavier says.

I think about the pictures in the ornament and the comments Jonah made about Salvador. He was angry about his death, frustrated the vicious man wasn't going to prison. But he also didn't seem convinced everything was exactly as it seemed.

"I'm not so sure," I say. I think for another second. "Dean, when you were talking about what you do remember about that day, you said you heard a gunshot. But you weren't shot."

"I just remember the sound," he says. "I don't remember anything else about it. I don't even remember if I was running or if I was at the arena."

"Could it have been the other gladiator?" I ask. "There had to be someone you were fighting against, and there hasn't been anyone found with injury patterns that indicate he was involved in the fights."

"Do you think I could have shot him?" Dean asks, his voice powdery with worry. "There were weapons in the arena when Mark and Eric were there. There could have been a gun during my fight. I might have used it to get out."

"Dean, right now you can't worry about that. We need to find the man who was in that arena with you. A more thorough search needs to be done of the area around the arena, and where you were found. If we can find him and figure out what happened to him, it might help us find

Salvador's accomplice after Serena," I say. "I'll call Wheeler and Simon in the morning."

Dean looks up at the big wooden clock sitting on the mantle. "It is morning."

Xavier leans back so he can look at the clock from his vantage point on the floor.

"It is. Eleven more hours of freedom. I should probably get some sleep."

Dean and I look at each other, then back at him and nod.

"We all should," I say. "I'll make breakfast in a few hours."

He stands up and looks into the fire for a few more seconds. "It really is beautiful, isn't it?"

"The fire?"

He glances over his shoulder at me.

"Freedom." He walks toward the door leading to the stairs. "Good morning, Emma. Good morning, Dean."

"Good morning, Xavier," we say and watch him walk back toward his room, lights in the walls illuminating as he goes, leading him along the way.

CHAPTER THIRTEEN

'M NOT SAD WHEN I WAKE UP A COUPLE OF HOURS LATER.

I expected to be. I worked so hard not to think about the whole situation yesterday that I figured I'd wake up this morning and have the entire weight of what was about to happen crushing down on me. I know this is happening because of me. Not because it was originally my idea, but because he's doing it for me. That's enough to make me want to call the warden and end this.

It's because he's doing it for himself that stops me. He wants this.

When I look at him sitting across from me at the granite island in the middle of the kitchen, trying to cut through the towering stack of pancakes he built up on his plate without knocking it over, I realize just how lucky I am. That's something I spent a lot of my life not feeling. In fact, a good portion of my life was spent wondering who had a hexed doll of me sitting in their bedroom surrounded by talismans and with a pin stuck through my heart. I was willing to accept it was the lot I had in life and the path that put me into the Bureau. I didn't pity myself or spend much time dragging around asking why it had to be me. I just knew that was my lot in life. But now, every single memory of struggle has just made me appreciate all the more the ones when my scars aren't the first thing on my mind.

With the tip of his tongue sticking out of the corner of his mouth in concentration, Xavier carefully slides his knife through the pancakes until it gets to the plate and goes to work on the other side of the wedge. Finally, he succeeds and grins as he attempts to lift the entire stack of pieces into his mouth. He pauses halfway and reconsiders, slipping several of the pieces from the fork so he can put the rest into his mouth comfortably.

I laugh to myself and go back to eating my own breakfast. We linger over the food for far longer than we usually would, then clean up together. Time is running short before we need to leave to get to the meeting point.

"This house is going to seem really big when he's not here," I say.

Dean nods, looking around. "It already echoes. Though, some of that might actually be him. Sometimes I'm not sure."

"Do you know about all of the gadgets and traps?" I ask. "If any of them surprise you and you don't have your phone on you, you might end up in a bad spot until someone stumbles on you."

"He gave me a list," Dean says. "I'm not totally convinced they're all on there, but it gives me a good overview. There are just parts of the house I'm going to avoid."

"That's good because I'd probably be the someone stumbling on you, and I'm just not up for all that right now."

"But you might be at some point in the future?" he asks.

"Meh," I tease, giving half a shrug, then a grin as I take a sip of my coffee.

Dean looks over my shoulder and I turn to see Xavier standing at the doorway. He's dressed and polished, looking like he just walked out of a courtroom, exactly as he should.

"How do I look? I went with the gray. Gray seemed appropriately remorseful. I was considering blue, but that seemed too festive. And the brown was too cuddly."

"Well, nothing is more festive than midnight blue," Dean nods.

"The gray is perfect. Do you want to go over your story again? Just to be sure?"

We've gone over his cover story with him several times. He has all the information he could possibly need to answer any questions an inmate might throw at him. His charge, his sentence, the name of his lawyer, the judge. All the dots were laid out so any inmate who wanted to go to the effort of connecting them could do it with abandon and end up with a perfect image of Xavier standing in a prison uniform.

He rattles off the story, then I ask him questions and he responds to them. Of course, it's perfect. I didn't expect anything less.

"I'll be there to visit you next week," Dean says. "And I'm sending money to put on your books as soon as they give me your inmate number."

"Thank you," he says. "You know what you need to do, right?"

"I've been studying the plans so I don't run into anything," Dean says. "And I stopped your catalogs. I already mailed a bunch of stamps so they should be showing up to you soon. And if you convince the warden to let you start your crochet club, I'll bring you yarn. I've already sourced plastic hooks in various sizes so they will be less dangerous."

"And?"

"And I promise I'll take good care of all the starters," Dean says. "I have their feeding schedules posted on the refrigerator, an order of four different types of flours are being delivered tomorrow, and I even got a set of brand-new jars for transferring."

"Just remember, Dough Derek is being dehydrated for survival purposes and will need to be flaked in a few days," he says.

That's when all the emotion of what's happening hits me. It crashes down on me and I gasp back tears. Xavier looks at me, bewildered.

"Don't worry, Emma. Dough Derek is going to be fine. Dehydrating just means we'll be able to bring the flakes with us if we are in survival mode and reconstitute it for baking." He crosses the room to me and rubs my arm comfortingly. "He's going to be okay."

I nod. "I know."

"Then why are you so upset?"

"I'm just going to miss you," I say.

"You are?" he asks, genuinely sounding surprised.

"Of course I am. Why would you ask that?"

"I'm easily forgotten," he says.

I scoff. "Xavier, that is not true. I don't think it's an exaggeration to say most people have never met anyone like you. It would be pretty difficult to forget you."

"What I mean is people don't tend to keep me for long. I'm forgotten about when it's convenient. People don't have space for me in their minds or their lives."

"Xavier..."

"No, Emma, it's true. I've accepted it. It makes it easier to admit that I don't really need people or think much about most of the ones I come in contact with. Most people stay away from me. The ones who don't see something in me they need. I'm adaptable that way. I'm useful until they don't have that need anymore, and then they can move on. I'm temporary. I always have been temporary. Andrew was different. He kept me until he couldn't. So did Millie. Everyone else leaves. I'm always there to see a phoenix burn, but I never see them rise from the ashes," he says.

"Xavier, I have burned a thousand times and you have always been there when I came back. I don't know if I could if I didn't know that you would be," I say.

"What she said," Dean adds. "I'm just not as good with words."

An hour later, the three of us are standing at the end of a rarely used road near the cornfields. I'm always brought back here. No matter how many times I've hoped I won't have to see it again, or how much it twists my stomach and squeezes my heart to remember everything that has happened in this place, it always seems to bring me back.

This time it's to meet up with the agent that Eric assigned to transfer Xavier into the warden's custody. He doesn't know all the details of what's happening, but Eric assured me he has discretion and will be invisible in the situation. That's exactly what we need. I can't bring him to the prison. And it isn't like we can put Xavier in a taxi and send him to the courthouse to grab a ride to the Big House. Getting him on the inside is one of the most delicate parts of this plan and it has to be handled carefully.

From here, the agent will escort Xavier to the prison. Today was chosen specifically because there are no cases on the docket at the courthouse that held the possibility of a prison sentence, making it possible to seamlessly filter Xavier in through prison transportation. The guards at the prison don't know about the court proceedings or who they might receive on any given day, so they won't be suspicious of his arrival. They'll process him in just as they would anyone else coming from the courthouse. From there, he'll be on his own.

The agent comes over and shakes my hand, saying the coded phrase Eric said he would give him to ensure he is the right person and knows what's happening. Maybe it's a step over what is needed, but it makes me feel better knowing for sure.

Dean and Xavier say their goodbyes, with Dean promising the same things he did, reiterating his intention to take good care of the sourdough starters taking up residence in a good portion of the house, to not forget to lock the doors, and to make a record of any socks that went missing in the wash so they know how many they will need to track down.

They hug and Xavier moves over to me. I open my arms to him and we hug.

"Take care of him," he whispers. "I'm worried he's not going to be okay. He needs somebody."

"I'll take care of him," I say. "I'll make sure he's alright. And he'll still have you. He'll visit and you can call him."

He nods. I want to offer for him to back out, but I don't. I know it wouldn't actually be an offer. It would be manipulation. This is a good thing, I remind myself. I've watched my friends go into many other undercover situations. I've done it myself. The work he's doing could be invaluable, not just for finding out how Jonah got out, but for improving the prison and protecting other people.

"I don't want to call too much," he says. "The other inmates might get suspicious."

I nod. "Do what you need to do. And remember, at any time, we can get you out."

"I know." He looks over his shoulder at the agent. "I've got to go."

"Bye, Xavier."

He walks away, turning back a second later for another tight hug.

"I will miss you, too, Emma."

Dean and I stand beside each other in silence until the car with Xavier in it disappears into the distance and the dirt from the road has completely settled.

"You want to come back to my house with me?" I ask.

Dean nods. We get in the car and make our way back to the big, quiet house to pack his bags, then head for Sherwood.

CHAPTER FOURTEEN

S AM IS ALREADY UP AND PACING THE LIVING ROOM FLOOR THE next morning when I get up. I'm surprised to have slept so well last night, but I figure my mind decided it needed to shut down for a little while to have a chance to process. After my first stop to the kitchen for coffee, I bring my mug into the living room and curl up on the couch, tugging a blanket down off the back to cover my bent legs.

"I'm going to call and see what I can get done. I don't know if they'll release it to me. You might need to be the one to make the request, and even then, they might not be forthcoming about it. We might have to try to get a court order." He goes silent and continues to pace. "I know. I'm going to do my best. That's all I can do." He listens again. "I love you, too. Bye."

He's off the phone before he notices I'm sitting there. I give him an apologetic cringe when he jumps back slightly.

"I'm sorry," I say. "I didn't want to say anything and interrupt."

THE GIRL AND THE LAST SLEEPOVER

"It's fine," he replies. He leans down to kiss me. "You seemed to sleep well last night."

"I did. I'm not sure if it was actual sleep or just a power down, but I'll take it. You didn't sleep much."

"I can't," he says, reaching down for my coffee and taking a sip. His face twists as he swallows. "Lord, that stuff is awful."

"It's the same thing you drink," I point out. "It just doesn't have all the cream and sugar in it."

"Which brings me back to it's awful," he says. "But it's caffeine. Anyway, Rose called me yesterday while I was at work, and I've been on and off the phone with her probably ten times since then."

"Was that her?" I ask, lifting my eyebrows and gesturing slightly toward his phone with my mug.

Sam nods. "Yeah. She's been trying to understand Marie's death and she isn't having an easy time with it."

"I can't imagine it would be," I note. "She lost her only child. That's a horrific thing for anybody to go through under any circumstances. But for a woman to find out her child was involved in heavy drugs through her death from an overdose is too much."

"And that's the thing. Her dying from an overdose just doesn't make sense." He holds up a hand to stop me before I start down the same path, I've gone down many times before, of trying to gently get him to accept the reality of his cousin's death and finally make the admission to himself. "I know. I know what you're going to say, Emma, and I'm not trying to pretend there isn't strong evidence Marie was involved in drugs. But it still doesn't make sense. No matter what anyone says, it doesn't add up.

"People don't just go from never having had anything to do with drugs, not even smoking pot, to suddenly having the contact information for a drug dealer in their phone and then dying from an overdose in an abandoned warehouse. There are five or six steps in there that are being skipped in this situation. The toxicology reports just came back and confirmed she absolutely had drugs in her system. A lot of them. Certainly enough to cause death.

"I know that means she must have been a part of that life. If this was a tragedy that happened after a first-time use, a miscalculation, she would have died in her apartment. Or in the bathroom of a bar or club somewhere. That drug den where they found her was somewhere for hardened users. She wouldn't have just found it or been invited out there by a dealer. She had to have been more deeply involved."

"It doesn't make sense, but it never does," I offer.

89

"I know," Sam nods. "But there's something wrong with this. You know it as well as I do. Even besides how out of character this would be for Marie, there are so many pieces that just don't fit. The officers who wouldn't check on her. The detectives who dismissed it as soon as the concept of her drug use came up. If she was so deep in the life, how could no one have ever noticed? How could she have never come up against the police?"

"What were you saying you were going to call about?" I ask.

"Marie's medical records. If Rose can access them, we might be able to identify when this part of her life started. Doctors aren't allowed to report drug use to the police under privacy laws, so even if she did go to her regular doctor when she was sick or for any other reason and they noticed signs of drug use, they wouldn't be able to say anything about it to the authorities.

"They could, however, put it in her records. I don't necessarily expect to open up her files and find 'drug addict' in big bold permanent marker with a date jotted down beside it, but maybe a doctor or a nurse made a note about a certain behavior or symptom or other sign. Or she could have shown up with health issues that are related to drugs or worsened by them. I don't know exactly what's in there, but maybe something," he sighs. "Maybe some answers."

"You're right about you not being able to access them," I say. "Remember even after death, a person is protected by health privacy laws and doctor confidentiality. Only the next of kin or power of attorney can access copies of medical records, and those have to be requested through formal practices unless the person signed a release giving a set person permission to access records and get information. It's possible Marie gave that power to Rose, but I doubt it."

"She was a grown woman," Sam says. "She didn't need to give her mother permission to look at her medical records and know what she was going through. But I'm going to try anyway. Rose has been trying to be so strong and get through this, but rather than getting easier with time, it's actually getting harder. She's really struggling with it and I need to take as much of the pressure off her as possible. I'll call the doctor's office and explain the situation. They might be willing to give them to me, but if they don't, I'll tell Rose she needs to do it and help her with the request."

"You should do the same thing with her financial records," I say.

Dean comes into the living room looking like he's not only been up for a while, but has spent the time he's been awake in the gym he made out of one of the spare downstairs rooms. At least it's good to see him being active. His mind is clearer and he's able to handle things so much better when he's been exercising.

"What are we talking about?" he asks.

He sits beside me and I explain the situation. Sam has gone back to pacing up and down the room and Dean's eyes sweep back and forth to watch him for a few passes.

"You definitely need to look into her financial records," Dean says in agreement. "They might be harder to get without a court order, but you need to get your hands on them."

"Makes sense," Sam nods. "A look through her finances might tell me if she'd been receiving any payments from anyone, or who she might have been transferring significant amounts of money to."

"Or even not significant," I chime in. "Drug sales aren't always huge. Look for steady expenditures that don't correspond with her usual habits. An uptick in cash withdrawals at odd hours of the night. Try to get copies of her phone records, too. If you can read through her texts or even access her email and social media through there, you might be able to notice patterns in the people she spoke with and the expenses on her finances. I could help you figure out when this all started and who had been helping her."

"I just don't understand why they didn't do their job," Sam says. "Why couldn't they have just done what they were supposed to do? A basic welfare check. It's nothing. That doesn't take any time, any effort. It's just a matter of going to the house and making sure the person is alive, healthy, and safe. And if you can't make contact, you go inside and try to find out what's going on.

"That's it. Rose wasn't asking them to do anything above and beyond. She, and I, eventually, were just asking them to make sure that she was doing okay. And they couldn't even be bothered to do that until after they got the 911 call from that neighbor who saw the man go into her apartment. If they had just done what they were supposed to do, they might have been able to find the information that would let them track her down. She might have survived.

"And I want to know who that man going into her apartment was and what he was doing there. What did he do and who sent him? Marie wasn't dating anyone, and even if she was, I highly doubt she would encourage the whole idea of her new boyfriend crawling through a window on her fire escape. He was there for something. But they weren't even able to find him," Sam says.

"So we keep looking," I say. "We keep looking until we find him and everything else we need to understand exactly what happened to Marie."

CHAPTER FIFTEEN

A FTER BREAKFAST THE THREE OF US SEPARATE OFF TO WORK.
Sam is doing his rounds of phone calls trying to track down any
information he can about his cousin. The death of the drug dealer
in prison after his interview with him seems far too convenient. It makes
no sense considering the timing of her disappearance, but the police are
giving him the runaround about that as well. He's driven to break the
situation apart and find the answers. I want to help him, but I also don't
want to get in his way. I'm here if he needs to bounce anything off me or
ask any questions, and he knows.

I'm in my office working on my preparation for the trial. I keep
going over my notes, making sure I have all the details straight in my
head so I'm ready for anything the counsel might ask me. As both an
expert and a material witness, I'm expected to not only speak on what
happened and what I experienced during my time with Marlowe Gray
and the rest of the production, but also what it all meant. I know the
entire case doesn't rest on my shoulders. There are more witnesses,

more experts, a host of evidence. But it's hard not to feel responsible. I owe it to Marlowe's memory, and to Lakyn's, to see this to the right end.

I'm rewatching some of the social media posts put up by Marlowe's assistant and the girl she considered her best friend, Brittany. These posts were supposed to highlight Marlowe and build her popularity to make her more desirable and enhance her career. And I believe they really did start out with that intention. But somewhere along the line, they shifted. The backhanded goal instead became to get Brittany herself in front of the fans and turn her into the desirable one.

The video on my screen is a shameless attempt at Brittany seeming charming, doing big theatrical laughs as she sings and dances alongside Marlowe, who is meant to be the focus. A knock on my open office door makes me turn around and I see Dean standing there with his own laptop in his hand. He's been wading through the Shawn Reichert case all morning, locked away in the bedroom that has become essentially his official room when he's here.

"Did you already find it?" he asks.

I pause the video on my computer. "Find what?"

He comes into the office. "What are you watching?"

I look at the computer again and sigh. "A whole bunch of vapid nonsense. This is supposed to be one of the candid videos of Marlowe Gray intended to make her relatable and seem like just a regular person to her fans. She's supposed to just be hanging out with her best friend and being silly singing."

He leans forward to look at the frozen image of the video on the screen, then straightens as he shakes his head. "Nope. No one just hangs out casually with their best friend with that much makeup on."

"Same with Brittany," I say, pointing her out. "She's barely even supposed to be seen, but look at her hair done up and her lipstick. Who looks like that in the middle of the night at a slumber party?"

"I'm not exactly up on the slumber party game, but I wouldn't think that number is terribly high," Dean says.

"Me neither," I tell him. I glance at his computer. "What did you think I found?"

"Oh," he says, turning his computer. "Nicole Sims, Agent Reichert's former fiancée, sent me this. She does regular searches of news, forums, social media, everything she can think of to try to find information about him. This video popped up on social media last night and had the right combination of captions to make it come up on her search."

He hands me the computer and I set it on the edge of my desk so we can both see the screen clearly. The still image in the middle depicts a teenage girl, but it's nothing like the video of Marlowe and Brittany I've been watching. It's a stark contrast to the heavily made-up, beautiful girls' vibrant energy intended to pull in attention. This girl is plain, quiet, and sounds almost unsure of whether she should be making the video at all.

Muted brown hair hanging down by a nondescript face and the hazel eyes looking back through the screen hold little light and emotion.

"Who is that?" I ask.

"Her name is Maya Cortez. She lives in Cold Valley and was just a little girl when Reichert went missing. None of the information we do have about his investigation mentions her family or anything having to do with her. But listen to what she says."

Dean starts the video. I watch Maya shift slightly in her seat before pushing some of her hair back away from her face and starting to speak.

"I don't know if anyone is actually going to watch this or if they're going to care if they do, but I needed to talk about it. Maybe it will mean something to someone." She takes a breath. "For the last few months, I've been having this memory. That's the only thing I can think to call it. It's not a regular memory. It's more like a dream, but I have it when I'm awake, if that makes sense.

"It's not even a whole sequence of events. It's just, like flashes. I don't know if I'm saying that right. Maybe this is completely stupid for me to be doing." She pauses like she's considering just stopping the video, then lets out a resolute sigh. "Alright, here it is. In this memory, I'm in the old park, the one out off Hollybrook. There are trees all around me and I can hear men's voices. Everything looks really big, so I'm guessing this is something that happened when I was little.

"I'm moving through the trees and see something off to the side. Then it's just flashes of images. I don't see any of the men's faces clearly, but it's like I know who they are. Or at least that I've seen them. I look around at the trees. They are just starting to get their leaves. But then everything looks dead. No leaves or animals or anything. There's something on the ground and when I look closer at it, I realize it's a body. There's a dead guy sprawled out on the ground. I try to go to him to help him, but I can't move. Then I see another man step up and lift his hands into the air like he's praying or something. Then the body starts moving.

"The guy is definitely dead. He's not sleeping or anything, but he's moving around on the ground. Then I must be running or something, because the trees are going by fast. The memory ends with a flash of light and something hot, like when you go outside into the sunlight for the first time since being in air conditioning and you shiver even though it's not cold anymore.

"Anyway, that's it. That's all I can get out of it and it keeps coming to me over and over. I have no idea what it's all about and I can't seem to figure it out. Does it mean anything to anybody? Does any of it sound familiar? I guess if you can think of anything, leave a comment below. Thanks."

She reaches forward toward the camera and the video stops. Dean takes the computer off the desk and looks at me with raised eyebrows.

"And Nicole thinks that has something to do with her fiancé's disappearance?" I ask.

"She's not sure. But she feels like it's worth looking into. This girl is about sixteen, seventeen? Maybe eighteen? She says she was little in the memory, so that would line up with the time."

"I mean, I guess. That's a bit hazy since there's no real definition of what 'little' is, but as you said, it might be worth looking into," I shrug.

"I'm glad you think so, because I was wondering if you would come to Cold Valley with me," he says.

"Come with you?"

"Yeah. I haven't actually been there since I've been investigating his disappearance, and now that this has come up, I feel like going to the town and trying to see if I can get some interviews with people who may have known him is the only way this investigation is going to go anywhere. You have a lot of experience with missing persons cases," he says.

"So do you," I point out. "That's kind of a big part of the whole private investigator thing."

"I know," he says. "But you're FBI. You might have some insights into what Reichert could have been doing there that might help us track his movements or figure out who he would have been talking to. Besides, it would be good to have you onboard just to have you around. I know you're busy with the trial and the other cases you're consulting on, but I'd really appreciate it."

"Of course," I say. "I'll come with you."

"Great. We'll make arrangements and should be able to head out there in a couple of days. I don't intend on staying very long. I promised Xavier I'd visit him as soon as they let me and the process should only take a few days to get me on his list and authorized."

"Even if you have to come back to visit and the investigation isn't done, I can stay," I tell him.

We both know how important that connection is going to be for Xavier. He's going to need the anchor points, reminding him that time really is passing and that what he's going through isn't his permanent reality.

"We'll see what we can find out," Dean says. "I don't know how much there is to uncover there. All the other investigations into his disappearance have turned up nothing."

"All we can do is try."

CHAPTER SIXTEEN

A FEW DAYS LATER DEAN AND I ARE ON A PLANE TO COLD VALLEY. It will actually land at an airport about an hour away from the rural town itself, so we'll be renting a car to bring us the rest of the way. I figure that's still better than doing the nearly nine-hour drive from Sherwood. This way we're able to get back to either Sherwood or Harlan quickly.

As soon as the plane is at altitude, I take out my computer and start going over the notes I've been taking down since the day I put the Christmas decorations away. Dean glances over at the screen.

"What's that?" he asks.

"My thoughts about the Emperor situation," I tell him. "I've been trying to figure out what Jonah is trying to get through to me with the pictures in that ornament."

"Have you reached out to him?" he asks.

Dean is one of the very few people who know I have maintained a line of communication with Jonah using coded comments on prescribed articles and blog posts. Jonah selects the post and lets me know what he wants the phrase to be, and if I need to talk to him about something, I just post that comment and wait for him to call me. The phones he calls from are always burners, untraceable, and calling the number back just gets endless ringing or a busy signal. It's frustrating, but it keeps up the link.

"No. I don't think there's much point in it. He sent that for a reason. It means it's something he's not going to tell me straight out and that I have to figure out for myself. It's just like Serena's murder. He wanted me to clear his name and prove Salvador killed her without giving me any of the relevant details because if I had his information to work with, the evidence I could offer up to the police wouldn't stand on its own. I need to get the answers on my own so that they are relevant in a formal investigation."

"That's a lot of weight to put on an oversized ornament full of bizarre pictures of a dead guy," Dean mutters.

"I know. But it fits. It means there's something there. It's not just random. He wants me to get something out of this, I just need to figure out what it is." I switch to another screen. "I took pictures of the pictures so I could have them to look at without needing to carry around the whole ornament."

"You are the only person I know who has pictures of pictures on their various devices," Dean says.

"Considering the number of law enforcement agents and officers you know, I highly doubt that," I say. I think about the folders filling up the desktop of my computer and give a half-shrug. "But I might have the most of them. Okay, look. Salvador alive, the foyer of his house, and Salvador dead. That's it. Those are the pictures he sent."

"Have you gotten anything out of them yet?" Dean asks.

"Not really. The one thing I've noticed is his bracelet." I point to one of the pictures of Marini when he was alive. "You can see it best there. I remember him wearing it when I met him. It's a gold cuff and has a part in the front that looks like a cage almost. It reminded me of the old-fashioned coal box my grandmother had in her bedroom when I was growing up. She told me her mother still used it right up until she died to warm up her sheets at night."

"I don't think one that small would do much good in the sheet warming department," Dean says.

"Probably a good assessment. But if you look here, you can see a little bit of it sticking out of his sleeve. Then when you look at the pictures of him dead, he's not wearing it."

"It was morning, maybe he hadn't put it on yet. Or maybe he decided not to put it on because he knew he was surrendering himself, so they were going to take it from him anyway," Dean offers.

"That's true. But look, in the pictures of his foyer, one of them has the bracelet sitting on the table in the corner. You have to look really closely, but doesn't that look like the bracelet?"

I point to a small shape on a round table in the back corner of the grand foyer. It's not very big, but the shape of it and the color look like it's the bracelet he's wearing in the other pictures. I didn't take much notice of the bracelet when I encountered him in person, other than to notice he was wearing it, but now it stands out in the pictures.

"It does," Dean nods. "But what do you think a bracelet has to do with anything?"

I shake my head. "I don't know. The only thing I can think to do now is to get in touch with the people who used to work for him at his house. They dealt with him every day. They might be able to give me some information about him or his habits that could make some of this make sense."

"So, you really think he might not have just had a heart attack? That he might have been murdered?" Dean asks.

"Right now, all I can say is I think things might not be what they seem. And we'll just go from there," I say.

The airport where we land is small, but not the smallest I've seen. I'm grateful to be able to get to the luggage carousel and then to the rental car desk without having to transfer three terminals and duck and dodge through heavy foot traffic. I've already reserved a car, so it doesn't take long to be piled in and on the road to Cold Valley.

Travel can make any day seem long and exhausting, but there's so much to do and both Dean and I are eager to get the investigation underway. We aren't staying in a hotel, but an old boarding house that has been in operation for well over a century. The massive old house is beautiful and well taken care of, with the added benefit of being directly connected to the investigation. There are more conventional hotels available just outside the edges of town, but we decided to stay at the boarding house because it was where Shawn Reichert stayed ten years ago when he was in Cold Valley.

Staying at the boarding house puts us right in the middle of what I guess could be considered the most bustling area of town. The main street running down the center of the town, referred to as Church Street, does indeed have a little white church with a big steeple at the end, as well as the boarding house, some shops and stores, and a couple of restaurants. It reminds me of an older version of Sherwood. The sprawling farmland and nearby mountains surrounding it give it a slightly different atmosphere, though.

There's definitely a different kind of feeling around here. It's like the sense of being lost in time, almost forgotten. The people living around here are obviously comfortable with life the way they have it and get along just fine. They don't want it to be any different, and just like Dean warned me, they don't seem particularly keen on having outsiders come in and interfere.

We don't intend on interfering. At least, I hope that's how the people of the town see it. It's part of the reason we chose to stay at the boarding house. We want to be right in the thick of things. We want to see what Reichert did, find the people he knew. That might give us a better understanding of what could have happened to him.

There's no real lobby inside the boarding house. Instead, a desk is set up in what had once been a formal parlor. There are still pieces of furniture set around the room to create a sitting area; Dean and I set our luggage down in the middle of it so we can approach the woman sitting behind the desk. She has a quilt in her lap and is carefully stitching decorative curves across the pieces.

It's almost hypnotic watching her, and I don't want to interrupt, but I do want to get into our rooms. We stand and wait for a few seconds before she notices us. She looks almost startled when she looks up at us and I smile at her.

"I'm sorry," she says, standing up and setting her project down on the chair. "I was distracted."

"Don't be sorry," I reply. "It's beautiful."

She looks down at the quilt almost like she forgot what it looked like between having it in her hands and standing up.

"Oh. Thank you. It's for my granddaughter. Can I help you?"

She says it not like she was offering the information in any effort to make a connection with me, but just because it fits into the context of the conversation. The detail just flows right into the question, pushing past any sort of personal chit-chat and to the business portion of the interaction.

"We have reservations," I tell her. "Mine is under Emma Johnson."

"And mine is Dean Steele," Dean adds from behind me.

She consults the computer sitting in the corner of the desk and nods, then reaches into a drawer and slides two cardstock registration forms toward us. I smile to myself when I see them. They remind me of the registration cards Mirna uses at her hotel outside of Feathered Nest. As I fill out the card, I make a mental note to send her a message. It's been a good while since I've talked to her and I'd like to check in and see how she's doing.

We return the cards and she hands each of us a key.

"Your rooms are right across the hall from each other on the third floor. Private bathrooms. On the main floor, you'll find the dining room. Breakfast in the morning at seven-thirty. Library and sitting room in the back. My name is June. If you need anything, just ask."

And with that, we are on our own. We gather up our luggage and tromp up the long flights of steps until we're on the third floor. I notice how quiet the rest of the building is, almost like there's no one else here. But that likely doesn't mean much. It is still early in the afternoon and most people would be out doing things rather than sitting around the boarding house.

Dean and I part ways to drop everything into our rooms with the plan to meet back up downstairs in ten minutes. I could have just thrown everything into the room and met right then, but Dean is highly opposed to living out of a suitcase, even for a couple of hours. When he checks in somewhere, he has to unpack his bags, put everything away where it's supposed to be, and make it seem like he's settled in to live for the long haul. He attributes it to his years in the military, though I'm inclined to believe he didn't have nearly as much luggage when he was on his tours of duty, and unpacking was a far more streamlined feat.

\

CHAPTER SEVENTEEN

NOT SURPRISINGLY, I'M DOWNSTAIRS BEFORE DEAN IS. I LOOK around the entryway and peek into the dining room. It's full of the kind of old, heavily crafted furniture I would expect. It wouldn't be a shock to find out this same furniture has been there since the place opened. These rooms have histories. I can feel it.

It's the kind of place Xavier wouldn't be able to resist touching. Any time we go somewhere with history or particular significance, I find him running his fingers across the surfaces like he's absorbing the energy of what happened there. I've always felt like there was something different about places that have seen particularly intense moments, thinking of those events as burning their image into the air of the space. It's that chill you feel when you go into an abandoned hospital or the unease of walking through a crime scene, even years after the crime was committed.

Xavier brings it to another level. I believe he can perceive something more and touching the surfaces is his way of experiencing it. He's drawn to what once was and seems to offer himself as a way for those moments to continue existing and having significance. It can be beautiful and heartbreaking at the same time.

It can also pose particular challenges, such as when we went to visit a tourist cavern and he felt the need to run his fingers through the water dripping down the wall. Or the time he felt called to connect with a mummy on display at the history museum. Not his finest moments.

Or maybe his finest moments. It all depends on how someone chooses to look at it.

"Mrs. Johnson?"

I turn around from where I'm gazing into a China cabinet filled with gorgeous crystal and delicate antique dishes. June is standing at the doorway to the dining room, holding my registration card in her hand.

"It's just Emma," I say, walking toward her. "Is everything alright, Ms. June?"

"Yes," she nods. "I was just wondering." She glances down at my card and then back at me. "You filled out your card as Emma Griffin Johnson."

I nod. "Yes. Griffin is my maiden name."

"So, you are Emma Griffin?" she asks. "The FBI agent?"

I'm surprised to hear the question come out of her. I'm not sure why, but it just wasn't something I would have expected her to ask. I nod again.

"Yes. That's me. How did … ?"

"I watch a lot of TV," she explains. "Ever since my Henry died a few years back, I've been spending my evenings keeping company with quilts and the TV. Leaving it running keeps the house from seeming so quiet."

"I'm sorry for your loss," I say.

Now it's her turn to nod. "I've seen you doing interviews about the crimes you've investigated. The killers you've found."

Before I can come up with a response, Dean comes down the stairs and into the room with us. June pulls back slightly and I gesture at him.

"Dean is my cousin," I say. "He's a private investigator."

The resistant posture shifts again and she seems to come closer even though she doesn't actually move from the space where she's standing.

"Then you came to investigate him, didn't you?" she asks. "That boy who went missing."

"Boy?" I raise an eyebrow.

"The one who was staying here about ten years back," she says. "Left without a word."

I realize the boy she's talking about is actually Shawn Reichert. Judging by the age she seems now, even ten years ago she would have been old enough to see the early-thirties agent as very young. Dean and I glance at each other. It seems our investigation is starting now. It's a good thing we didn't have any hopes of coming in and staying unnoticed. We would have already been burned.

"We are," I confirm. "Can we talk with you about him?"

June looks hesitant, but in the kind of way that the entirety of Cold Valley seems hesitant. Not overtly unpleasant. Not angry or rude. Just hesitant. But the moment passes and she nods.

"Yes. Can I make you some tea?"

"I'd love some."

She heads out of the dining room and Dean and I follow. She leads us all the way through the house to the very back and into the library. It's full of polished dark woods and tall shelves filled with books. June notices me looking around with what I can only imagine is a surprised expression on my face.

"This wasn't originally built as a boarding house," she tells me. "It was the private home of one of the wealthiest families in the original town. Then it was converted into a boarding house when the… clientele changed."

I'm assuming that is her polite way of talking about when the moonshiners murdered their way into control of the town. That probably isn't something she feels particularly comfortable saying to guests who have just arrived.

"It's beautiful," I say.

"Make yourselves at home. I'll be right back," June says and leaves Dean and me alone.

"I didn't expect her to be so open," Dean says, lowering his voice so he can't be heard even if June is lurking right outside to see if we started talking about her as soon as she left. "From what I heard, it's not always easy getting people around here to warm up."

"It's me," I tell him as I sit in one of the large wingback chairs set on a dark burgundy rug. He sits in the one beside me, leaving a settee across from us and a table in the middle.

He gives me an incredulous look. "Because you're so charming and people just can't resist you?"

"Because she watches a lot of TV and knows I've captured a lot of killers," I clarify. I roll my neck a little in acknowledgment of how that sounds. "Which may or may not bode well for this conversation."

June comes back into the library with a tray and sets it on the table. On it is a perfectly matching silver tea set and a plate of cookies. She pours each of us a cup and gestures toward the bowl of sugar cubes and creamer of milk. We augment our tea in silence and Dean is the first to reach for a cookie.

"What can you tell us about Agent Reichert?" Dean asks.

June gives him a strange look and I realize Dean's mistake.

"You probably know him by a different name," I say quickly.

Dean looks embarrassed. "That's right. I'm sorry. He checked in here under the name of Michael Forbes. Does that sound more familiar?"

"Yes," June says, lifting her cup to her lips and taking a slow sip. "I remember that name."

"What can you tell us about him?" I ask.

"He was polite. Quiet. He never caused trouble with the other guests. He always offered to help clean up after breakfast and never seemed to drink too much or cross anyone in town. Every time he saw me, he had a smile for me, which was nice considering how many people just seem to walk on by like I'm invisible once they check in. Unless they're looking for their breakfast or have something they want cleaned, that is."

"Did he ever tell you what he was doing in Cold Valley?" Dean asks.

"I didn't ask," she says. "Not really my business why anyone is here. Just that they are. I figured he was visiting someone he knew, or maybe he was from the city and just wanted some peace and quiet. I could tell that about him."

"That he was from the city?" Dean asks.

June gives a single nod. "It was just something about him that told me he wasn't from anywhere around here. But, again, it's not my business. He seemed to enjoy it here, but he didn't spend much time around the boarding house. He was always one of the first to show up for breakfast in the morning and by the time other guests had trickled downstairs for the meal, he was already finished and gone for the day. Usually, he wouldn't come back until well after supper. Sometimes I didn't see him again until the next morning because he came in after I'd already gone to bed and the night manager had to open the door for him."

"But you never knew anything about what he was doing?" Dean asks.

June looks at him like she's starting to lose patience. "No."

"And when he left?" I ask quickly to smooth over the interaction. "Did he say anything to you about when he was planning on leaving, or where he might go next?"

"No," she says. "When he checked in, he didn't give me a check-out date. He just said he was wanting to stay for a while and he would let me know when it was time for him to move on. That isn't all that unusual.

Some people come here and don't leave for years. That's the thing about a boarding house. For some, it becomes home."

"Did you think that was what was going to happen with him?" I ask.

"I thought it might," she says, sounding almost wistful. "He didn't wear a wedding band and he never spoke of a special lady. He didn't seem to have any plans or anything he was waiting for or looking forward to anywhere else. It seemed if he just settled here, he might find something he was looking for. But then one day I went upstairs to change the sheets on his bed and he didn't answer his door. I tried it and it was unlocked. It looked like everything he brought with him was still there except for the clothes he must have been wearing and the books and papers he always kept stacked up on the desk in there. But he wasn't. There was money sitting on the pillow, enough to cover his bill and a little bit extra.

"It seemed so strange that all his things were there. For a little while, I thought he was going to come back. Thought he was just paying himself up before taking a little getaway, but would be back. I left that room just exactly as I'd found it for days. Then Sheriff Boyd came around asking about him and said the police had reached out because no one had heard from him and some people were worried.

"I tell you, that's when I got worried myself. A day or so later, some people showed up saying they were from the police department where he came from and they were searching for him. They went into his room, searched around a bit, asked me all kinds of questions about him, then left with everything."

"With everything?" Dean asks.

"Everything," June nods, plucking one of the cookies from the plate and taking a bite. Pink sanding sugar breaks off and tumbles down the sides of the cookie onto the napkin draped across her knee.

"You said there were some books and papers he had on his desk," I say.

"Yes. They were always there. Sometimes one or a couple of them might not be when I came in to clean or to make sure he had everything he needed, but there were always some sitting there."

"And they weren't there anymore when you went in and found him missing," Dean confirms.

"Right," she confirms. "The whole desk was empty. I hadn't seen it that way since the day he started renting the room. He was a neat, clean boy, but he sure loved his papers and books. They were spread all over that desk from the first day he checked in. Then that day, they were all gone. Maybe I should have paid more attention. That should have been the sign he wasn't going to come back."

"Why do you say that?" I ask.

"You do this line of work as long as I have, you start to pick up on things. Doesn't matter who they are, once people get settled in, they stay settled in. They don't pick up just to pick up in a place like this; they wait until the last minute to pack it back up. He made himself at home with all those books and things, but then one day they were gone? I should have known for good he wasn't going to come back."

CHAPTER EIGHTEEN

"**D**ID YOU MENTION THE PAPERS AND BOOKS TO THE OFFICERS who came?" I ask.

"Yes," June tells me. "But they didn't exactly seem to care. Or, at least, they didn't seem to think it was something to care about. They said if those things were so important to him, that was probably why they weren't still there. He brought them with him. Wherever he went, he took those things along."

"But why leave everything else that belonged to him?" Dean asks. "Why would he bother to pack those up and even leave you the money for the room, but then leave his clothes and everything else?"

"I don't know," June shrugs. "But I don't think... I don't think it could end well for him."

"You think he's dead," I say, going ahead and filling in the silence with what she meant but didn't want to say.

"I can't see any other explanation."

"Do you think something might have happened to him?" I ask.

She looks at me with acid in her eyes and I feel I'm getting a glimpse of what this place is supposed to be like. I've used up the grace she was showing me and now I'm getting how she actually feels.

"I don't think he just walked off into the sunset and vaporized, if that's what you're asking. And I don't think he offed himself, either. That wouldn't make any sense," June replies.

"You think it's possible he was murdered," I say.

"I think if that man isn't still walking this Earth it's because of someone else," she says. "And it shouldn't come as a surprise considering who he really was."

Dean and I look at each other out of the corners of our eyes. It suddenly feels like we're walking into a minefield. We have to be cautious with what we say and what we confirm, but also give her as much space as possible to tell us everything she might know, or what she might have heard.

"Who he really was?" Dean asks. It's carefully worded and inflected to lead her into giving us more rather than questioning what she's saying.

"Yes," June nods. "You said it yourself. Agent. He was with the FBI."

"Yes," I confirm, nodding back at her, mirroring her so she feels recognized and acknowledged. "His real name was Shawn Reichert. He checked into the boarding house with an assumed identity."

"Because he was undercover," she says. "He was investigating."

I can't tell if we're volleying bits of information or if she's asking hidden questions and hoping I don't notice their silent punctuation.

"Do you know who he might have been investigating?" Dean asks.

She noticeably bristles. "We protect our own here."

"Of course you do," I say. "We're not asking you to name anyone or make any assumptions."

It's exactly what he was doing, but I have to guide him off that course.

"How about what? Do you know what he might have been investigating?" Dean asks, adjusting the question so it doesn't seem to cut too close to her loyalties. "Has there been anything going on around town, even any rumors about something that might have happened, that would warrant being investigated by the FBI?"

"There were some rumors," she says. She's treading lightly now. "Way back. Some people talking about money coming in and out of town. Some sort of shady dealings with one of the farms."

"What kind of shady dealings?" I ask.

June shrugs and shakes her head. "I don't know anything about that sort of thing. I heard someone say there was money laundering going on, but to be honest, I don't even know what that means. Every time I hear that all I can think about is how my Henry would always forget his cash in the pockets of his blue jeans and it would end up floating around in my washer. Always dried out nice and soft, though."

She laughs and we chuckle with her.

"Is there anything else you might want to tell us about Agent Reichert? About when he was here or if you noticed anything after he left?" I ask.

"I think he might have found something," she says.

"Why do you say that?" Dean asks.

"A couple of days before he went missing, he came back here looking bright-eyed and very satisfied with himself. He was full of energy that day. Gave me a big smile and ran up the stairs to his room. He never ran. But this time he bounded right up there. He came back down about fifteen minutes later with a couple of notebooks, you know the old spiral kind, that I'd seen sitting on his desk. I offered him some fresh cookies I'd made for an afternoon snack for the guests and at first, he said no, that he had to get going. But then he came back and took two. He put one in his mouth and grabbed another one."

She leans back and chuckles, fondly recalling the memory. "That's how I always want to remember him. With the cookie hanging out of his mouth as he thanked me and ran back out the door."

"Do you have any idea where he was going?" I ask.

"The library," she tells me. "Later that night the librarian, Vera, called up here to let me know he'd left his jacket. It was in the microfilm room. He wasn't back here yet, so I slipped a note under his door. I guess he had to have gotten it, because he had it the next day when he came back in."

"You say he was in the microfilm room?" I ask. "What kinds of microfilms does the library have?"

"All kinds," she shrugs. "It's a small place, but we hang onto our history here. We don't want it to disappear. Too much just disappears these days. Everything is always new and fast. It's like if it's not the newest thing it's standing still. We don't like that around here."

"I understand what you mean," I say.

"Speaking of new and fast," Dean says. "Would it be completely off base to ask if you do any kind of social media?"

"Son, for me, social media is a card at Christmas and the Sunday newsletter from church."

I giggle and even see Dean crack a bit of a smile.

"Alright," he says with a nod. "I hear you on that. So, I'm assuming that means you haven't seen the video by Maya Cortez?"

"Video?" June frowns. "I don't understand what you're talking about. Did Maya do something?"

"You know her?" I ask, surprised by the familiarity in her voice when she said the girl's name.

In a town like this, it's safe to say everybody knows just about everybody, and even if they don't personally know someone, they know the name. But that's not how June said it. She said "Maya" as if the girl is someone she knows well.

"Yes," June says. "Her family used to live next door to my sister. I got to know them a bit."

"She recorded a video of herself and posted it online where she's talking about a memory that keeps coming up. It's obviously very disturbing to her, and she's asking for help from anyone who might know what she's remembering or what it might mean," Dean explains. "I was hired by Shawn Reichert's former fiancée to investigate his disappearance and she sent me the link to the video after she found it. She thinks it might have something to do with what happened to him."

June shakes her head, looking bewildered and upset. "I don't understand. What kind of memory? What could she possibly know about what happened to him? She was only six, maybe seven years old when he went missing."

"That's what we want to find out. Would you mind watching the video? Maybe something she said will mean something to you," I tell her.

"I'm not sure I can be of much help. Like I said, I don't know what happened to him after he left here. But I'm willing to try. I want to know what happened to him. And if he really was investigating something that was going on here..." her voice trails off. She takes a breath. "Cold Valley might not be everyone's idea of the most wonderful place to live. But it is for me. It's been my home my entire life. My parents were born and raised here, and so were my grandparents. I want it to be safe."

Dean takes out his phone and goes to pull up the video. He makes a face.

"What's wrong?" I ask.

"The video was taken down," he says. "It's not there."

"I downloaded it," I tell him.

"Course you did."

Pulling up the video, I hand my phone to June so she can watch it. Her expression darkens and her eyes look sad and frightened at the same time as she watches. When it's over, she presses my phone back into my hand quickly as if she can't stand to hold it anymore.

"Does that mean anything to you?" Dean asks.

"I don't know what she's talking about," June says. "But the old park she's talking about. That's out past town, back behind a couple of the farms. It used to be a real popular place, but not as many people go there anymore. Some of the trails have been closed off. The ones she's talking about, off Hollybrook, are actually on private land."

"Private land?" I ask.

She nods. "There was a big dispute about it. The farm has been there for a very long time and when the town decided to open that park, they carved out a piece of the wooded area the family owns. But they never actually purchased it or even seized it. They just set up signs and assumed the family would go along with it. Which they did for a while, but when kids would sneak in there to party, or the moonshiners would run through there, more than families would use the park, they shut it down."

"The town tried to get in their way, of course, but they pushed right on ahead and brought them to court. The court decided the town was at fault and the land was rightfully the family's, so they could do with it as they please. Some people still go out there and use the trails."

"Does the family allow that?" Dean asks.

"Sometimes they do and sometimes they don't. It's up to them."

"Can you tell us where it is?"

CHAPTER NINETEEN

T HE RIDE OUT TO THE PARK IS SO PEACEFUL I ALMOST FORGET we're investigating possibly multiple crimes. I admire the farmland as the narrow road weaves through it. It's the beginning of February now, and the cold weather hasn't quite broken yet. On either side of the car, fields that will in a few months be vibrant green and full of growing crops are still dormant. Even in that quiet state, there is a raw beauty to them.

It isn't the kind of beauty that is easy and comfortable to perceive. It's a kind of beauty that demands more of you. It requires a willingness to overlook imperfections, to see more than what something will be, to accept and appreciate what it is right in that moment. Sometimes it's much easier to literally overlook something. To spend so long looking forward to some imagined future that you forget to appreciate what's right in front of you.

The sleeping fields are what they are. Vast, cold, matted with gray tangles of weeds and broken cornstalks, dotted with clods of dirt and farm equipment abandoned for the season. Far out to the edges, they tuck into the tree line with a deepening slash of charcoal tinged with green.

Seeing that isn't about thinking ahead into next year's potential. It's about remembering last year's abundance. It is beauty in fulfillment. In pure, unapologetic reality.

"Do you believe her?" Dean asks.

It's the first words either one of us has said since we got in the car and headed for the park.

"June?" I ask.

"No. Maya. Do you believe this memory thing she was talking about?"

"I don't know what you mean about believing her."

"Do you really think she saw those things? Do you think she's actually remembering that happening?"

"She remembers something. I can't tell you exactly what that is. But that memory isn't just something she came up with. It's in her," I say.

"Then why would she take it down? She went to all the effort of making that video to talk about this memory, but then she turned around and deleted the video. I didn't even get a chance to see if there were any comments on it or anything. Maybe that means she actually did make it all up and it either didn't get the kind of reaction she expected it to, or got too much of a reaction and she decided she needed to pull the plug on it."

"Or it could mean that just the act of making the video, of putting herself out there and sharing what she went through each time she experienced that memory was too much. You know as well as I do how difficult it can be to only remember little shreds of something that happened. And to not even know if what you're remembering is real. It can make you question yourself, not to mention what everybody else around you thinks. This is a teenage girl, Dean. Life probably already isn't easy for her every day. Sharing something like that could just make it worse."

"I didn't think of it that way," he says.

"I know."

I turn to look out the window again. I can't help but feel sympathy for the girl in the video. I don't know her. I don't know anything about her beyond what she looks like and the bits of information she shared. But when I watched her talk about her memory, I could see myself. I remember so distinctly what it felt like to be tormented by the scattered shards that made up my memories of my mother and her death. I struggled with those bits of memory and all the questions that came with them from the time I was a child until I was a grown adult, battling the world because I was still afraid of the boogeyman I couldn't remember.

I learned young that it felt far better to be angry than it did to admit to being afraid.

Maya still looks afraid.

The GPS directions don't seem to want to get us to anything resembling access to the park, but that's not all that surprising. In places like this, the roads and access points the locals are accustomed to using without a second thought aren't actually on the recognized maps and don't have coordinates that can be used in the GPS. There are places around Sherwood that have the same problem. People trying to find them have to go against everything they've been taught by society for years, abandon their reliance on technology, and just follow written directions for a while to get to their destination.

Which is why a small business popped up in recent years that is nothing but a woman who has lived in the area her entire life who goes out rescuing lost people and leading them back to where they're supposed to be. Right now her website and business card just say "I'll pick you up" as she workshops an actual name for the business.

Because Nanette is also an officer in Sam's department and a personal friend, he was tasked with the responsibility of telling her "Driver Nanny" is not a good choice, though still infinitely better than what she first attempted to call it. Nan with a Van.

We've gone up and down the same stretch of road a few times before we notice the little side road that apparently doesn't have its own position with the GPS. Going down it leads to an old parking area. It's not a lot. There isn't any pavement or concrete bumpers delineating parking spots. It's more just a rounded dirt area carpeted with pine needles that funnels into a trailhead.

"Is this it?" Dean asks as we get out of the car.

I tug my sweater closer around me against a cold wind and walk toward a brown-painted wooden sign near where the trees swallow up the barely visible path.

"Bike path, hiking trail, picnic areas," I read. "This seems to be it."

"This is private land?" he asks, looking around.

"I'm not sure this part is," I shrug. "But it must be somewhere around here at least. It doesn't look like this place is hopping with visitors."

"Where is the street Maya was talking about in her video?" he asks.

I pull up the map June used to show us where we were going and point out the short stretch of road that has the name she used.

"It's only this part," I tell him. "So we have to be at least on the right track."

Dean nods. "Then let's look around."

There are many unsettling things about being an FBI agent. The frequency with which I find myself walking into the complete unknown without even a clear plan of what I'm trying to accomplish is right up there in the greatest hits. Doing it as the afternoon is getting very close to evening in a densely wooded, partially abandoned park that may or may not be the site of a murder just adds bonus points.

But this is what I thrive on. I crave the tingling of energy on the bottoms of my feet and in the tips of my fingers. It's probably my survival instincts kicking in and telling my body to stop. There's something about the energy of not knowing exactly what's coming, but heading in anyway, that is completely life-affirming to me.

There have been times in my career when I thought I'd made a mistake by deciding to go into the Bureau and I questioned what I was doing with my life. Questioned if the FBI was still what I actually wanted. It was one of those crises of identity and life choices, the one that led to Bellamy encouraging me to go on the ill-fated vacation to the resort on Windsor Island, that led to me getting a private investigator's license.

I left that island knowing the FBI was absolutely where I was supposed to be and I wasn't budging any time soon, but I still got that license. I like knowing it's there, that I have another path if I want to follow it. It also lets me be more helpful to Dean on his cases. I don't always want to hide behind my badge when there are tough decisions to be made about how to handle a situation. And it means I'm not stepping on his toes by bringing the Bureau into everything.

For now, it's the perfect compromise.

We've been walking along the path for more than an hour, weaving on and off at random times and taking in all of our surroundings as much as possible, before we see another person. The first glimpse of her is actually pretty startling as she comes around a corner to stand in the middle of the trail and look at us. Her white coat flashes like the tail of a deer among the brown trees.

"Hello?" she calls out.

"Hi," I say, walking toward her.

"Can I help you?" she asks.

"Help us?" I ask.

As I get closer I realize she's younger than I thought. She's beautiful and put together, she carries herself like someone several years older, but she can't be more than a teenager.

"I'm sorry, I thought you might be lost. This is private land," she says.

"We're not lost," I tell her. "We were actually looking for this place. What's your name?"

She seems hesitant and I take out my badge. This is one of those times when it is very helpful.

"Genevieve McGuire," she says.

"Hi, Genevieve. I'm Emma."

"Are you a cop?" she asks.

"No," I tell her. "I'm an FBI agent. This is my cousin, Dean. He's a private investigator."

"FBI?" she frowns, looking back and forth between us. "What's going on? Did something happen?"

"We're just looking into some details about a case Dean is investigating and I'm helping with," I explain.

"A case? What happened?" she asks, sounding worried. "Did it happen here?"

"Genevieve?"

A man's voice calls through the woods and a second later I see a tall man with worn jeans and a work jacket coming toward us. The thick hat and gloves he's wearing instantly tell me he spends a considerable amount of time outdoors.

"I'm over here, Jim," she says.

There's nothing but suspicion in his eyes when they fall on Dean and me. He stops close beside Genevieve and I notice the protective, almost possessive way he places half his body between her and us.

"What's going on here?" he asks. "You folks out for a hike in the park?"

"They're law enforcement," Genevieve tells him.

The man's face hardens. I don't like the way he's standing, the strange way he seems to be simultaneously shielding and claiming the girl.

"I'm Dean Steele," Dean starts, stepping forward slightly and extending his hand toward the man. "I'm actually not law enforcement. I'm a private investigator."

"I am law enforcement," I say without hesitation. "Emma Griffin. FBI."

The man eyes me as he shakes Dean's hand. "Jim Calhoun. And it seems you've met my stepdaughter. Can I ask what brings you out here?"

"We're doing an investigation," Dean says.

"An investigation?" Calhoun asks darkly. "You must be in the wrong spot. This here is private land. My land. That's been proven in court already."

"We're not investigating your ownership of the land," I tell him. "The Bureau doesn't tend to interest itself in individual land disputes."

He looks me up and down, sizing me up. It's a look I'm used to—and one I despise.

"We're investigating a missing person," Dean says. "A man went missing from Cold Valley ten years ago and recent information suggests he might have been in this area."

"When it wasn't considered private property," I add.

Dean tenses up slightly beside me as if he's trying to send out a jolt of energy toward me to quiet me down. He does it all the time. It never works, but I admire his persistence and faith in himself.

"I don't know anything about a missing person being around here," Calhoun says.

"Well, if you did, he wouldn't be a missing person," I shrug. "Or maybe we would have different questions for you."

The man's eyes narrow at the same time the girls widen. They plead with me over his shoulder.

"Are you suggesting something?" he asks.

"I'm not suggesting anything other than that you let us do our jobs," I say.

"And what exactly do you think your job is on my property?" he asks.

"We need to thoroughly examine the area to determine if he was, in fact, in this location before he was reported missing, and if there is any surviving evidence of what might have happened to him after that."

Jim sucks his teeth. "You say ten years ago?"

"Yes," Dean says. "Early spring."

A look of realization crosses his face, followed by the slightest hint of a smug smile.

"You're talking about that other FBI fella. The one who was pretending to be someone else."

"He was working undercover," I correct him. "It wasn't a game."

"Yes, well, whatever you call it, he wasn't around here. And he definitely isn't now."

"How can you be so sure of that?"

"You should know," he says almost like he's challenging me. "Your people combed all over these woods. Disrupted the whole town trying to find him. They didn't find anything or you wouldn't be here."

This is a distinctly different impression than we got from June.

"Like I said, there is new information that needs to be followed up on," I say.

He wraps his arm around Genevieve, pulling her up beside and against him.

"Well, you can go right on ahead and do all the searching you want as soon as you have a warrant. Until then, you're trespassing. And upsetting Genevieve. I'd offer to show you back to your car, but I think I need to be getting my girl on home. I have a feeling you can find your way just fine."

He turns his back on us and walks away.

CHAPTER TWENTY

D EAN STORMS BACK TOWARD THE CAR AHEAD OF ME. I'M ABOUT TO
say something to him when he roughly opens the door and whips
around to look back at me.

"Damn it, Emma," he says angrily.

"What?" I ask.

"Can't you ever just keep your mouth shut?"

"Excuse me?"

"Why did you have to do that?" he asks, shooting his arm out to the
side to point toward the woods where we'd just encountered Jim and
Genevieve.

"Do what?"

"Talk to him like that."

"He was an ass, Dean. And did you not notice the way he was standing with his stepdaughter? That didn't give you a creepy vibe at all?" I
ask, surprised by his reaction to the whole situation.

"At that second, I wasn't thinking about the way he was standing or
if it seemed creepy. I'm here for a single reason, and that's to try to find

out what happened to Shawn Reichert. And part of that is going to the places he might have been. That guy was right. I've looked at notes from the initial investigations after he went missing. I don't have access to the full records, but I know a lot of people around town were interviewed. The search was thorough.

"I didn't know about the park, but there is mention of searching wooded areas and farmland. We need to be able to search these areas again, and you just managed to piss off the landowner so now he can completely block our access to it."

"Are you seriously blaming me for this? You're up against a missing person who might not be missing, and who, according to the vast majority of the people around here, didn't even exist. I'm sorry I didn't talk sweet and bat my eyelashes at the man so he would give us carte blanche to traipse around in the woods some more without any clear idea of what we're looking for. But the reality is, you don't know who we're dealing with around here. Neither of us do," I say.

"So guilty until proven innocent," he says.

"Suspicious until proven trustworthy," I counter. "You aren't just looking for a random man, Dean. You keep saying his name, but you're not thinking about who he actually is. The people in Cold Valley thought a man named Michael Forbes was visiting town for his own personal reasons and went missing. But you aren't looking for Michael Forbes. You aren't looking for someone who just disappeared when they were going about their normal course of life.

"You are looking for Shawn Reichert, an FBI agent involved in an undercover investigation into potential money laundering. That is extremely dangerous work. And it opens up far more possibilities. There's a chance he was identified and had to go into hiding while evidence is gathered to protect himself. There's a chance the people he was investigating got suspicious and neutralized the threat, so to speak. And, yes, there is a chance he just decided to walk the fuck away. The point is, in ten years there hasn't been a single sign of him. Hiding like that in this world is almost impossible and the chances he could do it on his own are next to nothing.

"If what Calhoun said is accurate and there actually was an extensive Bureau investigation and not just police, they believe he's dead. They wouldn't put those kinds of resources into a bogus search knowing he was being hidden. A brief search, some interviews, a dog and pony show for the media, maybe, but not an intensive search over the entire area. Either that man is lying about what happened after Reichert went missing, or we are looking for a dead agent and the people who killed him. Forgive me if that doesn't put me in a personable mood."

I get into the car and slam the door beside me. There are a few seconds of me being left alone with the sound of my fuming breath before Dean gets in. He sits silently beside me for a few long moments before speaking.

He takes a deep breath to say something, but I try to rush my own words out first.

"I'm sorry—"

"I'm sorry," he says at the exact same moment.

We let the awkwardness hang in the air for a second before we both let out a relieved chuckle.

"I'm sorry, Emma. I shouldn't have gone off on you like that."

"Don't worry about it," I tell him.

"No, I mean it. I'm just tense and this case really has me on edge. You seem to think I don't realize who I'm looking for, or the stakes that are involved with this. But I do. And that's what's making it so hard. This is the first time I've dealt with a case like this. I've had missing people. I've had confusing, complicated cases that seemed impossible. And I've figured them out. I found the people and did what I needed to do. But this one seems different.

"I want to find this man for his fiancée. I want to find him for him, if he needs to be found. But I have the weight of possibly compromising the work he did and putting people in danger sitting on me because of it. And if we get it wrong and any evidence we find is tossed out because of a technicality, or someone realizes what we're doing and makes sure we don't find any evidence, that's on me," he says.

"It isn't easy," I tell him. "This job, either of our jobs, aren't easy. You're going to do what you need to do, just like I've always known you to do. Keep in mind the Dean Steele I met was stalking me on a train while corpses were piling up and I was trying to stop everybody onboard from dying. You weren't following any protocols then. You didn't know who I was other than my name and that I was an FBI agent Jonah is obsessed with.

"And when I found that man stabbed to death in the empty car, you jumped right in to help in any way you could. You didn't panic, leave, and pretend you didn't see anything. And you didn't start demanding everything be handled specifically by the book. You did what you knew you needed to do, even if it didn't make sense right then. And that's all you need to do now.

"But as long as we're apologizing, I'm sorry, too. This is your investigation, not mine. I shouldn't be stepping on your toes and wedging myself into every situation. I didn't need to correct him."

Dean makes a sound like he's considering what I said and isn't quite going along with it.

"Yeah, you did," he admits. "Maybe not that way, exactly, but you did need to do it. And you're not stepping on my toes. I'm the one who asked you to be here because I respect you as a talented agent almost as much as I love you as my cousin. You kick ass and take names. And sometimes don't take names, and those might be my favorite times. I'm glad you're here. I appreciate you being here."

"Thank you," I say. We smile at each other. "So. Now that we've been kicked out of the woods and need to get some official permission to be there, what do we do next?"

"I reached out to Maya Cortez's mother Grace before we came to let her know we'd like to talk to her," Dean says.

"And she was receptive to it?" I ask.

He nods. "She sounded very willing to talk. I'm going to call her and see if she's available to talk tonight. I'd like to see if Maya is around, too. I want to talk to her about her memory, and about taking down that video."

A quick call later, Dean and I have plans to meet with Maya's mother in two hours. It gives us enough time to go back to the hotel for a quick change and bite to eat. Since there aren't any literal fast-food restaurants in the town of Cold Valley, we end up in one of the little diner-style restaurants on Broad Street.

As soon as I walk inside, I feel homesick for Pearl's back home in Sherwood. Just like the rest of the area, this place feels like a slice of another time, just a different one. Like Pavlov's FBI agent, my mouth waters and my stomach rumbles in response to the smell of the food. It's that kind of smell that tells you within the first two seconds of walking into the restaurant that the food is going to be amazing.

The hostess seats us and hands each of us a laminated menu. My eyes fall on the all-day breakfast menu and their offering of biscuits and gravy.

"Be still my heart," I whisper after ordering.

"You keep eating like that and your request just might be granted," Dean says.

"Look, cantaloupe and berries and cottage cheese sounds delicious. Just not as delicious as big buttery biscuits sopping up thick sausage gravy."

"That's a very cogent argument," he admits. "You know what, actually?"

He raises his hand to get the waitress's attention and it's all I can do not to burst out in laughter as he tells her he's changing his order.

Dean and I may have different approaches to following our investigations, but that just might be why we're such a great team. Not for the first time lately am I so grateful to have him in my life.

CHAPTER TWENTY-ONE

GRACE CORTEZ LOOKS WORN AND PALE WHEN SHE LETS US INTO her modest home and invites us to sit in the living room. It's the kind of worn that seems like she has probably been that way for a long time. Like a light within her was snubbed out and never ignited again.

"Thank you for coming to speak with me," she says. "Can I get you something to drink? Coffee? Tea? Water?"

"No, thank you," both of us reply.

She sits down and folds her hands on her thighs in front of her.

"We really appreciate you being willing to meet with us," Dean starts. "We're just looking into every angle and possibility, and the video your daughter made was brought to our attention."

She nods and takes a breath. "I'm glad you said something about it. I didn't even know she made it. She isn't usually very active on social media. To be honest, she's not very social at all. She has a couple of close friends she's had since she was a child, but not much else."

"Did you watch the video?" Dean asks.

Grace nods again. She looks like she's edging toward tears. The conversation has just started and it's already too much for her.

"I did. Just before she took it down. I think she might have taken it down partially because she knew I watched it."

"What did you think of it?" I ask.

"It was… disturbing. And heartbreaking," she says.

"Has she ever mentioned anything like that to you before?" Dean asks.

"No. A couple of times she's said that she has weird thoughts, but that sounded like a teenager thing to me. Like she was just saying her mind was filling up with all the crazy stuff that happens when you're seventeen. She never told me about this." She takes another breath and lets it out slowly. "But I think I might know what she's talking about."

I sit up a little straighter, surprised by the revelation.

"You do?" I ask.

"Her father's death."

"Her father?" Dean asks.

Grace nods. Now the tears are right at the edges of her eyes. I can see them glittering in the light from the lamp on the side table. Her hands squeeze together tighter like she's trying to find strength in herself. Now that I know Maya's father is dead, I can believe that is exactly what she's doing.

"He died when she was seven. It was… horrible. She's never talked about it. She never remembered that day. I've had her in therapy and counseling, but she's never been able to talk about what happened."

"Was she there?" I ask.

"Yes. They were out at the park riding their bikes. It was just starting to warm up a little and the trees were starting to get leaves. Maya always insisted that meant it was spring, and David always promised her they would start riding bikes again in the spring. She was always so upset when they had to put the bikes away in the winter because it was so cold, and he would tell her she just had to be patient because as soon as spring was back, they could go back out to the park together.

"I remember David thinking it was still too cold. It was overcast and getting later in the afternoon, but she was so hopeful he couldn't say no. Maya was everything to him. From the second he found out I was pregnant, that little girl was his entire life. He was so proud of her. Every little thing about her made him so happy. I used to joke that he thought he made her all by himself.

Seeing the two of them together was the most wonderful thing I ever experienced. When he died, I didn't think I was going to be able to go on. We'd been together since high school. I couldn't imagine a single day of my life without him. The only thing that kept me going was Maya. I had to take care of her. but it was so hard watching her not remember what happened and try to understand that her daddy was gone."

"If you don't mind me asking, what happened to him?" Dean asks.

Grace lifts her eyes to him from where they've been focused on the floor in front of her while she talked about her late husband.

"They were almost at the end of their ride and were about to head back to where the car was parked. There was a stretch of road that cut through their favorite part of the park. He would usually use that as a shortcut to get back to the parking area rather than looping all the way back around through the trails. I hated when he did it. It never felt safe. But he always assured me it was fine because they were inside a state park. He said people don't drive fast in the park like that.

From what the police told me, he had just pulled out onto the edge of the road and was hit by what they assume was a drunk driver who lost control of their car. They drove over him and hit Maya, then backed over David again as they were driving away. Both of them just lay there until another car came by and noticed them and called the police. He was already dead when the police got to the scene, but they were able to save Maya."

"I'm so sorry you had to go through that," I say.

"She woke up briefly while they were putting her in the ambulance, but went unconscious again before they got her to the hospital. The doctors put her under sedation to stabilize her and kept her that way until the next day. The first thing she said when she woke up was to ask for her father. I had to be the one to tell her what happened. She was so confused. She said they hadn't gone biking yet. It was still winter. It wasn't spring yet, so they couldn't have gone biking and he couldn't have been hit.

"Even after they released her, and we went home and he wasn't there, and then at the funeral, she just couldn't accept it. She kept saying it wasn't true, that it couldn't be. I put her in as much therapy as I could, hoping they would be able to tell me she was just acting out or in denial, but they all told me it was what she truly thought. She genuinely didn't remember any of it, so in her mind, it couldn't have happened."

"Are you talking about me?"

We were so locked in the conversation none of us had noticed the door open and Maya come inside. Now she stands at the edge of the room, glaring in at her mother from the same hurt hazel eyes I watched in the video.

Grace stands and takes a step toward her daughter.

"Honey, this is Ms. Griffin and Mr. Steele. They came to talk about that video you made."

Maya takes a sharp step back. Her face reddens and her jaw hardens.

"You saw that? How did you see it? I took the video down. I don't need to talk about it."

"It was sent to me by my client," Dean tries to explain. "I'm a private investigator and I'm investigating …"

"It doesn't mean anything," Maya cuts him off. "That's why I took it down. It's just a stupid idea that got stuck in my head. It doesn't mean anything."

She runs out of the room and Grace looks at us with embarrassment etched in her eyes.

"I'm so sorry. I didn't think she would react like that."

"It's not easy being her age," I say, feeling kind of ridiculous saying that to a woman older than me who has children when I clearly don't.

"Mrs. Cortez, can I ask you something?" Dean asks. "You said you think the flashes of memory she's having are the memory of her father's death resurfacing."

Grace nods. "She talks about the park and the location where they always biked. The trees going by. The body on the ground."

The last words are hard for her to say, but she manages to get them out.

"Right," Dean nods. "She says a body. She doesn't say her father. You said she doesn't remember his death, but she obviously remembers him."

"Of course she does," Grace replies.

"Then she would be able to recognize if it was him that she saw dead. And she describes going away from that spot and feeling heat. She didn't leave the accident site."

"No," Grace says, shaking her head.

"So, it sounds like that part is when the accident happened. Which means she is having flashes of seeing someone dead before that happened."

Grace's mouth falls open, but no sound comes out. She struggles with something, then shakes her head.

"No. Nothing like that happened. There was no one else in the area. No bodies were ever found in the woods." She pauses, her chin trembling. "You think it was that man. The one who everybody says was an informant."

"He wasn't an informant. He was an FBI agent. Shawn Reichert. He was here doing an undercover investigation when he disappeared."

"He left," Grace says. "He left town. That's what June said."

"We spoke to June," I tell her. "We're staying at the boarding house. She told us almost all of his belongings were still there when he went missing."

"Yes, but if he was undercover, doesn't that mean those weren't really his things? He just brought them for his cover?" she asks.

She's desperate to cling tightly onto these ideas and it hurts to watch Dean have to chip away at them.

"We don't know what happened. That's why we're here. I told you I was hired by his fiancée to find out why he never made it home, and that she found the video your daughter made and thought it might have something to do with the case," he says.

"It can't," Grace insists. "They searched for him in those woods. It was all over the news. They didn't say he was an FBI agent, but everybody knew who they were talking about. They didn't find anything. The park is big, but it isn't a huge, sprawling piece of land. It was carefully searched a couple of times."

"Can you excuse me for a second?" I ask.

I walk out of the living room and follow the hallway Maya went down, eventually finding a door with an M on it in purple scroll. My knock is met with a fairly surly response, but I call into her anyway.

"Can I talk to you?"

CHAPTER TWENTY-TWO

"I FIGURED IF THERE WAS GOING TO BE ANYBODY WHO COULD connect with her, it was going to be me. I remember being her age and still not knowing what happened to my mother. And then my father went missing right after that. It's a special kind of torture very few people will ever understand. I wanted her to know she isn't alone, and that having the kind of memory she has doesn't make her crazy. It means her mind is trying hard to bring back what was lost."

Dean reaches across the assortment of Chinese takeout containers spread across my bed and grabs up a sauce-coated sugar snap pea with his chopsticks. It took forty minutes of driving away from Cold Valley to find a Chinese restaurant open late, but it's worth it. Now we're holed up in my room at the boarding house, trying to stay quiet so our conversation doesn't become the nighttime entertainment for the other guests on the floor.

"What did she say?"

"She isn't sure how much of that memory is real and what it even means, but she feels like it's real. She's frustrated that she still can't remember anything about her father's death, but somehow she has clung onto this bit of information and it's just coming back to her now," I tell him.

"Her brain still needs to process through things before it can bring back those memories," Dean says. "Been there."

I nod. "The fact that anything is starting to surface means that she's processing. Just perhaps not in the way that people would expect her to. She's still not ready to face the moment of her father's death. I can't blame her. That must have been horrific. She was just a little girl and by the way the police described the scene to Grace, it looked like Maya tried to move closer to her father after the accident, which means she was conscious and could see him."

"That's not something anyone needs to have in their mind," Dean says.

"No," I say.

I am eternally grateful I have no memories of my mother's body. The only time I saw her after her death she was on a gurney and covered with a piece of cloth. I couldn't see anything about her. I don't have to remember her that way. But I do have memories of another murder: a bloody, gruesome death I carried within me for a long time because I was confused into thinking it was a memory of finding my mother.

The truth was my mother had been dead for five years by the time I stood in that kitchen getting blood on my shoes and staring down at the unrecognizable face of the blonde woman slaughtered on the floor. My father never explained it to me. I don't blame him for trying to protect me, but he doesn't understand how deeply that affected me, and how much I questioned myself when later I returned to that apartment and found the kitchen spotless, found my shoes clean, and there was never any mention of a murdered woman.

It wasn't until I was an adult that I discovered the truth. The dead woman really did resemble my mother. That was why Jonah chose her. She was his plaything until he bored of her and killed her, leaving behind the young son I wouldn't know anything about until we met on a train more than a decade later.

In another life, she'd have been my aunt.

"Did you ask her why she took the video down?" he asks.

"She said she decided she didn't want anyone at school to see it. I got the impression she has a harder time with the kids there than her mother was letting on. She isn't just not social. I think she's pretty outcast. And at first, she thought putting up that video would make it seem like she was participating in the same kinds of things as the other teenagers around, then she realized they might not take it the same way and instead turn on her even more because of it. You've seen how people have reacted to even talking about Shawn."

"It's definitely a heated issue around here. Speaking of which, I reached out to Eric and let him know what was going on."

"Why did you do that?" I ask. "You're doing fine. You don't need to have the Bureau's official involvement."

"Well, except that I do," Dean says. "You heard what Jim Calhoun said. That's his land and if there's going to be any investigating on it, we have to have a warrant. I have a feeling he's not going to be fooled by us pretending to go out there for a nice jog and a picnic."

"So, if Eric reopens the investigation into the disappearance of an endangered federal agent, it will be easier to get the clearance," I say with a knowing nod.

"Exactly. And since I already have the best of the best FBI agent with me here, the investigation can go forward without slowing down," he says.

"Are you sure you're alright with that?" I ask. "I don't want you to feel like I'm taking over control of your investigation."

"You aren't," Dean says. "I'm asking for you to be a resource for me."

The comment makes me think of Xavier and I smile and tear up at the same time.

"How long is it going to take for the case to be officially reopened?" I ask.

"Eric said it will probably be a few days. Maybe a week. I figured we'll go home and I can be at the prison for visitation. You can help Sam with Marie and work on Marlowe's case. We'll keep looking into everything going on here, and when it's ready to go, we'll come back."

"That sounds perfect," I nod. "I'll book the flight."

Even though we didn't have a set time when we were going to come back, it feels a bit odd to already be back in Sherwood. It's like my mind was preparing for a long stretch in Cold Valley, and now that I've broken that, it isn't sure what to do next.

Two days later, back in the quiet of my house while Sam is at work, I do what I promised myself I would do while on the plane to Cold

Valley. Searching through every bit of information I had access to about Salvador Marini, I find the contact information for some of the staff he maintained at his palatial home.

It doesn't surprise me that he had so many people serving him and taking care of his house every day. His delusions of grandeur and entitlement were so extreme they were almost funny. At least, they would be if they hadn't had such horrific consequences. He certainly wasn't the type of man who would clean up after himself or do his own cooking. Those are the kinds of activities he would see as beneath him. His station in society, the one he perceived himself as having, entitled him to extraordinary service and having all his needs handled by others. He should never have to lift a finger.

Which tells me that he not only had a considerable staff, he likely had a considerable *disgruntled* staff. People with that kind of attitude are rarely kind to the people who are serving them. Because they've put themselves on a pedestal and believe they deserve this kind of indulgence, it's easy for them to treat their staff as less than human.

That makes for hurt feelings at the mildest and deep, seething anger in others. I'm banking on both to encourage the staff to talk to me about the things they went through with him, and possibly help me understand what in the pictures could be of any significance.

I spend most of the morning seeking them out and then by early afternoon I'm in my car, heading for the new post of one of his housekeepers. She seems eager to talk to me, though I can't say the same for everyone I spoke to about him. Two more of his housekeepers, his cook, and a gardener all flat-out refused to even talk on the phone about him.

He's dead. Good riddance.

I've never actually heard a person say "good riddance" about another human being, but there it was. These people had been so mistreated by Marini they didn't even want his name in their mouths. He was off the Earth and they didn't want to bring him back even in memory. They were very content to just let him be gone and never have to think of him again.

I can understand the impulse. I certainly have people in my past who I am happy to leave there and would rather never consider again if I don't absolutely have to. But I'm glad I have at least one person who is willing to talk to me. I just hope she has something valuable to offer.

CHAPTER TWENTY-THREE

"HIS FITNESS TRACKER?" DEAN ASKS A COUPLE OF DAYS LATER while we sit in the living room, waiting out a cold rainstorm before running errands. He ran into the house from Harlan just before the downpour started and he'll be staying in Sherwood with me until we go back to Cold Valley.

I now have a kitchen full of sourdough starters again, and somehow that makes me feel better.

"Apparently that's what that bracelet is," I confirm. "I showed it to the housekeeper and she immediately recognized it. She told me that little cage holds his fitness tracker and he was fanatical about having it and keeping records of his physical activity."

"He did have an obsession with being in shape and physically superior to any other man," Dean notes.

"I just don't understand what it could mean, though. Why would Jonah want to emphasize the man's fitness tracker? Just to make us think harder about the possibility he had a heart attack?" I ask.

"People in exceptional shape have heart attacks all the time," Dean points out. "Marathon runners, swimmers, triathletes. People whose bodies are literally their entire lives can just drop dead of a heart attack right in the middle of one of their events."

"Let's be honest, most people would drop dead attempting to do one of those events, but I understand your point. He was in pretty good shape, but I wouldn't go so far as to say he was a super athlete or anything. And he lived a very indulgent lifestyle with his food and drink, drugs, smoking. All of it. That's going to put a strain on a heart. Not to mention he was facing some very serious stress in the form of several life sentences in a very less-than-glamorous prison," I say. "But the thing is, the medical examiner didn't see any particular risk factors in his heart. There wasn't any sign of serious heart disease or a stroke. He didn't seem like a candidate for a sudden heart attack like that."

"Which brings us back to there being something else going on," Dean says.

I nod, letting out a breath. "That's where we are." I roll my head across the back of the sofa to look at him. "How did your visit go yesterday?"

"It went well," he says. "Xavier is still in high spirits. He looks like he's been eating fine and there were no signs of injuries."

"Somehow mentioning he isn't starving and covered in bruises kind of takes the zip out of an update," I say.

"He is already building a list of the vendors and volunteers coming in and out of the prison, their schedules, and their routines. He hasn't been there long enough to figure out anything major yet, but he's optimistic."

"And he doesn't think anyone has caught on?" I ask.

"If they had, I don't think he would be in good spirits with no signs of injuries," Dean points out. "He did have the thrilling update that his counselor has officially taken the crochet club into consideration. He should hear back on a decision about it within the next couple of weeks."

"That seems like a long time to make a decision about letting some men crochet," I say.

"It's prison, Emma. Valuing the personal time of the inmates isn't exactly a priority. But at least it gives him something to look forward to while he's investigating."

"How long do you think he's going to need to be in there?" I ask.

"There's no way of knowing, and I don't think we can let ourselves think like that. He's going to be in there for as long as he needs to be to find what you need him to. If something happens, we'll get him out. If you think too much about when it's going to be over, it will make it more stressful for you, and you have other things you need to be focusing on," he says.

"I know."

Sam gets home just a few minutes after Dean and I get back later that evening. His eyes are bright and his expression looks excited, far more excited than he usually does after work. I know he loves his job, and he's proud to have followed in the footsteps of his father and grandfather as Sheriff of Sherwood. But the reality is, it isn't usually the most stimulating and thrilling of career options.

Sherwood has seen some devastating crimes over the years, but those incidents are few and far between. He's grateful for that. It's good to be the sheriff of a mostly peaceful and safe community. On the other hand, days of driving around the streets, telling teenagers to cross at the light, giving out the occasional ticket, and sometimes rescuing a puppy from a drainage pipe can leave him on the low end of the thrill spectrum.

Today, though, he looks pumped. My initial thought is that someone was either murdered or robbed the bank. Part of me wants to chastise myself for thinking it, but the other part of me is just glad he's happy.

"Is everything alright?" I ask, walking over to him and resting my hand on his chest.

"I just got off the phone with Marie's bank. It turns out, she had her mother as an authorized user for her account."

"Without Aunt Rose knowing?" I ask.

"Apparently. When she called to ask the bank manager what he would need in order to provide her with statements from Marie's account, he looked it up and said she was added months ago."

"Why would she do that?" I ask.

"I don't know. But it meant she had access to all the statements. They were able to give her online access and I went through her account. It hasn't been used since she disappeared, which isn't surprising, but what is surprising is a few of the transactions."

"What were they?"

"I'm not sure exactly. But it looks like she was being paid by somebody on a fairly regular basis."

"Was she dealing?" Dean asks.

"I don't think so. These were consistent payments done as a wire transfer. So unless she has joined up with an extremely financially responsible drug cartel that has her on a salary for selling what would be very small amounts of controlled substances considering the payment amounts, I don't think that's what was happening."

"Who was making the payments?" I ask.

"I'm not sure. It doesn't give full information. I'm looking into it. I also found payments she made to a cloud storage company. There's something she's protecting that she either didn't want to risk losing or didn't want to be found on her computer."

"Could be both," Dean says.

"Are you going to get access to it?" I ask.

"That's harder," he admits. "Rose and I tried to figure out her log-in credentials, but we haven't been able to. Even using the forgot password feature was useless because it said she didn't have an account under her email address."

"She used a different address specifically for that," I muse. "It must be something she really wanted to protect. Documents, audio files. Something she would be able to receive or create on her computer and then save to the cloud storage."

"I'm going to keep trying to figure it out," Sam says. "I've already reached out to the company to try to get them to understand the situation and provide us access."

"Have you shared any of this with the police?" Dean asks. "They could get a warrant to compel the company to give you that information."

Sam lets out a chortle. "The police have completely stopped caring about Marie's case. To them, calling it a straightforward overdose is the easiest thing that they do. It means they don't have to think too hard about it or try to find anybody who's responsible because to them, she's the one who did it to herself. Even though I keep bringing them new evidence and showing how ridiculous it is to think she went down that drug rabbit hole that quickly with nobody knowing, nobody is taking me or anything I have to say about it seriously."

"And remember, these are the same police who refused to do a basic welfare check," I add.

"Exactly," Sam concurs. "There's something else happening with that. Somebody knows something. They just don't want it coming out. I'm not going to get any help from the police. They aren't going to go out of their way to help me investigate this. I'm going to have to do it on my own."

"Not on your own," I tell him. "We'll help you as much as we can."

"I know you will," he smiles, pulling me in for a kiss. "But you have your own things to handle, too."

"We do," I say. "That doesn't mean we can't help. You have the best private investigator in the business right here in your home. I'm sure Dean has a couple of tricks up his sleeve when it comes to finding details like that about somebody."

"You might oversell me a bit there, but thank you for the sentiment," my cousin says. "But, yes, I've had to get access to things like cloud storage, online payment accounts, and hidden social media before for cases. Now, since you are technically The Law, with the big T and L, I'm going to go ahead and put down the disclaimer that not everything I am going to suggest is one hundred percent on the up and up. If you can deal with perhaps just a little bit of shady tactics, I can get you what you need."

Sam nods without hesitation.

"Do it."

CHAPTER TWENTY-FOUR

THE DAY BEFORE VALENTINE'S DAY, DEAN AND I MAKE OUR WAY back to Cold Valley. Sam and I aren't big on celebrating the holiday, but there's still a definite tug in my heart when I kiss him goodbye at the airport. I know he has more than enough with work and everything with Marie to wade through over the next few days, so it's not as if I'm leaving him to sit on the couch in his underwear and eat candy-themed pints of ice cream while watching sappy movies. At least he better not. We're supposed to be saving that for when I get home.

For now, Eric has officially declared Shawn Reichert's missing person's case reopened in the Bureau with me in the capacity of lead agent in the field. It means we can request the appropriate warrants to access the area of the park that is technically within Jim Calhoun's property and examine it with the new information we gathered from Maya's video.

The request is in and we're hoping to have approval soon after arriving back in town. It will give us a chance to hit the ground running and hopefully get some answers.

I'm disappointed when we go through the same routine of landing, gathering our luggage at the carousel, going to the car rental desk, and making the drive to Cold Valley without hearing a peep from the judge. I have more than enough experience with warrants and legal red tape to know things like this can get dragged out, especially on a weekend, so I tell myself not to get discouraged. There are other things we can do while we wait.

Just like before, our first stop is the boarding house. I called June when we knew we would be heading back and she seemed happy to have us returning, promising us our same rooms. That's a nice touch. The familiarity is comforting. But it also makes me feel like she has made at least some sort of connection with us. A connection like that can be invaluable during complicated investigations. Because she has lived here her entire life and has first-hand knowledge of Shawn and at least some of his movements when he was here, she can offer us insights and details we wouldn't be able to get otherwise.

That link to her, even if it is somewhat tenuous, makes it that much more likely she'll be helpful when we need her.

She's waiting behind the desk, sitting and quilting just like she had been the first time, when we arrive. I'm expecting her to hand us registration cards again. I know Mirna would. Instead, she just gives us back the keys we gave her the day we left.

"Thank you, Ms. June," I say. "We appreciate your hospitality."

We start out of the sitting room and I hear her coming around the desk behind me.

"Emma?"

I turn around to face her.

"Hmm?"

"There's something I forgot to tell you when we were talking about Michael... Shawn. I'm sorry. It's hard for me to think of him as anything else."

"It's alright," I say. "What did you need to tell me?"

"It's actually something I need to show you," she says.

"Okay. Let me bring my luggage upstairs and I'll be right back down. Is that alright?"

The older woman nods, her hands twisting in front of her body in a way that makes me a little nervous about what she's going to reveal.

"What do you think it is?" Dean asks as we drag our bags up the stairs.

"I don't know. She seems nervous," I say. "Which I really don't like. People who are nervous during investigations into missing people are usually hiding something, and I really don't like the kinds of scavenger hunts they send me on."

"Do you think she could have had something to do with his disappearance?" he asks.

I stop in front of the door to my room and give him a look.

"Are you asking me if I think she pulled a Dorothea Puente?" I ask. He raises his eyebrows and lifts his shoulders just slightly. "I highly doubt June has that kind of upper body strength, and I didn't notice much lawn space outside, but if what that woman forgot to tell me is that she killed Shawn Reichert ten years ago and she wants to show me the planters where she stashed him, it will make our job a lot easier."

I go into my room and drop off my luggage on the bed and floor, then head back downstairs, leaving Dean to his efforts of unpacking and getting settled back in. June is in the sitting room when I get downstairs, pacing in short passes as she waits. She looks up when I come into the room.

"I'm sorry I didn't show these to you earlier," she says. "They've been in the basement for ten years because I didn't know what to do with them. I found them yesterday when I was getting lightbulbs."

"It's alright, June. What are they?"

She walks over to the desk and two small cardboard mailing boxes that I assumed were just deliveries for the boarding house. Now that I look at them better, I notice their age. Rather than picking them up, she rests her hand on top of one of them and looks over at me.

"These were delivered to his room right before he disappeared. This one came first, the day before he went missing. This one came the day he left and never came back."

"Delivered to his room?" I ask.

She looks almost embarrassed. "I have guests who come and stay for a short time like you, but there are some guests who have this as their steady address. I want them to feel like they're home, and part of that is not having to come to me and sign for packages or mail when it's delivered. And to be honest, I don't want to have to be bothered to hold and store it, or to take responsibility for it. I'd rather them just get their packages and letters when they arrive.

"I don't usually have mail coming in for short-term guests, so I've never had a problem with it. For guests who are going to receive mail, they sign a slip saying they give permission for it to be delivered to the room. The mail carrier comes, gets the extra key for that room, and leaves the mail just inside the door if the guest doesn't answer."

"You let the mail carrier go into their rooms unattended?" I ask, shocked by the revelation.

"As I said, I've never had a problem with it. Otis has been carrying the mail around here for nearly forty years. I taught that boy piano when he was young. He knows I won't tolerate any funny business and the guests have already given their permission. They feel like they are getting more privacy out of their mail being dropped right inside than they would if it was kept up at the desk," she says.

There's a slight hint of defensiveness in her tone and I nod to try to smooth it over.

"I can see that," I say. "I guess it's not much different than the big online places where you can shop and they will deliver into your garage or your living room."

"Exactly. The guests get their mail as soon as they get back to their rooms and I don't have the clutter or the headache of keeping it straight. These were the only two things he ever had delivered. He was here for more than a month and he never got a single letter. Never a bill, a postcard, anything. Then just before his disappearance, he got these. When I went into his room to clear out his belongings, I found them, unopened. They were just like this."

She holds her hand out over them like she's displaying them.

"Why did you keep them?" I ask. "Didn't the rest of his belongings get turned over to the investigators?"

"No," she says. "He wasn't married and didn't have a next of kin. They said they couldn't take possession of anything that wasn't considered evidence. He didn't have a whole lot with him, but I donated what I could. I don't know what possessed me to hold onto these. I guess it just felt strange that he would receive packages and never even open them. It felt like they meant something. Like maybe they'd come in handy someday. I put them down there and didn't think of them again."

"Can I take them?" I ask.

She nods. "They aren't doing anyone else any good. And I figure you are FBI. It would be harder to convict you of Federal mail fraud since you are the Feds."

I decide not to answer that. Instead, I smile at her as I pick up the boxes. One of them is distinctly heavier than the other, enough so that after lifting the heavier one I nearly toss the lighter one with the excessive effort.

"Thank you. I appreciate you giving these to me."

"I hope they can help," she says.

I bring the boxes upstairs and take pictures of them from several angles, then write down notes about them and how they came into my possession before Dean and I open them.

Then I spend the rest of the evening wondering why someone with no return address sent Shawn Reichert a box of densely bound newspapers and one with just a few torn sheets of paper. And why they both have the same postage.

CHAPTER TWENTY-FIVE

I WANTED TO GO TO THE LIBRARY YESTERDAY, BUT BECAUSE IT WAS Sunday it was closed. It's opening soon and I intend on being there as soon as it does. I need to look at the microfilm and see if I can figure out what Shawn was looking at the day he went missing.

When I get downstairs, the house smells like pancakes and I think about Xavier and his careful wedges. I hope he's doing well and send him good thoughts. It's all I can do at the moment.

I knew I was going to miss him when he was gone, but I honestly didn't think about just how much I would notice his absence from moment to moment. We don't even live in the same town and there are stretches of weeks at a time that pass without us seeing each other. But we talk far more frequently, and now that Dean has gotten him used to video calls, it's almost like being together every couple of days.

The biggest thing is the same as it is with my father—just knowing I can get to him. Dad is undercover right now, but I know there are still ways I could get in touch with him if I really needed to. I have that reassurance, especially when he is just at home in his house outside of the DC area, that I can just pick up my phone and call him if I need to ask him a question or go over something that's confusing or bothering me, or even just because I want to hear his voice.

The same is always true for Xavier. I can get to him when I need to talk to him. Sometimes, I just need to know how he sees a situation or hear his interpretation of something that I'm trying to unravel. I might not always understand what he says at first pass, or even months later, but it's bolstering. And the times that he does come out with something I can understand often prove shockingly valuable. Even if that value is just a moment of clarity, of seeing a situation or a person, or even myself, through his eyes. I know my world is a better place for having him in it.

I don't think I really prepared myself to not have that.

When I come around the corner into the dining room, I find myself taken away from my thoughts of Xavier. Unfortunately, it's because I'm faced with June setting a platter of heart-shaped pancakes in the middle of a table decorated with hearts in various shades of red and pink, along with tall, thin vases of roses.

She looks up at me and smiles. "Happy Valentine's Day." Then her face drops a little. "Oh. I'm sorry. You're probably missing your husband, aren't you?"

I'd done a great job of being in denial about that this morning, but now I definitely was.

"Happy Valentine's Day," I tell her. "This looks really nice."

She looks over it and lets out a contented sigh. "Thank you. I like to try to make holidays around here special. Valentine's Day can be a hard one for just about anybody, but if you're alone or traveling, it can be that much worse. When my Henry died, I never wanted to see another heart or rose again in my life. He always showered me with sweet little gifts around Valentine's Day."

"That's sweet," I smile.

"Nothing extravagant, of course. But it didn't need to be. He made paper hearts and brought me flowers and my favorite candies. One year he caught on to a particular fabric I'd been admiring and bought everything the store had. I woke up Valentine's Day to yards and yards of that fabric. It was beautiful and I absolutely loved it, but it was so much more than I could use in a project. I put the extra away in a closet so I could keep going back to it when I was working on something new. You know, I still have some of that fabric."

She laughs and the sound is a familiar mix of happiness and sorrow. "Anyway, I didn't want to do anything around the holiday ever again. I thought it would hurt too much. Then one year I realized that doing nothing was hurting me just as much. Maybe even more. So the next year I brought out the decorations and little gifts Henry got me. I started making special breakfasts. Sometimes I even get enough to help put together special dinners or desserts for couples staying here. It's like I can still celebrate every Valentine's Day with Henry."

I'm glad June has softened and is opening up more, and her story is truly adorable, but I don't want to hear her say "Valentine's Day" anymore.

"My husband and I have never really been big on celebrating it," I tell her. "Not on the day itself, anyway. I do miss him, though. But I've got work to do. Speaking of which, you told me that Shawn was at the library the day he disappeared looking at microfilm."

"Yes," June nods, looking a little confused by the sudden shift in conversation.

"But you don't know what he was looking at?"

"No," she says. "He was in the room by himself. Vera doesn't like to crowd people when they are using the rooms like that. She thinks it's tacky."

"Thank you. I'm going to head up there and see if I can figure it out," I say. "Maybe what he was looking up has something to do with his disappearance."

"Don't you want breakfast?" she asks after me as I walk out of the dining room.

I nearly run into Dean as I head for the door.

"Hey," he says. "Good morning."

"Morning," I say. I turn around and wave at June. "I'll grab something while I'm out. Thank you, anyway. I'm just not in a pancake kind of mood."

"Where are you going?" Dean calls after me.

"Library."

"I'll meet you there later. I am definitely in a pancake mood."

There's no need to get in my car. The library is located on Broad Street only a few blocks from the boarding house, so it's an easy walk. I pull the collar of my jacket up over my ears and duck my head as I hurry down the sidewalk to warm up in the morning chill. A woman in a gray tweed skirt and jacket is just opening the doors when I get to the bottom of the stone steps leading up to the library.

She gives me a suspicious look when I get to the top. That's the kind of Cold Valley greeting I was anticipating.

"Good morning," I say.

"Good morning."

There's just as much suspicion in her voice as there was in the look on her face, but she seems to be doing her level best to contain any outright comments questioning the motivation of a woman showing up at the library this early on a Monday morning.

She steps out of the way to let me inside and I glance around. This is the kind of building I think of when I hear the word "library." It's an old building just like the boarding house, but has been meticulously maintained. Warm wood makes up the predominant material for the counters, tables, chairs, and shelves, and a high-polished marble floor adds grandeur to the space, even if it isn't a huge one. I'm drawn to the little green lamps in the corners of tables off to one side.

"Can I help you find something?" the woman, who I assume is the Vera that June has talked about, asks.

I decide to take the leap.

"Vera?"

She peers down her nose at me. "Yes."

"Hi," I say. "My name is Emma Griffin Johnson. I'm staying at the boarding house and June has told me about you."

The mention of June's name is like giving a password at a clubhouse. The tension on the librarian's face lessens and she pushes her eyeglasses back up to the bridge of her nose where they rightfully belong.

"Emma Griffin," she says. It comes out of her mouth slowly, in that way that means she's testing it out and seeing if it's actually what she thinks it is. "Are you that FBI agent?"

It seems Vera has been sampling the true crime as well. I like to imagine the two of them in pajamas with a giant bowl of popcorn bingeing seasons together.

"I am," I tell her. "That's actually why I'm here. I'm helping with an investigation here in town and I think I might get some valuable information from your library."

"I can show you to the books about the town's history," she says, starting in the direction of a small alcove toward the back of the library.

"No," I say quickly. "That's not exactly what I had in mind. I'm actually interested in your microfilm. June tells me you have quite the collection here."

"You can say that," she says. "I've been head librarian here for more than fifty years. One of my main projects has been to make sure as much of the town's history is preserved for future generations. I know microfilm is seen as outdated by some, but at least we have the records from years ago. Things you can't just find on the internet because they were only released on paper and only archived this way."

"I agree," I nod. "Preservation is vital."

She starts walking and I follow her. "What is it that you are looking for?"

"I'm actually looking for someone," I clarify. "And what he was looking at before he went missing."

"That man," she says. "Michael." She shakes her head. "No. That wasn't his real name, was it?"

"No," I tell her. "It wasn't. His name was Shawn Reichert. He was an undercover FBI agent."

She draws in a breath like she's steeling herself against the information I just gave her.

"I'd heard whispers he was something like that, that people came from Washington to find out what happened to him and told the sheriff who he really was, but he was sworn to secrecy. I just didn't know how much stock to put in that."

"Well, I don't know about anyone swearing the sheriff to secrecy, but some discretion was likely requested considering the sensitivity of the work he was doing. It's been ten years and there has still been no sign of him, so the investigation has started again. I think that whatever he was looking up on the microfilm could put us in the direction of what happened to him. Or at least give some insight into what he was investigating so we can dig deeper."

"I didn't ask him what he was looking at," she says. "And he didn't tell me."

"I know," I say. "But is there any way to find out? Do you have records, sign-out sheets? I know it's been ten years, but is there any way that you could trace which films he might have been looking at?"

"I have a logbook of everyone who uses the microfilm. They have to sign in and out and record the serial numbers assigned to each reel or each sheet of microfiche. I can look through the log with you and help you find the media he was using," she offers.

"It's the same logbook? Even after ten years?" I ask.

"The internet," she says, shaking her head as she walks away.

I don't know if it's a condemnation of the entire concept or just the use of it for recordkeeping, but I'm left with little choice but to sit there and wait.

CHAPTER TWENTY-SIX

NOT CONDEMNATION. EXPLANATION.

As it turns out, Vera might be the type of woman who wears gray tweed to the library she has worked at for fifty years and looks down her nose at people who don't appreciate the finer aspects of tiny duplication as a means of preserving media, but she's also a sharp old broad who knows her way around a computer. Including being able to implement internet-based tracking of library visitors and what they read, the materials they use, and the resources they take advantage of while they're there.

Not so enabling of privacy in the library after all.

She pulls up the database of information and uses a search feature to find the name Michael Forbes.

"There," I say, pointing out the name as it appears on the screen along with several entries. "He came in here a few times." The numbers beside his name don't mean anything to me, but I notice several of them are the same each time he visited. There was something specific about those items that kept his attention. "Can you help me find these?"

Two hours later, I'm sitting at the closest diner to the library when my phone rings.

"Hey, Dean," I say.

"I thought I was meeting you at the library," he says.

"You didn't get there fast enough."

"Where are you?"

"At the diner across the street. You can probably see me through the window when you come outside."

I lift up in my booth and look through the big window across the front of the diner to look at the library. Dean appears at the top of the steps and looks in my direction. I wave with my fork and he starts toward me.

"You're eating pancakes?" he asks as he nears the window.

"Yes, I am eating pancakes," I say. "And they are amazing. Would you like some?"

I offer a bite up to him as he enters the diner and hangs up the phone, but he shakes his head. "I'm still stuffed from breakfast. Why are you here? I thought you weren't in a pancake mood."

"Of course I'm in a pancake mood. Have you ever truly known me not to be in a pancake mood?" I ask.

"Then why didn't you stay for breakfast?"

"The pancakes were shaped like hearts, Dean," I say around a bite of the fluffy vehicles for butter and syrup.

"I'm sure that means something offensive," he replies, sitting across from me and grabbing my glass of juice for a swig.

"What took you so long to get to the library?" I ask. "How many of those pancakes did you eat?"

"Enough for several cardiac units. But that's not what actually took up all that time. I was at the park," he explains.

I pause. "You went back to the park? Even after Calhoun all but threatened to shoot us if we came back without a warrant?"

"Who says I didn't have a warrant?"

My eyes widen. "It went through? And you didn't call me?"

Dean looks hesitant. I know that look. It's the one he gets when he's trying to figure out exactly the right way to word something. No matter how he decides to do it, I'm not going to like what he says, so by now, he should have figured he should just say it however it comes to mind.

"I thought it might be better if I went by myself this time," he starts. "After the way you and Calhoun butted heads during the first interaction, I figured a little distance might do the process some good if I ran into him again. It would give me the chance to let him know about the official investigation so he could get used to the idea of having us out there."

"Since when do we care if someone is used to something before we do an investigation? Especially if they are an ass? Actually, let me reword that. Since when do I care if someone is used to something before I do an investigation, especially if they are an ass?" I ask.

The waitress who has been taking care of me makes her way over to the table with a smile that doesn't fully cover up the concern on her face.

"Is everything alright over here? Your pancakes good?"

"They're delicious," I say. "Thank you."

"How about your coffee? Can I get you a refill?"

"That would be great," I say, smiling up at her broadly.

As soon as she walks away, all starched pink dress, white apron, and polished tennis shoes, the smile drops away and I glare at Dean again.

"Emma, you know you care about people. Somewhere in there," he says. "But the point is, we're going to be on his land and we don't know how long we're going to be there or what we're going to need to do. Issues might come up that only he can fix, or questions only he can answer. It's going to make everything a lot easier if he's assuaged at least a little bit."

"And was he?" I ask.

"No," Dean says without a second of hesitation. "If anything, he was worse. Ranting about how he knew we were 'those kind' and that we were going to get anything we wanted."

"What is that supposed to mean?" I raise an eyebrow.

"I don't know. He didn't seem drunk or high or anything. Just angry," Dean says.

"But what is he so angry about? He can't be that worked up about us trespassing. There are still people who use the entire park, even the sections that are closed."

"Maybe it just offends him that the two of you are looking at his land as a potential crime scene."

The voice behind me makes my head snap around. Sam smiles at me, the same boyish smile I fell in love with when I was seven coming at me from a face that is most certainly not a little boy. A lock of his hair is hanging down over his forehead and his eyes look both tired and filled with happiness.

"Sam?" Dean asks.

"Happy Valentine's Day, baby," he grins.

I'm on my feet as fast as I can and throw my arms around his neck, pulling him close. He holds me tight, laughing as I squeeze him.

"What are you doing here?" I ask.

"I know we don't do Valentine's Day all that much," he says, sliding his arms away from my waist and sitting down in the booth beside me. "But I couldn't be away from you. We already spent so much of the last couple of months apart, and I haven't finished recovering after missing you."

I grin. "You know so many good words."

"And the right order to put them in," he says.

I lean my head on his shoulder as he reaches out to shake Dean's hand.

"Good to see you, buddy." He looks at the table and quirks an eyebrow at Dean. "Nothing for you?"

"I'm still full from breakfast at the boarding house," he explains.

"What did you have?" Sam asks.

"Pancakes," Dean says. "Emma wasn't in the mood for pancakes."

Sam looks down at my plate and then back up to me with a questioning look.

"They were shaped like hearts," I say.

"Ah," Sam says understandingly and I can't help but press another kiss to his cheek.

"Go on," I say to Dean as I snuggle up close to Sam's side and loop my arm in his to hold his hand. "Was Genevieve there? Was he weird about her again?"

I'm sure this is not what Dean wants to be witnessing at this moment, but I am invoking the Valentine's Day card. It is my naturally born right to make goo-goo eyes at my husband and throw my squishy feelings in the face of anyone within a several-mile radius. So help me Hallmark.

"She was there and so was another girl. Melanie, she called her Mel. He kept looking over at them and when I was leaving, he went over to them and stepped up in between them so he could wrap his arms around both of them to watch me go," Dean says.

"I get such a strange vibe off that man," I say.

"Well, fortunately for us, he no longer has the legal right to stand in our way. We can go back and investigate that area as much as we want. It's just a matter of figuring out exactly what we are looking for that the previous searches might have overlooked."

It's hard to imagine that all the searches over all these years have missed something, but we can't just ignore Maya's memory. It might be a shaky piece of evidence at best, but it's what we have to work with right now.

"What about you?" Sam asks. "What were you doing? I went by the boarding house to surprise you and met the woman June you told me about. She said you went to the library first thing this morning."

I nod. "I wanted to trace what Shawn was looking at on the microfilm the day he disappeared. I found out he was a pretty frequent flier of the microfilm room. Some of the materials he looked at several times."

"What were they?" Dean asks.

"News archives," I tell him. "He read several news articles about deaths that happened in Cold Valley and the neighboring rural area over the course of a couple of years."

"Serial killer?" Sam wonders.

"The articles didn't say the deaths were connected. They were reporting them as different, individual deaths and all as accidents."

"I don't understand," Dean says.

"Across a span of three years, seven farm workers died performing basic tasks. Falling out of the hay loft, accidents with the equipment, one even got into the pen with a bull and didn't make it out."

"Accidental deaths happen on farms," Sam says. "There are only a couple of working farms near Sherwood and I've had to respond to a couple of deaths at them over my career."

"Exactly. So why was Shawn so interested in these deaths? Why did he keep going back to the articles? I read through them a couple of times and noticed that it isn't just the fact that a farm worker died that links the articles. In each of the circumstances, the man who died wasn't from the area. He'd been hired from the outside and brought to one of the farms in Cold Valley or the next county to work."

"Migrant workers?" Dean asks.

"A few of them specifically mentioned that they were seasonal workers who came to the area before to work the farms during planting or harvest seasons. Another couple were men who had been hired on as permanent or semi-permanent labor through an online search. Different farms, different times, different manners of death. But each one of them came into the area from the outside. I know accidental deaths on farms happen. It's just a tragic reality. But is there something about being from the area of the farm that makes you immune to it?"

CHAPTER TWENTY-SEVEN

'M STILL TOSSING THE ARTICLES SHAWN WAS RESEARCHING AROUND in my head as we walk around the wooded area later. I am finding it a little difficult to continue to refer to it as a park considering it has more or less been converted back to a piece of Calhoun's backyard. Albeit a backyard with professionally created trails and the continued presence of signs and markers put up by the park.

There has to be something more to this place, though. Reichert wouldn't come all the way out here to do an investigation into a string of deaths without anyone at the Bureau knowing that's what he was looking into. All the information we have is that he was building a money-laundering case. But there was nothing in any of those articles that suggested involvement in anything criminal. I know I'm going to have to find a different angle. There had to be something about those deaths in particular that made them a focus in the agent's undercover work. We just have to find it.

"Previous searches were done all over this area," Dean tells me. "In fact, the entire park was searched a couple of different times. The police did a formal search. The FBI sent people to search. And there were a couple of citizen search parties put together to search."

"Search parties for someone who wasn't from the area?" Sam asks. "According to them he was just someone staying in town for a little while, right? Usually, search parties form when it's someone who is known in a community, or at least has strong ties to it. In this situation, I thought it was the accepted understanding that he just decided to leave."

"It was when he first went missing. That's why he wasn't even reported missing for several weeks. June found the money for payment for the room inside along with many of his belongings, so she figured he would be back. When he didn't come, she thought he must have just decided to move on. That happens around little towns like this. People drift in and out," Dean explains.

"So searches weren't carried out until his fiancée reported to the Bureau that he hadn't come home and hadn't had any communication with her, and they determined he was missing," I add. "That's a big stretch of time to pass before looking for someone. In all that time, evidence can be lost or destroyed, and even signs of a body or disposal can be far harder to identify."

"For right now, our focus is on this area," Dean says. "If we don't find anything, maybe we consider a larger search at another time, or request the FBI send in a larger team."

"Don't start going down that slope yet," I say. "Like you said, we focus on this area. What brought us here is that video. Maya's memory. So we take her words and what she described during my conversation with her and we try to narrow down where she might have been and if she did actually see something. We start at the beginning, Dean."

"The beginning is ten years ago, Emma," he says. "Things change so much during that time."

"One thing hasn't," I counter. "Shawn Reichert is still missing, and whatever he was investigating hasn't been revealed. There have been searches, yes. But maybe they weren't looking for the right thing."

"And what is the right thing to be looking for?" Dean asks.

"I don't know," I admit. "But that's why we keep an open mind when we search. Rather than trying to find something specific, we need to be looking for things that stand out, that don't seem to fit in, then go from there. But we also need to be looking at the things that aren't so obvious, that don't immediately jump out. Things that are supposed to be here and would go easily unnoticed."

"You want us to look for things that we don't notice?" Dean cracks wryly. "Things that should be here already? Like, there are trees. And a couple of signs. And a whole hell of a lot of leaves."

"Not just random things," I say. "Things that could be used to make actual evidence unnoticeable, too. There was a case years ago where a woman went missing on her own dairy farm. Her husband woke up in the middle of the night and she wasn't there beside him. She was known to have trouble sleeping, so he didn't think a lot of it and just figured she'd gone for a walk out in the fields."

"In the middle of the night?" Sam asks. "She just got out of bed and wandered off into the dark to stroll around with the cows?"

"Apparently it was something she was known to do on a fairly regular basis. She couldn't sleep well, she found peace on the land, so she would go off and walk. She was also known for getting tired and sometimes even a little disoriented while she was having these walks and would end up in one of the barns or other outbuildings.

"There was also a small house separated from the main house by several acres. It was their original home when they'd first bought the land. It had been there for many decades already by then, but they decided it was still in good condition so it made for a good guest house or place they could offer to new hands they hired. Sometimes when she went on these walks, she'd just stop there and fall asleep or read for a while.

"Even her two sons, who lived in their own homes on the property, said the only reason their father called them to let them know she wasn't in the house was that a storm was about to hit and he was worried she'd get caught in it. They didn't think it was strange that she was out walking and they weren't particularly worried about her.

"But by the next morning, they hadn't been able to locate her. They searched every building; they searched all the land. The police came and did their own search. Nothing. They even brought dogs with them to track her scent, but it didn't do anything. They weren't able to find her. Years later, her son was walking around the property checking for broken fences from the winter, just making sure everything was in good condition. He went into one of the fields and found his mother's body. "

"Holy shit," Dean says. "She was there the whole time?"

"Yes," I nod. "Now, that entire farm had been searched very heavily the morning she was reported missing. Officers, dogs, the whole thing. The family was out scouring it, finding corners and spots that other people might not think to look. But they didn't find her."

"How is that possible?" Sam asks.

"A combination of factors that were expected and already in place," I say. "Her taking walks around the land wasn't considered unusual behavior, so it didn't bring up any red flags immediately. Her husband even admitted he didn't start actively searching for her for a couple of hours after waking up and realizing she wasn't there. It wasn't until it seemed like the storm was going to start eminently that he woke up his sons and they started actually searching.

"But the main thing was the cows themselves. They weren't kept in one location on the farm. They moved the herd from place to place to make sure there was enough for them all to graze on, and allowing them to use different sections of the farm kept the ground naturally nourished. The son who found her body later told police the morning they were searching for his mother, his father asked him to make sure the cattle were moved to the next section on the rotation. He did what he was asked.

"He didn't think anything of it because that was something that they did regularly. It was one of the responsibilities of running the farm. Anyone who works the farm will tell you that chores and responsibilities don't stop for anything. No matter what else is going on, there are animals to be fed and work to be done. Rotating the cows was just an example of that work.

"But as it turned out, the cows distracted the dogs. They weren't able to accurately follow the mother's scent and none of those searching actually went into that field because of the animals there. The point is, her body laid there for years because completely predictable, already-existing factors made it difficult to see what was right there." I look at both of the men, making sure they were following me. "So, that's what we stay open to here."

They both blink, look at each other, and then look back at me.

"Should we start at the beginning of the trail?" Dean asks.

"Seems as good a place as any," I reply.

CHAPTER TWENTY-EIGHT

"**I**'M SORRY I STOLE YOU AWAY FROM WORK," SAM SAYS.

"I think I can forgive you," I say, smiling over at him.

He holds my hand, squeezing it just enough that no one would be able to see his hand moving, but I can feel his palm press against mine a little tighter. That's my favorite kind of squeeze. One that is just for the two of us.

"Good, because I don't think I could have lived with myself if I passed up the opportunity to experience a real live Valentine's Day carnival," he says.

"Have you ever heard of a Valentine's Day carnival?" I ask.

"Nope. But I'm feeling the hype."

"Well, I'm feeling dizzy from all the neon lights and the smell of body spray," I say.

"Oh, come on, you grump. Get into the spirit. I mean, seriously, how can you not be inspired by a balloon pop game called Cupid's Arrow? Are you trying to get the balloons to fall in love? While destroying them? Is it a metaphor? I don't know. Or the photo op where you can pretend you're standing on the deck of the Titanic. Kind of tragic and outdated theming there. And, look, the Tunnel of Love, but the lights in the L are dimming so it's just the Tunnel of Ove half the time."

"You know if Xavier saw that he would think it was a ride dedicated to the life of a Swedish man," I say.

"He would and he would be angry that it wasn't. Come on, babe. Let's go see what they've got in there." He leans down to snuggle his face into the curve of my neck. "I love you."

"Alright," I say, wiggling away from his pointy chin hairs. We walk toward the ride and I glance over at him. "Did you call me a grump?"

"You are a grump. But you're a cute grump."

I laugh and lean my head against his shoulder. Having him here with me is all the celebration I really need, but it's really nice to be out doing something special with him tonight. Getting out of the thick of the cases I'm working and just breathing with my hand in his restores me.

And I have to admit, if we're going to do the whole Valentine's Day thing, this is the kind that I'd go for. There might be more hearts, feathery boas, and sappy music around than I ever thought it was possible to stuff into one event, but compared to the stuffy prix-fixe dinners that were the standard of Valentine's Day dates in my younger years, I'd take it any year.

After the Tunnel of Love, we roam around taking in the atmosphere before Sam starts tugging me toward the Ferris Wheel.

"Do you have any idea how cold it's going to be up at the top of that thing?" I ask.

"I'll keep you warm," he promises.

That's all I need to hear.

We scurry to the loading dock and hand the attendant our tickets. He ushers us into a waiting gondola and a second later we lurch up away from the glowing neon carnival and toward the blanket of stars overhead. Just like I thought, the air feels thinner and sharply cold as we perch high above the midway and look out over everything, but the feeling of Sam beside me and the view is more than worth it.

He leans in and kisses me as we start to glide down toward the ground, but the moment is ruined by a terrified scream ripping through the carnival.

"What was that?" I ask, looking over the side of the gondola to try to see what was happening.

"I don't know," Sam says.

There's another scream and my instincts kick in, wanting to get me running toward the sound so I can help. But I'm still in a Ferris Wheel gondola many feet off the ground so there's nothing I can do.

"There's something wrong. Why is no one reacting?" I ask.

"Because we're at a carnival," Sam replies. "We're surrounded by games and rides and all kinds of things meant to make people get excited and act silly. And, if you haven't noticed, there is a very high percentage of pre-teen and teenage girls here. I'm sure it's just one of them getting scared on a ride or trying to get their date's attention."

He gives me a gentle pull on the back of my jacket, so I'll settle against the seat again.

"You're probably right. That was super misogynistic of you, by the way," I say. "But probably accurate."

"How is it misogyny to point out the number of young girls here and say it's probably one of them when we distinctly heard a girl screaming?" he protests.

"The date part," I say. I shrug. "But, again, probably accurate."

"Fair."

We get to the bottom of the ride and step out onto the metal platform. The attendant gives us a wave as we walk down the platform.

"Did you enjoy your ride?" he asks.

"It was great," Sam says. "The view is awesome."

"Thanks," he says as if he personally created the wheel and decided where to put it for maximum viewing potential.

"Did you hear that screaming?" I ask.

"Yeah," he says dismissively. "You get used to it when you work the carnivals. Probably just some girl on a ride hoping the boy she likes will put his arm around her and protect her."

He chuckles and my husband chuckles right along with him.

"Have you had enough Valentine's Day carnival fun?" I ask as we make our way away from the wheel.

Sam shakes his head. "Absolutely not. We haven't played any games, yet. And I need a red velvet funnel cake."

"It looks like intestines shaped into a heart," I say.

"Delicious and appropriate for Halloween as well. You should appreciate that." He sees that the balloon pop game has no one standing at it and pulls my hand. "Let's go."

"I'm so sorry you had to deal with that," Genevieve said. She reached up onto the top shelf of the closet and pulled down a stack of folded blankets. "Those guys are idiots."

"It's alright," Maya said, trying as hard as she could to pretend it actually was.

"No," Genevieve insisted. "It isn't. That was really mean of them. That's their stupid idea of a joke. I promise I didn't have anything to do with it."

Mel made a sound across the room and Genevieve looked at her, the tips of her fingers still pressed to the middle of her chest where she'd put them like she was giving a solemn oath.

"Mel, you don't think I would have done something like this, do you? That I would set all this up just for a cheap laugh at Maya's expense?"

"Dayton was there," Mel pointed out. "He was acting like he was the one who planned it all."

"Dayton always acts like he plans everything because he can't stand the idea of not being the center of attention and the most important thing around at any given moment. And you already know we broke up. Why would I have anything to do with some juvenile prank he was planning?" Genevieve asked.

Maya hated when people said things like that. Juvenile. As if Genevieve wasn't one herself. She couldn't shake the feeling of anger and humiliation.

It had all just been a joke. At least, that was how the group of guys that came tumbling around the corner of the Fun House, laughing so hard they could barely hold themselves up, described it. She had just run out of the building, still wracked with sheer terror that made it so she could barely even see where she was going. Mel caught her in her arms, shaking her to try to get her to calm down and tell them what happened. She'd been inside for so long and they heard her screaming.

That's when the guys bounded out, full of themselves and thinking what they'd just watched was the funniest thing they'd ever seen. Maya felt her stomach twist and her chest burn just remembering the sound of their cackling.

It had felt so real. Being followed. Being trapped. The flames crawling up the walls and into the car with her. Even now, far away from the carnival ground and in the easy light of Genevieve's bedroom, knowing her imagination had taken hold and made those horrific images and feelings bigger and stronger, it was difficult to convince herself they weren't what she thought they were. They weren't real. It was all a joke.

But the memories that flashed through her head when she was in the dark, struggling against the flames, were far from funny. The felt like torture. She would have done anything to get away from them.

"You're right," Mel said. "I'm sorry. I just hate seeing Maya that upset. You know what she's been through."

"You don't have to talk about me like I'm not in the room," Maya snapped. "You aren't sitcom parents. You can't have a conversation about me right in front of me and expect me to not hear you."

"I'm sorry," Genevieve said. "I feel like it's my fault. He was trying to impress me and ruined everything. I just wanted us to have fun tonight. We were supposed to go to the carnival and have a good time, then come back here and drive my mom crazy talking all night so we can't possibly get to school in the morning."

Maya couldn't imagine being allowed to purposely miss school. She wanted the conversation to be over. She'd had enough of reliving the humiliation. Standing up, she walked to the other side of the room to look at the massive bookshelves taking up nearly the entire wall. She'd never been in Genevieve's bedroom before. She'd tried to imagine it. She'd watch Genevieve gliding through life and wonder what she was like away from school. What color were her sheets? Her curtains? Did she have posters on her wall? Was there a desk or a TV?

Of course, she never told anyone that. Today she discovered they were purple. The curtains were white and gauzy even though it was still winter, and she had both a desk and a TV. There were no posters, but the calendar hanging by her window was old and open to the wrong month. Porcelain dolls and puppies.

Maya was surprised by the handmade dollhouse sitting in the corner. It obviously hadn't been touched for many years, but it was there, like it was waiting for Genevieve to come back. Maybe it was like the drawings in Maya's storybooks and they were watching.

She ran her hand along the spines of the books filling the middle shelf. None of them looked like they'd ever been opened. Show books. Just there to take up space and look good. Maya didn't have any of those. She did have plenty of ones that looked like the stack on the next shelf. They were worn and bent like they'd been read through a dozen times. She took one out and turned toward Genevieve.

"I love this one," she said. "I used to read it all the time."

She didn't see Genevieve moving to stop her from flipping through the pages. When Maya got to the middle of the book, something fell out of the spine and fluttered down to the plush cream carpet.

"Maya," Mel said. It sounded like she already knew what it was, but Maya wanted to see.

She reached down and picked up the paper. There was a year scribbled on the back, ten years before. Turning it over, she saw an image that made her feel like her throat was closing, like she was back in that car in the carnival ride.

"What is this?" she asked, turning the picture toward Genevieve.

"It's the three of us," the other girl responded. "At our group."

Maya shook her head and looked at the picture again. "I don't know what this is." She looked back up at Genevieve. "Why do you have this?"

"Because that group was a big part of my life," she said. "It made a difference for me. And it did for you, too."

Maya shoved the picture back into the book and returned it roughly to the shelf.

"I don't know what that is," she insisted.

"Then why are you crying?" Genevieve asked.

Intense eyes fell on her.

Maya wiped away tears she hadn't realized were sliding down her cheeks.

"Maya, you have to remember some of it," Mel said, coming closer to her. "Something."

"No. I don't remember any of it."

But she felt like part of her did. Not the part that could see it or remember the smells or sounds. Not the part of her that could put words to it. Only the part of her that still felt it.

"Then how did you have that memory you talked about in the video?" Genevieve asked.

"I took that down."

"I saw it," she said. "A lot of people saw it. That was a memory of your dad dying."

"Genevieve," Mel said. "Stop."

"She needs to hear this," Genevieve said. "Maya, that memory is of the day the car hit your father and you. That's the trees and the man lying on the ground. The heat is the car."

"No," Maya said. "That's not what I remember. And I don't remember that picture."

How quickly eyes can change to being filled with fear.

Just half an hour later, maybe less.

And in that moment, Maya remembered her. She remembered all of them.

She remembered everything.

CHAPTER TWENTY-NINE

I NEVER LIKE BEING WOKEN UP IN THE MIDDLE OF THE NIGHT BY someone knocking on my door. But tonight, the sound of the pounding just a few steps away from the bed where I'm curled up sleeping next to my husband is especially unnerving.

The sound is so loud and intense my heart is in my throat before my feet are even on the floor. I can hear Dean's voice along with the slamming of his hands against the door.

"Emma, get up! Emma, you need to get up now."

Tugging a bathrobe on around me, I cross the room and open the door, instinctively trying to shush my cousin so he doesn't wake up all the other guests on the floor of the boarding house. I haven't moved fast enough though. There are already open doors down the hallway and people grumbling and complaining.

He doesn't care. He pushes past me into my room and opens my dresser.

"What are you doing?" I demand.

"Dean?" Sam asks groggily from bed. "What's going on?"

"I'm still trying to figure it out. He hasn't told me," I say.

"I'm finding you clothes. You need to get dressed. We've got to go."

June appears at the doorway. Her eyes are narrowed, her arms crossed over her chest.

"Do you have any idea what time it is? You're disturbing the other guests," she scolds. Dean ignores it and throws a handful of clothes at me, which only seems to make June angrier. "I run a respectable place. This type of behavior is unacceptable. There better be an explanation."

Dean's eyes turn to me with a stare that chills my blood.

"How did this happen?"

The air is thick with the smell of ash, wet burned wood, and melted plastic. Around us, people move around in seemingly random routes, as if they don't know what they are supposed to be doing next even though it's their job to handle things like this. I don't blame them. The first sight of the house reduced to a pile of blackened debris took my breath away. Worse was finding out who was inside.

"We don't have any theories yet," the police chief tells me. "It could be anything. The fire burned hot and intense. The investigation is going to take some time."

I nod. "Thank you."

He leaves and walks back to some of the other firefighters. A few have gathered off to the side to take off their helmets and gulp in breaths of the cold fresh air. Spotlights set up to provide light in the inky night blackness illuminate the streaks of ash on their reddened, sweaty skin. I shake my head and turn to Dean, but before I say anything, a man approaches us. He's in a suit with a winter coat thrown over it, a knit beanie pulled down over his blond hair.

"Are you Emma Griffin?" he asks.

"Yes," I say.

He extends his hand to me. "Sheriff Jeffrey Boyd. I believe we had a meeting scheduled for later this week. I'm sorry to be meeting you here instead."

"Me, too. Sheriff Boyd, this is my cousin Dean Steele. He's a private investigator."

THE GIRL AND THE LAST SLEEPOVER

"Yes, Mr. Steele. I believe you were mentioned for the meeting as well." He shakes his hand too, completing the compulsory transaction of encountering new people, even in a situation like this.

"Sheriff, what can you tell us about the fire?" I ask, wanting to cut right to the chase.

"Emergency dispatch received a call just after two A.M. to report a house fire in progress. Vehicles arrived within ten minutes, but the house was already fully engulfed. There was no possible way of saving the structure."

"Ten minutes?" I ask.

"Unfortunately, it takes some time to get out this way. The station house is in town for the more densely populated neighborhoods."

I've seen the neighborhoods near the main area of Cold Valley and I don't think they really qualify to be referred to as densely populated, but I understand what he's getting at.

"That means the fire had been burning for quite some time already," I note.

"That's how it would seem," he nods.

"Who made the call?" I ask.

"Someone driving past on their way home from a Valentine's date. They noticed the smoke and drove up to get a better look."

"Are they here?" I ask, wanting to talk to the caller to find out what they might have seen or witnessed before or while making the call.

"No. They didn't want to be involved and left before responding officers arrived. The call was too short to trace, so we don't know who made it."

"Are there any survivors?" Dean asks.

"As of right now, none have been located. We know there were five people in the home last night. Jim and Sara Calhoun, the homeowners; Sara's daughter, Genevieve; and two of her friends, Melanie Donovan and Maya Cortez."

My heart squeezes in my chest at the mention of Maya's name. When Dean told me he'd heard over his police scanner app, a favorite nighttime activity for him when he's having trouble sleeping, that the Calhoun house was on fire, he didn't mention the possibility of anyone other than the family inside.

"How do you know about the girls?" he asks now, obviously as shocked by the news as I am.

"One of the firefighters has a son who goes to school with all three of them. He mentioned to me that his son said Melanie and Maya planned to spend the night here. We've tried to reach both of them through their cell phones and their social media and haven't heard anything back from either of them. We can only assume they were inside."

"Did you call their parents before you started posting about this online?" I ask.

The thought of one of them stumbling on this kind of news without some sort of preparation is horrifying.

"Yes. Both mothers reported that they haven't seen or spoken to their daughters since they left for the carnival tonight. They've reached out to them and I've told them the best thing they can do right now is stay home and wait just in case they didn't come here and will go home later. I didn't want them to come here and see this."

"That's good," I say. "This isn't something either of them needs to see."

"Can I ask what you're doing here, Ms. Griffin?" he asks. He gets a sheepish smile and turns slightly to gesture toward another officer. "I have to admit, one of my officers recognized you and told me you were here, that's why I came over to introduce myself. But he didn't know why you, or your cousin or husband, are here."

"Our current investigation involves some of Mr. Calhoun's land," I explain. "We've encountered him a couple of times and just today got a warrant to search through this land. Dean heard about the fire. We wanted to see what was happening."

"And you are in Cold Valley investigating that disappearance ten years ago?" he confirms. "I believe that's what we were supposed to meet about."

"Yes," I say.

He shakes his head. "I remember that happening. It was so surreal. People don't just go missing from around here. And to find out he wasn't actually who all of us thought he was? It was… surreal."

"That's one way to put it," I nod.

"I honestly never would have pegged him for an FBI agent. I guess I had an image of what those people look like." He pauses awkwardly. "You people. I'm sorry."

He shakes his head and lets out an embarrassed laugh. It's an uncomfortable reaction considering the scene in front of us, and he seems to realize it almost instantly. The smile drops from his face and he shoves his hands deep into his coat pockets.

"That's an important characteristic of an agent who is doing undercover work in the field," I say.

"What is?" he asks.

"Not looking like an agent who is doing undercover work in the field."

He lets out a chuckle. "That's a valid point."

From the hazy area at the edge of where my eyes can handle the intense brightness of the spotlights, a uniformed officer runs toward us.

"Sir," he says as he approaches.

Sheriff Boyd nods his acknowledgment. "What's going on, Harrison?"

"The firefighters found remains," the officer says.

CHAPTER THIRTY

I STAND BACK AS A GURNEY MOVES PAST US TOWARD THE WAITING ambulance on the grass. There are no lights, no sirens. It's the dark, empty silence that I've always found haunting. A screaming ambulance racing down the street, blaring its horn, lights blinding at every angle, can be startling. It can even cause chaos as drivers scramble to get out of the way. The blocked intersections make the horn and sirens just seem louder.

But that means hope. It means there's someone who still has a chance to be saved.

When the ambulance is slow and there is no sound to get people out of the way, it means the hope is lost.

That hangs heavily over everyone gathered at the destroyed house as we watch the black body bag bearing the body of Sara Calhoun.

While the sheriff talks to the officers and the firefighters, coordinating with the fire chief to continue the search for the rest of the bodies, Dean and I take the opportunity to slip away and look around the area.

People are everywhere, trying to figure out what to do next. The situation is hard to fathom. I'm glad not to be the one tasked with bringing it under control.

The firefighters had been fighting the blaze for a while by the time we got there and the flames were still raging. Now the structure is reduced to ash and rubble, there is one person dead, and four more are missing. The risks associated with trying to recover them are extreme. What's left of the house might look dead, but it is highly likely there are still glowing embers and pockets of melted metal deep within the debris. It will take time and digging deep into the remains of the home, breaking it apart, exposing the still-burning pieces to air and water, to finally end the fire completely.

They will continue to search. They will go back in and fight to stop the flames from resurging and to look for the four people who were inside and haven't been seen since the blaze was reported. It's their duty. What they have dedicated themselves to do. But that doesn't mean it's without danger. They have to pay attention to every step, be aware of everything around them, and do everything they can to get out of the rubble, to get back home.

"I'm going to call Sam and let him know what's going on," I say. It took some convincing, but I got him to stay put in the room until we found out what was going on.

Dean nods. "I'll keep looking around." He glances over at officers looking at him suspiciously. "Unless they decide to make me leave."

"They let us in," I point out.

"Because you showed your badge," Dean says.

"This is instrumental to an official FBI investigation. We're legit. Just look around, take pictures. Get as many details as you can."

He nods and walks away as I take out my phone. Sam sounds worried when he answers.

"Hey, babe. I was hoping you would have gone back to sleep," I say.

"My wife went to a burning house and wouldn't let me come," he replies. "I'm not going to be getting any sleep after that."

"I'm sorry. It's part of the investigation and I didn't know how long we would be out here," I say. "It's cold and I wanted you to be comfortable."

He sighs. "You make it really difficult to be upset with you when you didn't do anything wrong and you're really sweet about it. What's going on? Was the fire bad?"

"The house is completely destroyed," I tell him. "The fire chief said it looked like it had been going for a long time before they even got there."

I tell him about the girls being at the house and Sara Calhoun's body being found.

"They haven't seen any sign of any of the others?" he asks.

"No. They have a team going in again, but for now, she's the only one accounted for."

"And they're sure the girls were there?"

"As far as anyone knows. The sheriff's department called all three of them several times, their parents have called them, and they put a message out on social media announcing the fire and asking for any of them to reach out, but there's been nothing. The only word is that they were set to come back here after the carnival for a sleepover," I tell him.

There's a pause.

"Emma? What is it? What are you thinking?"

"Jim Calhoun," I say. "Sara's husband and Genevieve's stepfather."

"The man Dean was talking about from the park," Sam says.

"Yes. There's been something about him since I met him. I never want to make assumptions about anyone, but I couldn't help but feel put off by him. And the way he interacted with and talked about his stepdaughter was really strange."

"Dean mentioned that it was weird the way he was interacting with the girls when he was in the park."

"Exactly." I take a breath. "What if he took them?"

"Took the girls?" he asks.

"It's possible. Sara's is the only body that has been found. What if he killed her, lit the house on fire, and took the girls somewhere?"

"It's definitely something to consider."

"I'm going to look around some more with Dean and see if we notice anything. I'll be back soon. Try to get some sleep. I love you."

"I love you, too."

I hang up knowing he probably won't sleep. Mostly likely as soon as the phone touched the nightstand, he picked up the remote and turned the TV on to keep him company until I get back.

Putting my phone away, I look around to find Dean. He's walking slowly along the perimeter of the front yard, looking between the vehicles parked on the grass. I walk up to him.

"Notice anything?"

"I'm pretty sure these cars belong to the girls," he says. "But there are also other tracks over here. They look like they were here recently."

"Like a car came and left while those cars were sitting there?"

"Yes," Dean nods. He brings me over and shows me the tracks. "There's not enough definition to make an imprint or anything, but look at that."

He points a few feet away in the grass and I see something white.

"What is that?" I get closer and lean down to get a better view. "It's an invoice for a car repair." Picking it up, I snap a picture of the front with my phone, then read it. "This information isn't for any of the cars that are here. And it's for a repair shop in Virginia."

Cold Valley is more than an hour from the border, making it unlikely anyone at the house routinely went over to Virginia just for car repair.

"Do you think it could be from someone who is involved in this?" Dean asks.

"I don't know, but we're going to give it to the sheriff so it can be investigated."

"And then we're going to investigate it?" Dean asks.

"Of course."

The sheriff is talking to one of the emergency responders, but she walks away as I approach. He looks at me through heavy, tired eyes and rubs his face with one hand.

"I thought you had left."

"No," I say. "We were just looking around. Dean found some car tracks over in the grass by those cars. We think those cars belong to the victims. But we found this as well."

I hand him the invoice and he looks it over. He makes a sound that's somewhere between a grunt and an acknowledgment, and I figure that means he's noticed the strange details on the paper.

"Thank you for bringing this to my attention. I'll make sure the investigators see it," he nods. I start to walk away, but he stops me. "Are you going to be in town for long, Ms. Griffin?"

"I don't have a set plan for when I go back to Virginia. Dean and I will stay as long as we need for our investigation," I tell him.

I'm expecting him to make a veiled threat about not interfering, or to suggest I stay out of his way so he can do his job. It would be far from the first time that happened, and I am under no delusions it's not going to happen many times in the future. Instead, he smiles.

"Good. I'm glad you're here. Your reputation precedes you, as I'm sure you know."

"I'm familiar," I reply.

He lets out what is supposed to be a short laugh, but ends up a sound that is dry and tense. "The truth is, I am running for mayor of Cold Valley. I've loved my time as sheriff, but I feel I could better serve the people of this town I adore by making the jump into politics. I'll be better positioned to help bring Cold Valley into the twenty-first century without losing what we love so much."

"That's very inspirational," I say. "I'm sure you'll do well."

"That's the thing. I very much hope I do. And I believe showing strong cooperation with people such as yourself will help that. I want to show that the people here are safe from crime. That Cold Valley will remain the type of town where people don't lock their doors and children have the freedom to ride their bikes and explore without worries. I would greatly appreciate any assistance you can offer."

"Assistance?" I ask.

"In resolving the missing persons case," he says. "And in this investigation as well."

"So, you think this was arson," I note.

"Haven't made any official rulings yet, but there are apparently signs of suspicious burn patterns. That combined with the heat and intensity the flames reached so quickly, it seems likely this was intentional."

"I'm happy to help," I say.

"Thank you," he says. "Can I use the contact information my secretary gave me to get in touch with you if I need to?"

"Absolutely," I say. I hesitate for a second. "Has anyone gone over to see Grace Cortez or Melanie Donovan's mother?"

CHAPTER THIRTY-ONE

GRACE IS CURLED IN ON HERSELF. HER HANDS ARE CLUTCHING A damp, wrinkled tissue and her elbows are perched on knees drawn in tight together as her feet bounce enough to rock her entire body.

"I'm so sorry this is happening," I tell her. "Can I get you anything? Maybe a cup of tea?"

She doesn't respond, just continues staring into the distance, so I take it upon myself to go into the kitchen and dig around in the cabinets until I find tea bags. I put a kettle onto the stove to heat up and go back into the living room.

"How can she just be gone?" she whispers. "Where is she?"

"I don't know," I say. "The investigators will continue to search through the fire site for any further remains…" She cringes and I push forward, "…but it's important we find out what actually happened. Until we know for certain what happened to her, I consider Maya a missing person. And when someone is missing, I search for them. That's what I will do for her."

Grace draws in a shaky breath and nods. "Thank you. You're being so kind."

"I see a lot of myself in your daughter," I explain. "And I want to know what happened. I know this is a horrible time, but it would help a lot if you could answer some questions."

"I'll answer anything you need. I just want you to find my daughter," she says.

In the kitchen, the kettle shrieks and I go to prepare the tea. When I come back, Grace is setting her phone down on the table in front of her.

"That was Shelby Donovan," she explains.

"Melanie's mother?" I ask.

"Yes," Grace nods. "We've been friends since the girls met. I hope you don't mind, but I asked her to come over."

"I don't mind. That's actually perfect. I wanted to speak with her, too, and I think it's good for you to be together right now."

She nods and a fresh wave of tears starts down her cheeks.

"I just don't understand. It doesn't make any sense. This all happened so fast," she says.

That comment throws me. "What do you mean?"

"I didn't even know that Genevieve McGuire was friends with Maya and Melanie. The two of them have been inseparable since they were very small. M and M." She manages a hint of a nostalgic smile. "They have a lot in common, but I think the fact that they both lost their fathers really bonded them."

I'm surprised by the revelation.

"Melanie's father died, too?" I ask.

She nods. "Mel was five. She and Maya were just getting close when it happened. When David died, I could see that Maya wasn't coping. She just wouldn't accept it. So I put her into a grief group for children who had lost a parent. Shelby thought it would be good for Mel also. Even though her father had already been gone for nearly two years, she was still having an incredibly hard time with it, and Shelby thought it would just get worse as she got older and became more aware."

The doorbell rings and Grace calls out that it's open. A tall, strong-looking woman with deep red hair and piercing green eyes rushes into the room and instantly scoops Grace up in her arms.

"I'm so sorry," she murmurs.

"I am, too," Grace says. They step apart and she holds her hand out toward me. "This is Emma, the agent I was telling you about."

Shelby nods but doesn't say anything.

"Can I get you a cup of tea?" I ask Shelby.

"No, thank you," she says.

Grace sits down with her own cup and stirs it absently.

"I was just telling Emma about the grief group," she says.

"That was an amazing thing for Mel," Shelby says. "It helped her so much."

"I wish I could say the same for Maya," Grace adds, earning a soft rub on her back from Shelby.

"Maya didn't respond well to the group?" I ask.

"She doesn't remember it," Grace explains. "At the time, I thought it was doing good things for her. I thought she was getting a chance to talk things out and work through her emotions in an age-appropriate, constructive way. She was even interacting with the other children more. Then I realized she was looking at the group like a playdate. She didn't seem to understand what was supposed to be happening. Then when the group stopped meeting, it was like the whole experience was wiped from her mind. She doesn't remember anything at all about it."

"You said you had her in therapy," I say. "Did the therapist ever talk to her about the group?"

"Yes," she says. "I didn't want to say it, but I thought maybe she was just acting up when she said she didn't remember it. Like she was trying to get attention or being dramatic. I wondered if maybe I was too focused on my own grief for my husband and wasn't supporting my daughter enough. But the therapist said that wasn't what she was doing. She genuinely had no memory of it. She said Maya blocked out that entire time in her life. She didn't remember her father's death, the funeral, the grief group. Any of it."

"I remember how much it upset Mel the first time she realized that Maya really didn't remember. It was the beginning of middle school and she saw Genevieve. Mel said Maya said she wished she was as pretty as her and wondered what her name was. Genevieve had been home-schooled when she was in elementary school, so it had been a couple of years, but she was in the group with them. She should have remembered her," Shelby says.

"Genevieve was in the group, too?" I sound like I'm several steps behind everybody, but that's exactly the way I feel. I feel like just as I am racing to catch up, my feet get tangled beneath me and I stumble.

"Yes," Grace confirms. "Her father died a little less than a year before David. He was also hit by a drunk driver. It was never solved. They had video of the accident and everything, but they were never able to trace the driver. I thought that would be something she and Maya would connect over. I didn't like the idea of them dwelling on the causes of their fathers' deaths, but it was something they were going to know, and at least this way they would have felt like they weren't so alone. They would know someone else who went through something similar."

"But it didn't work," I say.

"No. The three of them got on really well during the group, but then after it was over, Genevieve didn't stay in touch. I know that's her mother's doing more than hers. Not that she is a bad person. Was a bad person. Oh," she covers her face with her hands. "I didn't mean to say that. I don't want to speak ill of the dead."

"It's alright, Grace," I say. "You don't have to worry about that. Tell me what you were going to say."

She lifts her head and tries to breathe in her tears. "Sara doesn't do well on her own. All of us struggled with our husbands' deaths. Obviously. We were in happy marriages and were looking ahead to many years together. More children. Happiness. Then it was all taken from us in an instant. Shelby and I grieved. We went through really dark times. It sounds horribly morbid to say it, but I am so grateful the deaths happened at different times so we could help each other survive.

"I had been there for her when her husband died, and then she did the same for me. Cooked meals, cleaned the house, took care of the girls. It was hard, but we did it. When we met Sara, my first impression of her was that she couldn't stand on her own. She wasn't a person who had ever imagined herself without a partner."

"And it didn't surprise us when we found out she never really had been alone," Shelby adds. "She'd gotten married really young and they were together for years before they had Genevieve. While the girls were in the grief group, we tried hard to get to know Sara. We wanted to include her and have her be a friend."

"But she seemed completely focused on Genevieve and finding a man to be in her life. Genevieve was homeschooled and I believe a big part of that was because Sara wanted her at home with her. We found out she had started dating just a couple of months after her husband's funeral and hadn't been without a relationship since. There's nothing wrong with that, of course. It just felt very fast. And a little strange," Grace tells me.

"And they never worked out. The relationships always fizzled and she'd be right back to looking for someone else to pay attention to her. She needed that constant validation," says Shelby.

"Then she found that with Jim Calhoun," I say.

"Yes. They got married five or six years ago."

"So right when she would have been going into middle school," I say.

The women nod.

"I didn't even know they were friends again," Grace says, hanging her head. "I had no idea."

"Mel and Genevieve have a couple of classes and activities together, but she never talked about her like they were friendly until a few weeks ago. It's not that Genevieve was mean to them or anything, they just weren't in the same circle. Then all of a sudden Mel started talking about going to her house to hang out with her, and then it was that she wanted the three of them to go to the carnival together as a single-girl solidarity thing. I thought it was good they were getting to know each other again."

"I was more hesitant," Grace admits. "Again, as Shelby said, it's not that Genevieve had ever bullied them or was mean or anything, she just wasn't part of their social group. And she was known for being very popular, and I worried that Maya would feel out of the loop or pressured to try to be more like her. I didn't want her to go through any of that. I just wanted her to be careful. But I let her go because she wanted to go so much. Part of me thought maybe…"

"Maybe she was starting to remember something," I finish her thought for her quietly.

Grace nods, starting to cry again. Shelby wraps an arm around her friend.

"Why does all this matter?" she asks. "Do you think the fire had something to do with the girls?"

"The early assessment does indicate a strong possibility of arson," I say, deciding it's best to just be straightforward with them rather than trying to sugarcoat anything and have it be that much harder later if things don't turn out well. "And three girls who have lost their fathers in tragic ways being involved in any kind of incident is unusual. It could indicate they were being targeted."

"Targeted for what? Why?" Grace asks.

"I don't have answers for that yet," I say. "But I promise I am going to do everything I can to find out."

CHAPTER THIRTY-TWO

"HOW MANY TIMES HAVE YOU READ THROUGH THOSE ARTICLES?" Sam asks the next day when he shows up to the library.

I've been here since opening again and now he's bringing me lunch. I know I only have today with him before he has to go back to Sherwood, but I have that feeling in the pit of my stomach, the sensation like I've swallowed a burning rock that says something more complicated is happening here, that I'm right on the edge and if I stop it could all get worse.

It's an instinct I always follow. Sam understands that. It sometimes makes me feel guilty just how understanding he is. I never forget to be grateful for him and the warm arms that will be waiting for me when each case is over.

"Enough that I know they changed the way one of the victim's names is spelled in the third sentence of the fourth paragraph of this one," I tell him.

"That's useful information," he says. "Want to take a break and come eat? The librarian made me put the food out on the picnic table in the courtyard instead of bringing it in."

"Don't upset Vera," I say. "She holds control of the library. She could stop me from being able to find out more about Isaiah Faro. Spelled with an 's' or a 'z' depending on which sentence you're on."

I put the microfilm I'm reading away, notate it on the logbook, and follow Sam outside. He leads me around the building to a small grassy area and a patio with a single picnic table. Dean is already sitting there, eating a hamburger with the gusto of someone who has never touched real food.

"Did June not feed you this morning?" I ask, sitting down across from him. It's a warmer day today and I'm grateful to not have to bundle up so much.

He shook his head. "She did. But I slept for an hour last night. I need this to keep me awake."

I nod. "Alright. Did you find anything?"

Sam hands me a container with a veggie burger, fries, and an extra pickle.

"I ran the information for that invoice. Nothing. The guy who the car is registered to lives in Virginia. He was at home all day, night, and the next day," he says.

"Is that confirmed?" I ask.

"He was doing an online watch party with fifty other people and at least half of them have full recordings of it. You can clearly see that he's in his house by the background. He even walks around with the computer a couple of times, goes outside, talks to his girlfriend. He was there. The watch party lasted until three in the morning. The next morning at seven he was at a dentist appointment."

"Well, I guess sleep deprivation is one way to manage a dentist visit," Sam says.

"Damn. So that eliminates him. But how did that invoice get into the yard?" I ask.

Dean shrugs. "He says he doesn't know. It's from a couple of weeks ago, and he was sure it was in his glove compartment, but he hasn't looked for it since, so it could have fallen out of his car and gotten picked up. Things can travel."

"I guess. How about you, Sam? Did you work your sheriff magic?" I ask.

"I'm not so sure it was about me being sheriff and not about me being your husband, but I'm going to go ahead and take credit for being able to get the record for you," he says.

He presses his finger into the middle of a manila envelope on the table and slides it over to me.

"We'll say both," I smile. "Thank you."

I open the folder and look over the accident report for David Cortez's death. It's fairly sparse, which I was expecting by the way Grace talked about the investigation. But there are pictures and I spread them out in front of me. Sam noticeably turns his back so that he can eat without looking at the death scene images. I don't really blame him. They aren't the most graphic images I've brought home and spread out on a table, but a couple of them are very difficult to look at.

Captions describe exactly what I'm seeing, which is important for a few that are taken very close or at strange angles. A couple of them highlight the road and the presumed point of impact.

"Look at this," I say.

"I'd really rather not," Sam says.

I flip the pictures with David's body and the ones that show Maya broken beside him back over.

"You can't see anything. It's just the road and the woods." He turns as Dean leans across the table to get a better look. "This is where they believe the car actually hit David Cortez. You can see the broken headlights and glass from the windshield on the ground. He landed over here a bit, just out of frame. You can actually see the bottom of the bike. But what aren't you seeing?"

They both look at the image for a few seconds.

"Skid marks," Sam says. "The car didn't skid."

"Which means unless the driver was fully unconscious for just those few seconds, they didn't lose control of the car. If they did, they would be slamming on the brakes, turning the wheel, trying to get it to stop. There would be some sign of resistance."

"It wasn't an accident," Dean says.

"It doesn't look like it," I agree. "I just don't understand why someone would want to hit a man out with his little girl at a park." As soon as the words are out of my mouth, cold realization settles into my brain. "Unless that little girl and her father saw something they weren't supposed to."

"Maya's video," Dean says. "She really did see something."

"And they tried to kill her and her father to stop them from saying anything," I say.

"But what does that have to do with the other girls? Or Genevieve's parents?"

"I don't know," I say, gathering up the record and stuffing what remains of my lunch back into the bag so I can bring it with me. "But I need to know more about what Maya saw."

It doesn't take me a lot of research to find the right address. It's too far for me to walk, so I drive the rental car out of Cold Valley and to the small city half an hour away. The office is small and nondescript, but as soon as I walk inside, light filters in from the ceiling to shine on bright murals and play centers in the corners. It's obvious that this is a place designed to appeal to children.

I walk up to a curvy desk built with a massive fish tank embedded inside. I can only imagine how fascinated little ones are when they come in and see the brilliantly colored fish swimming around seemingly freely within the desk. A young man with very straight teeth and eyes so blue they look like he was chosen specifically to match with the water theme offers me a warm smile.

"Good afternoon," he says. "How can I help you?"

"May I speak with Olivia Bragg, please?"

"Give me just one second to see if she is available." He picks up the phone beside him and makes a quick call. "Dr. Bragg? There's someone here to see you. Are you available?" He looks up at me. "Your name please?"

"Agent Emma Griffin," I say. "FBI business."

If he's fazed by my credentials, he doesn't show it. He simply relays the information through the phone, pauses, then smiles. "Great. I'll send her back." He hangs up, then gestures toward a hallway at the back of the lobby space. "You can go on back. She's in the meeting room at the very end."

"I appreciate it."

I head down the hall without a single doubt that Dr. Bragg is using the time I'm walking to look me up. That's fine. I looked her up before I came, so it's only fair for us to be on even ground.

The door is standing open when I get to the meeting room and I see an older woman walking around inside, seeming to carefully arrange toys in different areas of a large carpet. Her silver hair is braided to the middle of her back and she's wearing a long, flowing floral dress that reminds me of my elementary school art teacher.

"Hello," I start, stepping into the room.

She looks up and smiles. "Agent Griffin. Come in."

"Emma, please."

"Emma. And you can call me Olivia."

"Thank you for being willing to talk to me. I know I don't have an appointment," I say.

"Not a problem. You're welcome here. What can I do for you?"

She's so gentle, I almost feel bad about the conversation I am here to have with her.

"Ten years ago, you led a group for children who lost their parents," I say.

"Yes," she nods. "That's a group I lead regularly. Unfortunately, there's always a need for support of that kind."

"I know. Three of the girls who were in that class were involved in a house fire this week. Maya Cortez, Genevieve McGuire, and Melanie Donavan."

The media hasn't released their names because they are minors, so I figure she doesn't know what happened. Her mouth drops and she lowers herself slowly to a nearby chair, her face blanching with emotion.

"I had no idea. I— are they alive?" she asks.

"Right now, we don't know," I say. "The fire was at Genevieve's house and her mother was found dead the night of the fire. Her stepfather and the three girls are currently still missing."

"Oh, my god, Sara," she says, bringing her name right out of the air as if ten years hadn't passed. "I can't believe that little girl doesn't have either of her parents now."

"She's not so much a little girl anymore," I point out. "They are seventeen years old and I'm afraid if they are still alive, they are in very serious danger."

"This is horrifying news," Olivia says, "but I don't understand what it has to do with my group."

"I need to know more about the girls. What they went through when their fathers died. How they reacted to their therapy."

The doctor shakes her head. "I'm sorry. I can't divulge that information. My clients may be children, but they are still people and deserve privacy. When they come here, they're promised a safe place where they can talk about how they are feeling or what they went through and it won't go anywhere else."

"I understand that, and I appreciate that you do that for them. But this is incredibly important. I've been investigating the disappearance of an FBI agent in Cold Valley and I believe he may have been murdered. His death could be linked to these girls," I explain.

"I'm sorry. I can't reveal anything about what they said. These were very vulnerable children who had experienced horrific things. Two fathers lost to drunk drivers and another to a brutal work accident. They were not equipped to cope with that, or how much their lives would be changed because of it. I don't know what their work here with me could have to do with that agent," she says.

"Maya had a memory," I say.

Olivia had stood, but now she pauses and looks at me. "Of her father's death?"

"Not exactly. She isn't sure what the memory is of. But I think it's the agent."

I already know how shaky my argument sounds. I'm still hoping she will be willing to help. Instead, she shakes her head.

"I'm sorry."

CHAPTER THIRTY-THREE

A S I DRIVE BACK INTO COLD VALLEY, I CATCH A GLIMPSE OF A CAM-
paign sign for Sheriff Boyd. He's grinning at the camera with his
arms crossed over his chest, turned to the side so one shoulder
is tilted down toward the ground. The text simply reads "Mayor." It
doesn't even have his name on it.

Bold choice.

But what's really on my mind is what Dr. Bragg said about the
fathers' deaths. She mentioned two drunk drivers, which have to be
Genevieve and Maya, though in neither case was the driver found so
they can't really prove they were drunk drivers. But it was the mention
of a work accident that really got my attention.

Up until now, I haven't known what caused the death of Melanie's
father. Shelby didn't mention it when we were talking at Grace's house
the other night, and I haven't sought out the death record for him yet.
Now that I know he died in an accident, my curiosity is running wild.

I drive back to the boarding house and go up to my room. Sam is sitting on the bed reading and he smiles as I come in.

"How did it go?" he asks.

"Not well. She refused to talk about the girls and what they said during their group," I say.

"Well, that was kind of to be expected. It was still therapy."

"I know," I acknowledge. "But she did give me some interesting information. I don't know if she even realizes that she gave it to me."

"What?" he asks.

"She told me Melanie's father died in a work accident."

"A work accident?" he frowns. "What does that mean?"

"I don't know yet, but I'm going to find out."

I sit down with my computer and search Melanie and Shelby's names, hoping that will trace me back to her father's name. It brings up an article talking about his death.

"Is that him?" Sam asks.

"It's talking about Mel and Shelby, so I think it is. 'Bryan Donovan died Sunday afternoon after a piece of farm equipment he was working on lurched from the supports and fell on him. Donovan was no stranger to farms or the equipment. Growing up helping with his grandfather's now-sold farm, he felt most at home working the land and was excited to have started work at the Gilley farm just two weeks before his death. Donovan leaves behind his wife, Shelby, and their daughter, Melanie.'"

I stop reading and look at Sam.

"He was crushed," Sam says. "Working on farm equipment."

He shudders, but I'm not focused on the cause of death. I'm thinking about his name.

"Bryan Donovan," I say. "Bryan Donovan."

"What is it?" Sam asks.

"I know that name. I've heard it or seen it somewhere." I keep thinking about it for a second before it hits me. Getting rid of the article, I pull up the transcripts of the information Shawn Reichert sent to headquarters or had on his computer that was available after his death. I find what I'm looking for and point to it. "Right there. Bryan Donovan." I read the rest of the entry and my jaw clenches. "Let's go."

Shelby looks like the stress of not knowing where her daughter is has worn her down when she answers the door, but I can't be swayed by it. This is a conversation I need to have.

"Emma," she says in a cracking, painful-sounding voice.

"I need to talk to you," I say. "Why didn't you tell me about your husband?"

"Excuse me?"

"Why didn't you tell me that your husband was Bryan Donovan, one of the deaths being investigated by Shawn Reichert as an element of the money-laundering scheme? You knew I was here investigating that man's disappearance, but you leave out the important part that your husband was a focus of his undercover investigation," I say.

"What would have been the good of telling you that? I have no idea why his name would show up in anything having to do with money laundering. My husband was good. Driven. Honest. He would never sell himself out like that," Shelby says.

"I am investigating Agent Reichert's disappearance and possible murder. It is critical I have all the information available, and I just found out that you are withholding this essential piece of evidence. Your husband didn't just die in a work accident. He was one of seven farm workers who died in and around Cold Valley over the course of a couple of years. But every one of the others was from out of town. They were somewhat unskilled, preferring to learn on the job.

"But your husband was from here. He already had tremendous skill on a farm. So, why him? What linked him to the others? Agent Reichert had your husband's name in his notes. He was zeroing in on something."

"And then he abandoned us," Shelby snaps.

"He did what?" I ask.

"He abandoned us. I knew he was investigating. My father was a detective. I can sense someone like that as soon as they step through a door. I knew there was something about that man and the secret wasn't just that his name wasn't Michael Forbes. I told him everything. About how my Bryan's death didn't make sense. He never would have worked on a piece of equipment the way they say he was when it fell on him. He knew far better than that. About going to the funeral home and having them tell me they'd already cremated him."

"They cremated his body without your consent?" I ask.

"No. It was just a mistake. But it was horrifying when I heard it. That agent wanted me to help him figure out exactly what was going on. He thought he had a good idea of it, but he wasn't positive and he needed more details. I was going to help him. But then he just left. He left without saying a word, abandoning me with Melanie, feeling completely vulnerable and unsafe."

"He didn't abandon you," I tell her. "He was working hard for your daughter and your husband, and I am going to need your help starting up where he left off."

A sob ripped out of her chest. "What good would it do me now? They're both dead. My entire family. The love of my life and my only child, gone. Why do anything now?"

"We don't know what happened to Mel, Shelby. We don't know what's going on with her or the others, and that's why I need your help so much," I say.

Her tears suddenly stop like she's so shocked she forgot how to cry. "Oh my god. You haven't heard."

That simple sentence burns through my chest.

"She was ten yards away from the house. Looks like she was shot," Dean says.

"Shot?" I ask, shocked.

"I think we can now conclusively say we are dealing with murder."

We get to the sheriff's department and I dial his number as I'm passing through the parking lot to let him know I'm here and need to speak with him. He's about to have an important conference call, but says it shouldn't take long and I can wait inside the lobby for him. His voice is thinner and more drawn than the last time I talked to him. I wonder if it's because of what is happening or because I'm there.

Just inside, I go to the desk where a woman in uniform flips absent-mindedly through a magazine. Clearly this is not the part of her job she enjoys the most. But at least she looks up at me without a sense of disdain when I get to the desk.

"Hi. I just spoke with the sheriff. He's expecting me. He said to just wait out here," I say.

She gestures toward the seating area. "Make yourself comfortable. There's a coffee machine over there if you'd like some."

She starts to say something else but stumbles over the words as she forces herself to stop.

"What?" I ask. She shakes her head. "Go ahead. What were you going to say?"

"I was about to offer you a doughnut, but then I remembered there aren't any. Jim always used to bring them in when he came for visitation." Her eyes reveal a haze of sadness. "I guess that's probably not going to be happening anymore."

My head tilts to the side curiously. "Jim? Jim Calhoun?"

She nods. "He came in here every week for visitation." She points off to the side where a cold gray door in the wall bears a painted sign. Jail. "He was so nice. Brought doughnuts every Tuesday and Thursday."

My head is spinning a little and I'm not sure what I'm supposed to say next. Fortunately, Dean steps in.

"Who was he visiting?" he asks.

"Anyone who was here and needed a visit," she says. "Especially the new people. Ones just being held for a couple days or those waiting for trial. A lot of times people think inmates only need visitors if they have long sentences or if they have been there for a long time, but I really think it's that first week that is the scariest and having someone to talk to helps them get through it."

"I'm not sure I understand," I say. "Why would he visit?"

"Jim…" she sighs like she isn't sure how to word what she wants to say, considering she doesn't know the current status of the person she's speaking about. "Jim has ideas about police reform and incarceration. He's one of those big activists for the falsely accused. He is always talking about sentencing and treatment even for criminals."

I nod. I've met the type.

"We would always joke when he visited that Jim is everyone's lawyer even without a formal law degree. He came and gave advice or offered help. Above all, he listened to what the inmates had to say. I think that was really valuable to them."

"How many inmates do you have in the jail?" Dean asks.

"At any given time, around fifty."

The door behind the desk opens and Sheriff Boyd steps out.

"Emma. Good to see you. Come on back."

CHAPTER THIRTY-FOUR

"I'M SORRY TO MAKE YOU WAIT. I WAS TALKING WITH MAYOR Galloway about my campaign. I know the election is still months away, so I'm in this strange position of feeling like it's far too early to be doing such a push, and yet everything is coming up so fast and I don't have enough time to do it all," Sheriff Boyd tells me as he leads us into his office.

He gestures at the chairs across the desk from his and invites us to sit.

"I can imagine it's particularly stressful trying to do all of that while also handling such a complicated case," I say. "Murder and missing teenagers is pretty salacious, especially for somewhere like Cold Valley."

He briefly pauses in mid-sit as if my words stunned him. Good. That's the reaction I want. I need him to know I'm not going to be charmed by the smile, and sheen, and good ol' boy bullshit like others might. His campaign means absolutely nothing. I'm not here to be his poster child or his prop to show how connected and serious on crime he is. I'm in Cold Valley to find out what happened to Shawn Reichert. And now, for three girls whose lives seemed destined to spiral out of control from the beginning.

"Yes," he says when he can move again and lowers himself the rest of the way into his chair. "I suppose that means you have heard about Melanie Donovan."

"I have," I nod. "She was shot."

"She was. At least once, but possibly more. Her body was lit on fire after she was killed and the medical examiner hasn't finished a full autopsy."

"Was there any sign that Sara Calhoun was shot?" I ask.

"No. She died of smoke inhalation."

"What's being done to look for the two remaining girls and Jim Calhoun?" I ask.

He looks at me with a slightly taken aback expression, like he can't believe I'm being so bold with him.

"It's a continuously developing investigation, Emma. I'm sure you understand that."

"I do," I say with a nod. "I understand it extremely well. I also understand how critical it is to make sure the investigation moves faster than the crime. You asked me to help you look good and assist you in any way I can. That's what I'm trying to do."

He nods, his lips twisting slightly into a smirk. "Alright. Go ahead. What do you think I should do next?"

"Did you get the impression he was toying with me?" I ask. "Like he sees me as a kitten he's dangling one of those feathers on a stick in front of and enjoying watching me bat at it?"

"He strikes me as the kind of guy who sees just about everybody that way," Dean says. "Not a bad guy, just one who really likes to feel powerful and in control. And you intimidate the living hell out of him. Why else do you think he wants you on his side?"

I turn a corner onto the road outlined by the GPS and look around for the right address.

"Yeah, what is that? When was the last time I had a sheriff or police head enthusiastically ask me to team up with him?"

"I mean … Sam," Dean offers.

"That doesn't count. I've had plenty of departments cooperate with the Bureau taking over or assisting with investigations. It's not like on TV where they never trust me. Believe it or not, I have actually had good relationships with local LEOs. But I don't think I've ever been scooped up quite like that."

"Or used for a political campaign," he points out.

"That's definitely not my favorite thing," I say. "We need to get the hell out of Cold Valley before the ticker-tape parades and campaign speeches start."

I pull into a parking lot and into a spot.

"What I'm wondering is why Mayor Galloway is apparently so enthusiastically endorsing Boyd for the next term. From just the little bit of research I've done, it's not like the two of them see eye to eye on a lot of the issues."

"Really?" I ask.

He nods. "Especially things like crime and public policy. You would think that a sheriff running for mayor would have that as a primary platform."

"I think he does. He rattled off some sort of public relations statement to me the night of the fire. It was all about keeping the people of Cold Valley safe and showing them that crime wasn't going to take over their beloved town."

"Which makes sense for him as a candidate. But the current mayor may not be completely opposite, but they don't exactly line up. His approach to addressing crime is far more hands-off. He's more focused on things like public programming, diversion, and helping those who have recently been released assimilate back into society as a way of reducing recidivism.

"I guess it's the same basic goal, but from really different perspectives. Unless Boyd is running against an anarchist, I don't really understand why they are teaming up." I take off my seatbelt and he looks through the window. "Where are we? I thought we needed to get back to the McGuire house to meet the crime scene analyst."

"We do," I say. "But I wanted to stop in here really fast. I have a quick question."

It doesn't take long before I'm back in the car.

"What did you find out?" Dean asks.

"They aren't just a funeral home. This is kind of a one-stop-shop for managing death. They'll handle everything from removal of the body from the death scene to preparation for burial or cremation, to the actual cremation or burial. Cremation is a big part of their business,"

I say. "Which doesn't really surprise me. Choosing to be cremated is becoming increasingly popular these days.

"But the operative word there is 'choosing.' The woman I spoke with was adamant that there is no default when it comes to handling a body. They can keep the deceased in cold storage for several days while the family makes final decisions. They also offer prepaid plans that allow a person to put down a flat amount before death to cover expenses like the casket, preparation, and viewing.

"I also saw a couple of boxes being handed off to a mail carrier. Apparently, those who do choose to be cremated can have their remains shipped to their loved ones in their urn to take another stress off their lives. I asked whether it ever felt uncomfortable weighing the package because maybe the person inside had a weight problem and hated scales."

Dean makes a disgusted face at me. I don't blame him. It's very similar to the internal look I gave myself as I asked the question.

"Emma," he says. "That was distasteful even for you."

"Thank you for that. I needed to ask about the weight because I wanted to know how they handle postage."

"And what did you find out?"

"Prepaid postage," I tell him. "Everything is standard depending on whether the ashes are already in an urn or just in the bag so that the family can choose the urn. To take out the step of having to weigh each package, which is apparently just as unpalatable and uncomfortable to do as it is to inquire about, they took a basic weight that is on the higher end of an average range for men, women, or children, then apply that standard postage to the package. If they know for sure one is going to weigh more, they just add an extra stamp of the same amount."

"Doesn't that mean they are overpaying for shipping fairly often?" Dean asks.

"They absorb it," I say. "It's worth the convenience and efficiency."

"Both things that are top priorities when it comes to giving a fellow human being their final farewell," Dean remarks with acid in his voice.

We drive in silence the rest of the way to the McGuire property. The crime scene tape is vibrant, garish yellow against the backdrop still fairly monotone at the end of winter. An officer steps up to us as I roll the window down and show him my credentials. He nods and lets us through.

I pull up behind the cars and a couple moments later, a sheriff's department car pulls in beside us. We get out and greet the man Boyd assigned to go through the cars with me. I'm not sure what I'm looking for, but it's one of those situations where I'll know it when I see it.

CHAPTER THIRTY-FIVE

"A DRIED-UP ROSE, A TEDDY BEAR, SOME LINGERIE, AND A BUNDLE of clothes," I say. "Mel's car had some books, an emergency roadside kit, and first aid supplies. Very prepared."

"You said those things were in Genevieve's trunk?" Sam asks.

I nod. "Maya doesn't have a car, so it was the two to look through. The parents' cars were clean."

"Why would she have them in her trunk?" he asks.

We're having dinner over a video call. It's nowhere near as satisfying as having dinner with him in person, but I'm still thankful for the technology that lets me still see him when we're apart.

"Hiding them, I'm guessing. I doubt many seventeen-year-old girls want to put lingerie like that on display for their parents to see. The rose and the teddy bear are pretty standard, but that lingerie is a bit much."

"You said she and her boyfriend just broke up," Sam says.

I nod. "A couple of weeks before Valentine's Day. It was one of the reasons she invited Maya and Mel to go to the carnival and sleep at her house. She didn't want to be alone and sad on Valentine's Day."

"Alright. So maybe those things were gifts from her ex and she wanted them out of sight, but hadn't had a chance to return them to him," Sam suggests.

"It's possible, but I don't know. The rose doesn't seem dried out enough to be from weeks or even months ago. And the lingerie isn't something a teenage boy would pick up at the nearest big box store. This stuff is expensive. None of it really means anything right now."

"In your text earlier, you said something about Jim Calhoun visiting the jail. What's that all about?" Sam asks.

I tell him about what the officer said.

"I looked into it and it turns out she was being gentle when she said he has ideas about police and incarceration. He is an activist against police corruption and abuses of the legal system. I'm not just talking about the falsely imprisoned. We've run into that before. This man has been aggressive in speaking out against the inequalities in how crimes are approached and rampant corruption in the jail system. I found his blog and read some of the posts that he made.

"He talks about specific cases of people who he believes were railroaded and ended up with ridiculously long sentences for what seem like fairly minor crimes, or combinations of crimes that shouldn't have been prosecuted the way they were. And then other people who were very clearly guilty of major crimes who got little to no jail time and were able to just walk away. He isn't subtle in his suggestion that those are the people doing favors for the ones in charge," I explain.

"Like Sheriff Boyd?" Sam asks.

I nod. "He seems very familiar with the concept of libel because he doesn't specifically call him out by name, but he also doesn't try to hide the fact that he's talking about the sheriff involved in those cases, which is Boyd. I dug into some of the cases more and from what I see, every one of them came back to either Boyd or someone with a personal connection to him.

"But the post that stood out to me the most was his story of meeting Sara. They met at a gathering for people who believed in creating a mutually cooperative community that doesn't require any police force. A place where people live harmoniously and there is no crime because there's equality and support for everyone living there."

"So, a commune," Sam says.

"That's a nice way of trying not to call it a cult," I laugh.

"You really think he believed in that?" Sam asks.

"He talked about being a father figure for the lost. He believes there's so much pain in this world and corruption and conflict make it worse. That when people are able to subjugate each other arbitrarily, there can never be peace. But that he could create a perfect community where that wasn't a problem. With just a small amount of land, he could make something new and wonderful, and in his ideal version of the community, he would gather those who need him close and love them as his children and his wives."

"Oh, holy hell," Sam says.

I point at his image on the screen. "And there it is. This man is obsessed with privacy and fights to reclaim control over his land. He envisions a world that is completely corrupt and where the law is a complete failure because the people in charge manipulate laws and charges to fit whatever they want and keep people in jail, or never punish them for what they do and allow them to continue hurting other people. He has three girls who all lost their fathers right at his fingertips. Maybe he just couldn't resist."

"But what about the one who is dead?" he asks.

"Melanie," I say. "She wasn't killed in the fire. She was shot and then lit on fire away from the house."

"That and the man you described talking to in the woods doesn't sound like the same man. Someone who wants to create a peaceful commune where there is no crime and everyone is healing everyone's past hurts, but then he gets aggressive and threatening when you approach him and kills one of the girls he is trying to start his flock with?"

"Ever hear of Waco?" He goes silent and I know the reality of what I'm saying is sinking in. "It's too dark now, but in the morning, I'm going out there."

"Emma," Sam sighs, already knowing it won't convince me.

"I have to do this, Sam. If he has those girls out on that land somewhere, they aren't safe. There's already one dead. We have to try to protect the others."

The woods are quiet when I walk into them the next morning. I know in the logical part of my brain I probably shouldn't be here alone. It's exactly the kind of thing Sam hates that I do and that landed me in suspensions and desk duty in the past. I should have backup with me.

Someone else to make the situation safer and help if things get out of hand.

In a perfect world, that is what I'd have. But despite Jim Calhoun's idyllic beliefs and best efforts so far, he hasn't been able to create that world. Which means I have to work with what I have. Dean is busy this morning and this can't wait. I'm not afraid to be here alone. It's not like if I do find where he's hiding with them that I intend on rushing in guns blazing to free them and take him down in one fell swoop. Even I know better than to attempt that.

I'm just here for some reconnaissance. To get an idea of the land and see if there are any signs of them passing through this way or creating any kind of annex away from the rest of the park and the house. In particularly shocking or disturbing cases, the ones that are difficult for anyone to look at fully in the face, it's dangerously effective to simply hide in plain sight. When you're trying to observe something out of the corner of your eye to stop from having to take it all in, or just because you don't want to see what you know you do, it's easy not to see what's actually there.

The drugs being pedaled from the child's lemonade stand on the corner in gangland.

The dutiful servant who was actually trafficked as a slave, has never been paid, and is regularly abused.

The girl who is kidnapped as a preteen and held captive for decades, but is trotted out in public and used as a broodmare for the kidnapper's wife, all the while staying silent.

It's easy to see only the child's lemonade stand, the prestige and elegance, and a live-in nanny. That's what people want to see.

I'm here to stare Jim Calhoun directly in the eye.

Using the map Dean found that outlines what area of the land was formerly the park but is owned by Calhoun, I determine a course and start walking. Everything stays quiet and still, nearly lulling me into a peaceful sense that I'm just taking a morning stroll. It isn't until I see something familiar carved into a wooden sign that my mind goes to steel again.

Bike path

I look down at the GPS on my phone screen, comparing my location to ensure I am where I think I am. The blue bubble indicating approximately where I am standing hovers near a curved road. It's too far from the path at this point for me to be able to see it through the trees, but the map indicates that not too far in the distance, in less than a mile, this bike path will intersect with Hollybrook Road.

Instantly, my mind is taken from everything else and I am in the middle of Maya's memory. This was where she was riding her bike with her father the day he died. It's what she sees in the flashes of horror that led to her making that video. I know it has to look different than it did ten years ago, but I start to scour the area, trying to take any details I remember from what she said and pair them up with what I'm seeing.

I pull up the video on my phone and watch it again and again, listening to every word she says. Something stands out to me and suddenly I stop. My hand drops down to my side and buzzing in my ears blocks out even the sound of the video still replaying on my phone.

All around me the trees are struggling to find their grasp on spring. The cold weather from when I first arrived here has softened; the earliest buds of leaves are showing up on the tree branches. All but the one in front of me.

A tree with no leaves.

I walk up to it and turn around to see how far I am from the path. The break in the trees that indicates where the path cuts through them is subtle enough it would be difficult to notice if you didn't know it was there. It's far enough away to not be right up against it, but close enough that someone riding their bike would be able to see the tree clearly.

But in the winter, no one comes here. Grace told me herself that no one uses the bike path until spring. Even with the path right there, someone at this tree at this time of year would think they were completely alone.

My breath is heavy in my chest as I look at the tree, my mind superimposing the images Maya describes. The body on the ground. It starting to move and rising up into the air.

It sounds like a child's imagination getting the most of her.

I scan the tree. No leaves means this tree is dead and it was dead then. It hasn't grown and likely hasn't changed much even in those years. I examine it carefully until I see it. Above my head, the branches fork and spread out, and in the juncture where they meet is a dark gap.

Putting my phone in my pocket and taking off my jacket to give me more freedom of motion, I walk up to the tree. It's been many years since I've climbed a tree, but crawling up walls and buildings during investigations has kept my skills intact. Thankful for the combat boots I'm wearing, I brace myself and hope the dead branches sticking out of the tree still have enough integrity to hold my weight.

It takes several long, painstaking minutes, but finally, I get to the gap. Taking my phone out of my pocket, I turn on the flashlight feature and shine it down into the darkness. The tree is completely hollow. Nothing but a shell that looks whole from the outside.

And at the bottom is a mound of cloth and bone.

CHAPTER THIRTY-SIX

M Y PHONE RINGS AS I'M MAKING MY WAY BACK DOWN THE TREE. When my boots hit the ground, I take my phone out of my pocket and look at the screen. It's Dean.

"Hey," I tell him. "I need you to get out to the park."

"Emma, I need to tell you something."

"Okay, but this needs to happen first." I hear something crunch behind me. It's footsteps. Someone is in the woods. "Dean, I need you to hang up and call the police."

"Emma, what's going on?"

I move away from the tree and start back toward the path. I've only taken a few steps when a gunshot rings out.

"Call them!" I shout and take off running.

The footsteps are following me and I duck and weave to make myself a more difficult target in case my pursuer wants to take another shot. Finally, after what feels like miles, I come out on Hollybrook Road. This is the spot where David Cortez died. The spot where Maya nearly lost her life. But I can't take the moment I want to. I don't hear the footsteps anymore, but that doesn't mean they aren't there.

My phone rings again. I know Dean's custom ring, but this is not the moment to answer. I run down the road for several yards, then head down the dip on the other side and into the trees. Concealed behind a tree, I take a second to try to orient myself. My phone keeps ringing and I press the button on the side to silence it so I can't be found through the sound.

Once I've caught my breath, I start moving again, purposely traveling in the opposite direction the traffic would flow down this street. It's harder for a car to turn around to chase someone going the other way than it is to just pursue them.

When I'm a good distance away, I call Dean.

"Where are you?" he demands.

"In the woods beside Hollybrook Road. Jim Calhoun just shot at me. Did you call the police?"

"I'm on Hollybrook. Come up on the road so I can find you," he says.

This would be the moment in any movie where I would do what he says and it would turn out to be a trap. But there isn't a single fiber of my being that believes Dean would ever let that happen. He wouldn't comply, and if he was forced to call me, he'd use one of the codes we've established. He'd tell me to do something else. He would ensure I stayed safe.

I have enough confidence in that belief that I climb up the embankment and back onto the street.

"Where on Hollybrook are you?" I ask.

"I'm coming around the curve. Do you hear me?"

"I hear a car. I hope to God it's you."

The car comes around the curve and skids to a stop just past me. I let out the world's biggest sigh of relief when I see Dean's face behind the wheel. I run to jump into the passenger seat and he takes off before the door is all the way closed.

"Are you alright?" he asks.

"He shot at me. Jim Calhoun saw me in the tree and he shot at me. I was searching through the woods and I realized I was on the bike trail that Maya was on with her father. Calhoun must have seen me. The place where he took them must be close to there. Or he just knew I was there and followed me. He took a shot at me and followed me when I ran."

"Emma, you have to stop for a second," Dean demands loudly.

My head snaps toward him. "What?"

"Jim Calhoun didn't shoot at you," he says.

"Yes, he did," I say. "Do you think I imagined it? I know what a gunshot sounds like, Dean. Unfortunately, I've been on the receiving end of quite a few of them in my time."

"Jim Calhoun's body was just recovered from the fire site. He's dead, Emma."

I swallow hard, trying to process what Dean just told me.

"Jim Calhoun is dead?" I ask. Dean nods. "So is Shawn Reichert."

Dean gets me back to my car and for the first time, I realize this is not our rental.

"Where did you get this car?" I ask.

"I borrowed it. When I heard about Calhoun, I knew I needed to get to the park to find you. There is some serious shit happening here."

"I know." I realize my hands are stinging and I look down at them. I brush away bits of bark and splinters. "We need to get the CSU out here. Quickly."

I feel like I'm juggling as the next several hours blend into each other. As I supervise the examination of the hollow tree and work with the team to determine how to best remove the body, I am also answering questions about the shot taken at me and chasing the new development of Jim Calhoun's death.

This is all connected. It has to be. But right now, I can't get them to come together. So I keep juggling.

It's late by the time I get back to the boarding house and take the longest shower I can before the water starts to cool. Sam looks exhausted when his face appears on the screen for our call. He's already heard about all the events of the day through a series of texts from me and calls from Dean. I would have rather been able to talk to him about them face to face, even through a screen, but I didn't want there to be a chance of him hearing about any of it over the news or through any of his law enforcement contacts, so I kept him up to date.

"I can't believe you went out into those woods by yourself," he says.

"And I can't believe the first thing you're going to do is scold me like a child," I reply.

"Not like a child. Like my wife who I love and worry about when she decides to go off into the woods chasing a potential serial killer by herself."

"It turns out I wasn't," I say. "He's dead."

"That doesn't change that you thought you were," he says. "And you went."

"I had my gun."

"That won't help you when someone is shooting at your back. Which also happened even though the man you thought was the one who would come after you couldn't have, as you just pointed out," he says.

I don't answer and Sam lets out a sigh. "Babe, I don't want you to feel like I'm trying to treat you like a child, but you scare the hell out of me. And not in a fun way. I can't lose you. You've promised me before that you wouldn't go into situations like that by yourself. "

"When I could help it," I clarify. "And this time, there wasn't another option. Dean was busy with another part of the investigation and this needed to be done." I groan and run my fingers back through my damp hair. "I really thought it was him, Sam. Everything is spelled out right there. I thought that had to be the answer. I really thought I was going to go into those woods, find him with the girls, and be able to get them home by tonight. And it would be over. Now I know I've put all this energy into something that was wrong right from the beginning."

"I don't think it was totally wrong, Emma. He might not have taken those girls and brought them away to start his dream reality, but maybe it's just because he didn't get the chance. Those blog posts still exist and they are still incredibly damning even if he didn't have the opportunity to actually follow through with them," Sam points out.

"Are you saying I should be glad he's dead because it hypothetically stops him from brainwashing women and girls and raping them?" I ask.

"I'm saying what you thought was happening might still have happened. And now it won't. And what you did today wasn't for nothing. You got the answers you were there to get. You found Shawn Reichert."

"I know. At least, I presume it's him. The remains are skeletal. But he's wearing clothes that match descriptions of him from early in the original investigation. The bones look to be from someone of the right age and size. I believe it's him," I say. "But that only means he's not missing anymore. We still don't know what happened to him. I have to rethink the entire way I've been approaching this. But, fortunately or unfortunately, I think it is pretty obvious who I need to focus on now."

"Who?" Sam asks.

"Who would want Jim Calhoun silenced? He was a budding cult leader, yes, but he was also an outspoken advocate for jail and prison reform, eliminating police corruption, and legal equality. He spent at least two days every week visiting inmates at the jail, and he just kept getting more fired up about the corrupt system, people getting railroaded, and special favors and promises buying criminals' way out from behind bars. If he was getting that angry about how these inmates were being treated and they were in the Cold Valley jail, who do you think was responsible for putting them there? Who would he blame for all this injustice?"

"The sheriff," Sam says.

I nod. "That's not going to look very good for an aspiring mayor. He needed to end that threat while he had the chance. The girls were just the perfect conspiracy to cover it up. They were unfortunate collateral damage, just like the innocent people he kept in jail, or the petty criminals he railroaded into getting heavier charges and long sentences.

"I've been reading through the records of inmates in the jail and the blogs Calhoun wrote about their stories. Boyd gets a lot of prestige for being extremely tough on crime. As long as he's been in office, he's made that a consistent pattern of his messaging. Remember he is running for mayor on a platform of making the area safe again. He wants to be admired and to have power, money, and influence. Getting into politics could serve that up to him on a silver platter. He just couldn't have anything or anyone standing in his way."

"Do you think he was involved in Shawn Reichert's death?" Sam asks.

"Maybe both of them were," I say. "He was found on Jim Calhoun's land. And Sheriff Boyd knew who he was, and wouldn't have liked how it looked for the Bureau to come in to do an undercover investigation into money laundering and potentially murder, when he's so much about making Cold Valley safe. It would have been a huge black mark on his record."

"Murder?" Sam asks. "When did the money laundering start involving murder?"

"I'm still figuring out the details," I say. "But he knew. He must have."

"Or maybe he wasn't intentionally hidden on Calhoun's land at all and it's just a coincidence you'll figure out when you unravel the money laundering."

"You've always said there's no such thing as coincidences," I say, my fingers running along the edge of one of the boxes that I now realize Shawn Reichert mailed to himself.

"I've been wrong before."

CHAPTER THIRTY-SEVEN

D EAN KNOCKS ON MY DOOR AND POKES HIS HEAD IN JUST AS I'M
getting off my call with Sam. I gesture for him to come in. I climb
up on the bed to free up the chair and he sits down.
"Did you get in touch with any of them?" I ask.

"I did," he confirms. "It took some calling around, and not everyone was
willing to talk to me, but I got through to four of the families."

"That's amazing. What did they tell you?" I ask.

"Pretty much the same story each time. Their loved ones were
extremely hardworking and good husbands and fathers. The migrant
workers loved their freedom and their ability to experience different
parts of the country. People, food, everything, as the seasons changed
and they went from place to place to work on farms. The ones who were
supposed to be permanent were thrilled to have found good-paying

jobs. They were looking forward to a fresh start, even if it meant moving away from their homes, families, and friends."

"They were preying on vulnerable people," I say. "People who were vulnerable because of their circumstances, needing jobs and wanting to build better lives for themselves, or vulnerable because they were so full of life and adventure they wouldn't turn one down."

"That's what it sounds like. Every one of them said pretty much the same thing about their loved ones' deaths. They were on the job for a little while, but obviously not enough time to be fully trained yet. They were working and there was a horrific accident. Equipment malfunction, miscalculation, user error. However they decided to formally describe it, the families just heard things like run over by a combine and fell out of a hay loft. But each and every one of those workers loved their jobs and Cold Valley so much they didn't want to ever leave. Even in eternity," Dean says.

"What do you mean?" I ask.

"Each family told me when they inquired about getting the body back for a memorial service and burial, they were told that wasn't possible. The worker was required to have end-of-life papers filled out before starting the work. They all recorded that they wanted to be buried in Cold Valley.

"And the funeral home was so understanding about the family's inability to travel all that way to attend the funeral and burial. They so appreciated the kindness of the funeral home helping them to make all of the arrangements right over the phone, including paying for it. Then they received a package in the mail, including a picture of the funeral service, a map of the grave, and a picture of the area. It was touching and felt like they cared. Really," Dean explains.

"Am I safe in assuming that package was a part of a bigger package that is usually pre-paid, but was offered at a special rate for them because of the urgent nature of the need?" I ask.

"You know, my high school social studies teacher always used to say you shouldn't assume, but I'm going to go ahead and say you can," Dean says.

"Your grandfather used to say that, too," I tell him. "Alright. It's getting late. But I have one more thing I need you to do."

The next morning, I meet June downstairs for coffee and some perfectly normally shaped pancakes. Wanting to make sure I don't offend her, I eat way more than enough before putting my plate aside and asking where I can find the best donuts in town.

An hour later, I walk into the Sheriff's Department with a massive box of pastries in my arms. The same officer who I spoke to the other day is sitting behind the desk and she looks up at me, her eyes widening slightly. I hold the box out to her.

"I hope this isn't distasteful or anything. But I thought I would bring these and say I'm sorry for your loss."

She takes them and thanks me with tears in her eyes, proving not everyone does their research. As she selects a pink glazed with sprinkles, at least demonstrating exquisite taste in pastry, she calls in to the sheriff to let him know I'm here. He comes to the door almost immediately.

"Emma," he says. "I wasn't expecting to see you today. Come in."

"Enjoy those," I say to the officer as I start around her desk.

We enter Boyd's office and I sit down. Rather than sitting in the chair across the desk from me, he sits in the one beside me. He clasps his hands and leans toward me, seamlessly following every trick a body language expert would say shows interest and compassion. I do my best not to recoil.

"What can I do for you? Did you think of something else about yesterday?" he asks.

I spent a lot of time talking with him yesterday about finding Shawn's body, about the shot, about Jim Calhoun's death. I couldn't think of anything else I would possibly be able to say to him about it. But I need to get a conversation started.

"I was just thinking about Jim Calhoun, wondering how he could have been missed in the rubble," I start.

"There was a lot of destruction," Boyd shrugs. "It was a large house and the entire thing collapsed."

"I guess I know that," I say. "It just seems so horrific to think his body has been out there this whole time and no one was able to find him."

"Well, he was located in what would have been the basement. It was under a huge amount of debris. So it would have been extremely difficult to see. The only reason he was found was because of the crew coming in to clear away what was left so it wouldn't be dangerous. It's going to take the medical examiner a lot of time and effort to pinpoint a cause of death."

"Oh?" I say, feigning surprise at the comment. "Don't you think it would be smoke inhalation, just like Sara?"

"Finding Melanie Donovan's body with a bullet wound forces us to consider different options," he counters.

"That's true. I just don't understand why someone would kill a father, allow a mother to die of exposure to the fire, let two teenage girls escape, and shoot one and light her on fire. It seems very chaotic," I note.

"Is murder ever calm and straightforward?" he asks.

"Yes," I reply without hesitation. His eyes widen slightly and I shake my head, brushing away the comment. "It just has me thinking about what time this all could have happened. I know the girls were at the carnival, but how about Sara and Jim?"

"It was Valentine's Day," he shrugs. "I'm assuming they were on a date."

I nod. "Probably. Is that what you were doing? I just realized I never even asked you if you had a nice Valentine's Day."

He smiles. "It was very nice, thank you. And, yes, I was on a date."

"What did you do?" I ask. I force out a short laugh in response to his quizzical look. "I'm a hopeless romantic. My husband surprised me by coming into town. We went to the carnival. It was adorable. I just love hearing about how people celebrate being together."

"Oh," he says. "Well, I brought her to her favorite restaurant. Mulberry. They were doing a Valentine's Day special menu. We were there until around eleven, then we went dancing in the city. I didn't even get a chance to go home before I was called out to the fire."

"You must have been exhausted," I say. "But at least you had a nice night first. And I'm sure your special lady understood."

"She did," he says.

I stand. "Alright. Well, thank you for letting me talk through this with you."

"Absolutely. Any time you want to talk through something, or if you think of anything that might help with the investigation, you just come by or give me a call," he smiles. "Although, now that you found that man's body, you'll probably be leaving so the investigation team can come in and handle it from here."

I shake my head. "Oh, no."

"No?"

"No." I take a step closer to him. "You see, Sheriff Boyd, I am the investigation team. And I will hunt down whoever is responsible for Shawn Reichert's death, and for the fire, and for Melanie's death, and I will deconstruct them piece by piece until all that's left is the truth and hopelessness." I take a step back and let out a sigh. "Well, have a nice day."

He doesn't move or speak as I leave the office. I say goodbye to the officer behind the desk, who by now has courageously made her way through three more donuts, and head back to the boarding house.

Rather than going upstairs and holing myself up in the same room, I go to the library. It's empty, giving me the perfect environment to continue my research. My computer in front of me, I search for the restaurant the sheriff mentioned, then the next city. I pull up maps and input directions to triangulate routes. By the time Dean comes in with two cups of coffee and a folder under his arm, I have what I need.

"Thank you," I say, taking one of the cups of coffee and sipping it.

"What did you find out?" he asks.

"That Sheriff Boyd is not a creative liar and should really double-check what he's going to say before he says it. He told me he went on a date at a restaurant called Mulberry and was there until about eleven, then went dancing. He supposedly went straight from the dance hall to the fire. But Mulberry was closed by eight that night because of a burst pipe. It's right on the social media page. And the nearest place to go dancing would have made it impossible for him to get there, dance, and get to the fire by the time we got there."

"So, what was he doing?" Dean asks.

"That's a good question. And we can actually thank him for giving us part of the answer."

"What do you mean?"

"Remember how we talked about his big push to end crime and make the city safer? One of his initiatives was to implement city-wide surveillance. Some of the bigger cities around the world have it. Some even use audio/visual systems to record what people are saying and doing around the town. His isn't quite that complex. It doesn't do video. But there are time-lapse cameras positioned on nearly every street corner. Including this one." I turn my computer toward him. "Which shows what I would very strongly argue is Sheriff Boyd's dark blue personal sedan sitting in front of the hardware store, which is suspiciously close to Maya's house."

"What the hell?" Dean says.

"Sums up my thoughts. I just need to find out exactly why he was there. How about you? Did you get them?"

"It wasn't easy," he says. "I've gone a whole lot straighter in my tactics since I've been hanging with you."

"You flatter me."

"Blame, actually. I'm out of practice breaking into places. Especially ones who have people on duty twenty-four hours a day. Because, you know, death doesn't stop."

"Somehow I don't think that's entirely true," I say. "The part about you being out of practice. Not the death part. That one is definitely true. What did you find out?"

He takes a swig of his coffee, trying to perk himself up after being out most of the night finding a way into the funeral home.

"Alright. I got everything you asked for. You were right about the filing cabinet in the corner. I didn't even know people kept those anymore."

"Tiny places like this do. And the way Vera talked about people using the internet like it was witchcraft then revealed herself as the coven lead with her virtual login book, I figured there was a good shot," I say.

"Well, you were right. There wasn't just one filing cabinet. There was an entire moving wall of files. I think more people have died here than live here," he says.

I give him a strange look. "I'm pretty sure that's how it works in most places, Dean. People are not reusable."

"Then the funeral home got into the right market. In more ways than one. Remember what I was saying about the families of the farm workers who died paying for their burial?"

"Yeah," I say. "The men supposedly recorded that their final wishes were to be buried here. A place they barely knew."

"Exactly. Well, according to the financial records for the same time, people by those names were cremated. Urns were purchased for them and their remains were mailed, using the prepaid postage system, to their loved ones."

"Why would they mail the remains of someone who was buried here?" I ask.

"A very good question. Goes along with, why would they record receiving payments for the cremation package, but not the burial package the families say they paid for?"

"Did they just take the money and then not send them anything?"

"Something got sent," Dean says. "There are confirmation numbers proving packages were mailed. It doesn't say they were necessarily mailed to the home of the family members, but they were sent to the same general area."

"PO boxes?" I ask.

"Yes. The USPS is the only shipping service that provides legal shipment of human cremains. It's the only method they could use to ship ashes, so it's the only one they could use to fake ship ashes."

"That's why Shawn Reichert shipped those boxes to himself. He wanted to test if having the same amount of postage on packages of the wrong weight would cause any difficulty."

"As long as the postage paid is equal to or more than what is required for shipping the package, it's not going to make any difference," Dean says. "The question is, what were they sending?"

"I'm going to go out on a limb and say some of the boxes had cash. The lighter ones could have had money cards, even phone cards. Both of those are popular instruments for money laundering. Now we just have to figure out exactly how deep this operation goes and who all was involved."

"How are we going to make sure this evidence is admissible?" Dean asks.

I look over the papers, knowing no court would touch them because of the way they were obtained.

"We'll figure it out," I say. "But for now, there's more we need to do."

He's putting the papers back into the folder when June rushes into the room. She's crying, her hands shaking as she presses them to her face.

"Emma," she says.

I stand and cross the room to her, reaching for her hands.

"June, what's wrong? What happened?"

"Nothing's wrong," she says, shaking her head. "It's a miracle."

"What?" Dean asks.

"Genevieve is alive."

CHAPTER THIRTY-EIGHT

THE STORY OF THE FIRE AT THE FARM AND THE DEATHS THAT HAVE been discovered afterward spread even faster than the fire itself, so the parking lot of the hospital is crowded with media when we arrive. Fortunately for Dean and myself, I've needed on many occasions to get into hospitals without being noticed, or at least without having to fight my way through reporters and TV crews. Finding a back entrance that hasn't yet been staked out is a piece of cake.

I called the sheriff on the way and he told me the floor to go to. He's pacing a hallway when Dean and I get upstairs.

"What the hell happened?" I ask. "You just found her?"

"She called me," he says, sounding like he hasn't fully processed what's going on. "Apparently she escaped wherever she was being held and got to a house on the other side of the park. She called me and I went and picked her up and brought her here."

"How is she? What has she told you?"

"You can go in and talk to her yourself. She's awake. She's shaken up and the doctor wants to give her something to make her rest, but she's refusing it until she speaks to you."

"To me?" I ask. "Why to me?"

"She asked specifically for you."

I nod and walk into the room he indicates. Genevieve is reclined in the bed looking tired and dirty, bandaged in a few places, but in better condition than most people could have hoped. And certainly far better than Melanie.

"Genevieve?" She turns to look at me, lifting her head slightly off the pillow. "Hi. I'm Agent Griffin. You can call me Emma."

She nods. "I know who you are."

I come closer to the side of the bed. "You asked to speak with me."

"You are the only one I want to tell my story to," she says.

"Alright," I nod. "Why is that?"

"I know you're with the FBI and that you've handled some really serious cases," she says.

"That's true."

"And you'll be able to tell everybody what really happened and they'll believe you."

"Why don't you tell me what happened? What do you remember before calling Sheriff Boyd?"

"I've been in a shed since the night of the fire, hiding. I must have passed out from one of my injuries because I woke up nearly frozen and didn't know what day it was or how long I'd been there. I was afraid to get out, but I knew if I stayed, I would die. So I ran. I ran until I wasn't able to anymore, then I collapsed on the front porch of a house. The man inside wouldn't let me in, but he brought me a phone, so I called the person I knew would protect me and make sure nothing else happened to me. Sheriff Boyd," she says in a shaky voice. "He came and rescued me."

I take another step closer. I'm trying to ease my way toward her, not wanting to overwhelm her.

"Genevieve, do you know what happened at your house? To the people in it?"

"I ran. I ran as soon as I could. Everybody got out, right? Everybody else is okay?" she asks.

This shouldn't be something I'm responsible for telling her, but I'm not going to leave her alone in the room knowing something terrible has happened. She needs to know now.

"I'm sorry," I say, my heart breaking as I say it. "Your mother, stepfather, and Melanie didn't make it."

She gasps, her hands flying up to cover her face as she shook her head.

"No. Not Mom, not Mel. They can't be gone. How did they die?"

I don't want to get into specifics with her, but I understand the compulsion to ask. A lot of people say they don't want to know what happened to a loved one when that person is killed, but that isn't the case with me. I want to know the details. I need to have that connection of knowing what they went through so I can properly work through it.

And know how I am going to make it right.

"Your mother died of smoke inhalation. They believe she was asleep and didn't know anything was happening. Melanie was shot outside the home and her body was burned."

It feels terrible saying the words to this young girl. I don't want to put those images in her head. But it's possible giving them to her will help to jar her memory and she'll be able to tell us what happened.

"Oh, my god. I can't believe she did that. I can't…"

"She?" I frown. "What do you mean? Who did this, Genevieve?"

Her eyes look wild as they meet mine. "You don't know? You haven't found her?"

"Found who?"

"Maya. Maya Cortez."

I can't speak. I don't know how to react. My mind is spinning.

"Maya?" I ask. "Maya did this?"

"Yes," she says, starting to cry harder. "I got away from her, but I've been hiding from her since. I knew if she found me, she would kill me. I thought since no one said anything about her or was trying to protect me from her, you'd found her."

I shake my head. "Genevieve, this isn't making sense. No one has been trying to protect you from her because we didn't know we should be. She's still missing. I need to understand exactly what happened. You need to start from the beginning and explain to me what she did and why."

"She just went crazy. I know I'm not supposed to say that, but it's the only way I can describe it. Everything was fine. It seemed normal. Then she saw a picture I have of when we were kids and in that grief group together. She said she didn't remember it. But I couldn't understand how that could possibly be true. We spent weeks going to those meetings. We were friends. Then she just started acting like she didn't know who I was and it took until this year for me to reconnect with her.

"Then she saw that picture and part of me hoped she would say she remembered. That we could pick up again like we used to be. But she was angry. She yelled and it was like she shut down. She wouldn't speak to either of us and she just sat there, staring out the window. We tried to talk to her. She wouldn't even look at Melanie, and that was her best friend.

"Then a little while later, she picked up her phone and looked at it. She walked out of the room, which I thought was really strange for her to do without saying anything. When she came back, she had that guy with her."

"What guy?" I ask.

"The guy she hangs out with. I can't remember his name. I've never spoken to him. He came in and he had gasoline and a lighter. They started screaming and taunting us. She said I was a horrible person who ruined her life and she was going to teach me and all my friends not to treat people that way. I ran. She tackled me and hit me, but I got away. I thought Mel was following me. I don't remember anything after that until I was running into the shed. I must have blacked out."

"Why would she do that?" I ask. "What would make her act like that?"

"She must have found the video," Genevieve says.

"The video of her talking about her memory?" I ask.

"No. The one from the carnival."

I shake my head. "I don't know what you're talking about."

She asks for my phone and I hand it to her. In a few seconds, she has a video pulled up. It's dark and grainy, and it takes me a few seconds for me to realize I'm watching security footage of what looks like a cheap amusement park ride.

"It's the Fireball," she says as if that will mean something to me.

"The what?" I ask.

"The Fireball. It's one of the rides at the carnival, but it's usually only open in the summer and for Halloween. They always close it at the Valentine's Day one and put the Fun House in front of the show building. I guess they don't think it fits the theme enough."

A second later, a terrified-looking Maya runs out of a door onto the ride platform. She desperately tries to find her way out and ends up sitting in the ride vehicle. I feel my stomach drop as the car lurches forward.

"A couple of the guys from school did this. They found out she was going to the carnival and planned to scare her. When we went into the Fun House, they followed her and made sure she got confused and scared. They made all kinds of sounds and screams. They made sure she found the emergency door that goes out onto the platform. It's usually covered and only the staff knows how to find it. The guys work there during the Halloween carnival, so they know about it.

"They chased her out there and then locked the door behind her. One was hidden in the control room, which is really just an alcove to the side, but it's painted black and has a curtain, so it's really hard to see unless you know what you're looking for. They started the ride, then stopped it at the part where there is a fire effect. The flames aren't that big, but by the time she got there, Maya was completely panicking. I've never seen someone so scared as when I watched the video that night after it was posted.

"They let her out and she got out of the building, but she was really shaken up about it. I was furious with those guys. I couldn't believe people I'd once considered friends, one of them was even my ex-boyfriend, would do something that cruel. We ended up leaving. I thought it was over. That they got their laughs and that was it. But then they posted the video. They said it was a 'memory' they would never forget."

"Making fun of her video," I whisper.

Genevieve nods. "I knew it would hurt her, but I never would have…" she pauses and lets out a sob. "I didn't think she would do something like this."

CHAPTER THIRTY-NINE

"EMMA, I'M SORRY. I KNOW THAT I TOLD YOU THE FIRST TIME YOU came here I can't talk about anything that happened in the support group. All I can do is confirm the details that law enforcement already has. I can't discuss anything any of those children talked about or what our therapy entailed. It would be unethical," Olivia insists.

"But not illegal," I counter. "They were, and still are, children. Minors. Which means they don't have inherent confidentiality. Their privacy belongs to their parents, which means if their parents consent to you discussing the group, you are within your rights to do so."

"I'm familiar with the regulations, Emma. That's not the point. I want to create a space where children don't feel like they're being judged by their parents or burdened by expectations from them. Studies have shown countless times that children respond better and are more honest, straightforward, and reliable witnesses when they are not with their parents.

"And I feel that is exactly what they are doing when they are with me. They are witnessing to their own experiences and perceptions. And when they have the freedom to communicate without having to seek validation or approval from their parents, they are more likely to do so authentically," Olivia says.

"What good is that if you don't protect them later? If they are so broken and scarred by what happened to them they can't face life?" I ask.

"What do you mean?"

"Genevieve McGuire is alive. She was found earlier today and is now telling a horrific story blaming Maya for all of it," I say.

"What?" Olivia gasps, her voice now low and powdery. "That can't be true."

"She says that when she saw a video some guys made to bully her, she flew off the handle, called a friend of hers, and they attacked Genevieve and burned down the house. She ran and didn't know what happened to the rest of them. Now, I need to know if you ever saw anything from Maya that would suggest something like that would be possible from her. Grace Cortez has given you permission to tell me anything you need to. Both for me to find out what happened, and try to make sure Maya gets through this," I tell her.

She hesitates and I lean toward her imploringly.

"Please. When I first came here, you said there would always be a need for groups that support children through the grief of losing their parents. I know that personally. My mother was murdered when I was eleven years old. I didn't know the truth about it for another nearly twenty years. I am still trying to recover from it. I see so much of my own pain and torment in Maya. I don't understand how she could do this, but I don't want anything worse to happen because of it. Please. Help me."

Olivia nods.

"Maya was a sweet girl. Most of the time. She didn't like to participate in the group conversations, but that isn't so unusual. Some children just don't express their grief well through words. That's why we do other activities like drawing and theater. Things that enable the children to process their emotions and communicate them in a way that feels safe and nonthreatening.

"She really enjoyed participating in those. But there were times when she would show a really dark side. She could suddenly become combative and aggressive. She didn't want anyone near her and the art therapy she created took on a really disturbing element. Pictures of blood and broken glass. A body hanging from a tree. Horrible things.

"She developed an extremely intense obsession with law enforcement. It was nearing hero worship. Especially the sheriff. She believed he could make the dead live again and cause them to rise up into Heaven," Olivia says.

"She said that?"

"Yes. Seven years old, and those were the thoughts she was having. It was terrifying. But if she was given the opportunity to get that out, she went back to being calm. I figured this was just a phase that she needed to work through, and when she felt validated and heard, she would move past it. I told her mother about the outbursts and suggested she put her into more intensive therapy if she got older. Over the years I've kept up with her from a distance and it seemed she was doing fine. Perhaps not a charmed, glistening life like Genevieve, but a normal teenage experience," Olivia says.

"Thank you. I appreciate you sharing that with me," I say, moving toward the door.

"What's going to happen to her?" Olivia asks, following me with a step. "What's going to happen to Maya?"

"I don't know," I tell her honestly. "Right now, the first thing is to find her. Then we go from there."

"Aiden Jones?"

A skinny boy too tall for his weight and his face with scraggly dark hair and thick glasses over expressive dark eyes looks across the cash register counter at me.

"Yes," he says.

"My name is Agent Griffin. I'm with the FBI. I need to have a word with you."

His face goes paler than it already is and he looks like he might faint. "Is this about Maya? Is she alright? Have you found her yet?"

"Please come with me. We'll go somewhere we can speak privately," I say.

"I'll have to ask my manager," he says.

"I've spoken with him. You need to come with me."

He finally comes around the counter and follows me into the back room the manager cleared to give us a place to talk.

"What's going on?" he asks when he sits down. "Please tell me Maya is alright."

"Her mother tells me the two of you have been friends a long time," I say.

"Since we were really little," Aiden says. "I know she has Mel, but she's my best friend. Can't you please just tell me she's okay?"

"When was the last time you saw Maya?"

"At school on Valentine's Day," he says. "We were having lunch and Genevieve McGuire walked by with a rose. She ran it along Maya's face and made her laugh. That's when she told me she was going to the carnival with her."

"You don't seem to like that idea," I say. "Do you have a problem with Genevieve McGuire?"

"Not a specific one. I just don't like people like her. She's one of the nicer ones, I'll admit. But she's still one of them. Popular. Rich. The world gets handed to them, and they don't even seem to realize it. She wouldn't give Maya the time of day up until just a couple of weeks ago. Then all of a sudden, she starts being friendly with her? I just didn't understand it."

"You didn't understand why somebody would want to be friends with Maya?"

"No. That's not what I meant. Maya is incredible. She's the most amazing girl I've ever met. She has her problems, sure, but I don't think you're really an authentic person unless you have a couple of problems. It's what lets you actually connect with the world. I mean I don't understand why she would go from not wanting anything to do with her to wanting to be close so quickly."

"She told Maya she wants to better herself," I tell him, relaying part of the conversation I had with Grace.

"She would definitely be able to do that with Maya as a friend," he says. A tear falls down his cheek. "I'm so worried about her. I tried to call her after the carnival when I saw that video, but she didn't answer and then I found out about the fire."

"You didn't see her after school?" I ask.

"No," he shakes his head. "I wanted to go to the carnival so that if she started having a bad time, she would have someone else to hang out with, but my boss wouldn't let me take the night off."

"The grocery store closes at eight," I point out, having noted the hours before coming inside.

"I know," he says. "I'm talking about my night job. At the hotel near Oak Bridge. I work the desk at night. I know I'm not supposed to because I'm not eighteen, but my family really needs the money. My boss pays me under the table. Please don't get him in trouble because I told you that."

"I'm not worried about your boss. I'm here to talk to you. I'm going to be completely straight with you right now. And I need you to be honest with me."

He nods and I tell him what Genevieve told me. I'm not even finished talking and he's already frantically shaking his head.

"No," he says. "No. That didn't happen. None of that happened. Maya would never do something like that. And I couldn't have been there. I was at work. I stayed at the desk until almost four in the morning, then I slept in one of the rooms for a couple of hours before I went to school. I was expecting to see Maya there, and then I found out about the fire."

"You are being totally honest with me?" I say.

"Yes. You can check the surveillance. You can ask my boss. I even made a note in my book to remember to tell Maya." He digs in his pocket and pulls out a small notebook with a pen sticking through the coils. He opens it and shows me the page. "February fifteenth. Midnight. I guess Maya is unsupervised tonight. Sara McGuire just checked in."

"He didn't have anything to do with it," I tell Dean when I get back in the car.

"You're sure?"

"This kid was afraid his manager was going to get mad at him for stepping away from his register to talk to an FBI agent. He asked about Maya like twenty times. And he has an alibi. He works a second job to support his family and he was there all night. I had him call his boss right in front of me and I spoke with him. I had to promise I wasn't going to turn him in for illegally employing a minor off the books, but he verified Aiden was at the hotel all night. And guess who paid a visit that night?"

CHAPTER FORTY

"**Y**OU LIED TO ME."

"No, I didn't," Genevieve protests with wide eyes. "I told you everything."

"Let's try this again, because I know what you told me the other day isn't what happened."

"I don't understand. I told you the truth. Maya snapped and that guy came and I guess they lit the house on fire."

"That guy's name is Aiden and I already spoke with him. He has a rock-solid alibi. He wasn't at your house on Valentine's Day night. Try again."

"Maybe it was a different guy," she says.

"Like your boyfriend?" I ask.

"I told you Dayton and I broke up."

"Is that why you have gifts from him in your trunk?" I ask.

She stumbles slightly, surprised I know about the items in her car. "I was bringing them back to him. He gave them to me months ago for our anniversary. He made that video, but he didn't have anything to do with this. It was Maya."

"Genevieve, my patience is getting thin. I want to know what the hell is going on," I say.

"I don't know what to tell you. I was in my bedroom and Maya completely snapped. She started threatening me and I was scared. Maybe I didn't actually see a guy, but I saw her texting somebody and then a car pulled up into my driveway. I heard voices. I know somebody was there. I got out of there as fast as I could and I ran for all I was worth. Then I sat in a shed until I figured I was going to die either way, so I might as well try to get out."

"Alright," I say. "I get that you're scared. You went through something really horrific. But I need you to be straight up with me. Don't make guesses. Don't come up with stories because they sound good. I need you to tell me what actually happened. What you really saw and experienced."

"What do you think?"

"I don't know. She lied about Aiden being there. Why would she do that if she wasn't lying about the entire story? The thing is, I think she knows that we know Maya could not have done all of that by herself. So she came up with somebody who could help the person she's blaming."

"So, you don't think Maya did it?" Dean asks.

"No. I did. I thought it was possible. But it doesn't make sense. She wouldn't hurt Mel that way. She remembered her. Even through such intense trauma that she blocked out an entire segment of her life, but the one thing that she remembers other than her mother is Mel."

"I know what that's like," he nods.

"I know you do. And so you can appreciate how valuable that makes Melanie to her. It wouldn't matter how angry she got or how much she wanted to lash out at Genevieve for representing something that hurt her, she wouldn't do that to Mel. And she especially wouldn't let Genevieve escape while she was taking the time to shoot Melanie and then light her body on fire. That's not her."

"Genevieve is injured and has been hiding out since the night of the fire," Dean points out. "Is it possible Maya really did chase her off? But then someone else came behind her and actually killed the others and torched the house? What good would it do her to lie about Maya?"

"There's only one person I can think of who would benefit from this fire and from those deaths. I need to go have a chat with the sheriff."

The sheriff isn't at his office and none of the officers on duty know where he is, so I set out to find him. The town isn't big enough for him to truly hide. At some point, I will stumble on his car, and I think I might have a good idea where it is.

Turning down the street where Maya and Grace live, I drive past their house and down to the corner. The dark blue sedan isn't sitting in front of the hardware store, but it doesn't take me long to find it. Diagonally across the street and two buildings down, it's up against the curb and I see a familiar figure behind the wheel.

Sheriff Boyd gets out of his car as I approach. He looks angry and he storms over to me, blocking me from looking at his car or anything beyond it.

"What are you doing here?" he demands. "Are you following me?"

"What are you doing here?" I fire back. "Is it the same thing you were doing Valentine's night? Are you watching Maya's house to watch her or are you waiting to see if someone comes for her?"

"What are you talking about?" he sputters. "I told you I was on a date that night. Just like many other adults in this town, including you."

"Yes. But the difference is I was on a date somewhere that was actually open. Mulberry closed early because of a burst pipe. So, you couldn't have been there having their special Valentine's Day menu until eleven. And if you actually did leave the area at that time and go dancing, there's no way you would have been able to make it back to the McGuire house before Dean and I got there. Which tells me you completely made up that date. You weren't going to dinner and dancing. You were sitting right here."

"No, I wasn't. I don't know what this is, but I'm not here for anything having to do with Maya Cortez. I'm here because that's my parents' house. My father is an invalid and my mother is the only one who can take care of him when I'm not here, but she's in terrible health. So I come and help. But I wasn't here that night. Not that it's any of your business if I was."

"See, but I think it is. Because the problem right now is that Genevieve is telling a story about Maya snapping out of reality and chasing her down, then apparently disappearing. And sometime after that happened, a teenage girl was shot and lit on fire, and a house was torched, killing two people inside," I say.

"I know what happened. I was there. You seem to forget that this is my investigation. One I invited you to stay to be a part of, by the way," he says.

"I know you were there. And I think you were there earlier as well. You were waiting. I'm not sure for what, but I promise I will find out." I take out my phone and show him the image I found of his car parked in the corner the night of Valentine's Day. "Your surveillance initiative is really fantastic, you know. It will really help to clean up the town. I bet you didn't expect for it to tell on you, though."

Sheriff Boyd looks at the image and scoffs. "You think I'm stupid enough to let my own surveillance program catch my car parked somewhere if I was lying about being somewhere else? For what reason? So I could commit some casual arson?"

"So you could kill the activist who uncovered your corruption and was going to reveal it, ruining your credibility and your chance at becoming mayor. Jim Calhoun knew you were getting kickbacks and favors. He knew you pulled strings and trumped up charges to make sure people who treated you right and promised you favors got a get out of jail free card, while others spent long sentences in jail for minor things. You decided who you wanted to punish and how, and you let free the ones you wanted under your thumb. He was going to reveal it all."

"Jim Calhoun," Sheriff Boyd says slowly, his voice slick, "was a burned-out right-fighter whose first wife was murdered and the guy who did it was exonerated. He never got over it. He's been looking for corruption everywhere he goes since then, which is pretty ironic when you think about how he saw his stepdaughter and all her little friends. Anyone who knew him well knew he was going to crack one day. He was either going to off himself or try to go out in a blaze of fucked up glory because he kidnapped a bunch of women and tried to make them be his wives. No one would have believed him.

"But you're right. I did lie about my date that night. I was trying to protect someone, but I guess I don't need to do that anymore. I spent most of the night with Sara McGuire at the hotel near Oak Bridge. I have a standing room there. One of my kickbacks. I fell asleep there while she went home because her husband was going to be getting off his computer and would notice she was gone. I'm sure if you look at the timestamps of his blog, you'll see it."

"Why would I hurt her? I loved her. She and I have been together since before she even met Jim. But I was too stupid to commit to her when I had the chance. We stayed away from each other for a while, but then we found each other again when her marriage started to go bad. I would never have hurt her, Ms. Griffin."

He furrows his brow and glares at me intently. "And just so we're clear, let me help you out with this clue. If you look at that picture, you see a dark sedan. You can't tell what color it actually is, but I'll even give you the pass of saying it's blue.

"But you can't see any of the license plate. Do you know who could see the license plate? The officer who would have given that car a ticket for sitting there at that time. You see, another of my initiatives is to keep the city more beautiful, and there was street cleaning that night. Now, I might not be the smartest man in the world, but I can assure you I wouldn't let myself get a ticket on top of everything else. Those fees are a bitch."

He walks away and gets in his car.

"Shit," I mutter as he drives away.

I can't believe I was that far off. I missed it.

Suddenly, I stop. I snatch my phone out of my pocket and I call Dean.

"I need you to do something as fast as you can," I tell him. "I'll be at the boarding house in ten minutes."

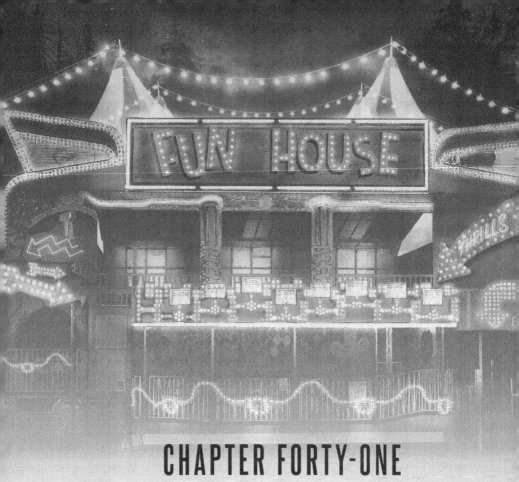

CHAPTER FORTY-ONE

"Hayden Carl Brunswick," Dean says, showing me the scan of the parking ticket given out on Valentine's Day. "Ticket for parking on the street during street cleaning."

"It's the same car as the invoice from the yard the night of the fire, isn't it?" I ask.

"It is. Dark green sedan. Almost a match for the sheriff's car. It belongs to this kid's mother's boyfriend. He was so busy with that online watch party, didn't even know Hayden had it that night."

"I'm sure he didn't. I need the contact information for the kid," I say. "I need to find out why he was in Cold Valley that night."

"What can I do?" he asks.

"Get in touch with Eric and have him send you the best satellite images of this entire area he can. We need Cold Valley, the park, and whatever is beyond it. As clear as possible."

"What are you looking for?" Dean asks.

"The day Maya and her father were hit, the car that hit them would have been smashed up and bloodied. It wouldn't have been able to just go down the street without someone realizing there was a problem. Which means they found a different way out of that park. I want to see all the different roads, paths, clearings, anything that would get them somewhere they could get rid of or fix that car and not have anyone know about it."

"I'm on it," he nods.

"Thank you."

I take the contact information he gave me for Hayden Brunswick and call him. It takes a few tries before he answers.

"Look, you son of a bitch scammer, I don't have a fucking desktop or a car so you can stop calling me to tell me my phony warranty is expired or I have a virus."

"Hayden Brunswick, this is Agent Griffin from the FBI. That would be the Federal Bureau of Investigation. And I assure you I don't give a damn if your computer is patient zero for the coming virtual apocalypse. I need to talk to you about Cold Valley."

"I—I..."

"Just let me start with a simple question for you. Did you receive a parking ticket for parking on a street during street cleaning in Cold Valley, Tennessee the night of February fourteenth?"

"Yes," he gulps.

"Alright. We're off to a good start. Now, let's try a slightly more difficult one. Did you go to Genevieve McGuire's house in your stepfather's car that night?"

There's a pause as he seems to try to decide what he's going to say. I'm waiting for a denial and to have to try a different approach.

"Please don't tell her I told you," he whispers, taking me off-guard. "I promised her I wasn't going to say anything. She didn't want anyone to know about us yet. It's really complicated. She says the guy she's with wouldn't understand, and it would end up looking really bad for him, and for her family, and for mine. She just wanted to see me for Valentine's Day. All she asked was that I park on that corner for a while, and then go to her house to see her."

"You didn't think it was strange she wanted you to sit at a corner for no reason?" I ask.

"I didn't care. Do you have any idea how long I've been dreaming about her? I never thought she even noticed me. Then she's the one who started flirting with me. She wanted to be with me. I would have done anything for her. Soon enough, we'll be able to be together."

I cringe at the desperation in his voice. His craving for her attention sounds so familiar.

"You said you've been dreaming of her for a long time. You live in a different state. How could you know her that well?" I ask.

"My father lives in Cold Valley," he says. "That's how I met her. She interned at his office. But that's also part of why it would be complicated for us to just come out with being together."

Bells are starting to go off in my mind.

"Who's your father?"

"I'll be back," I tell Dean as I run through the library and toward the front door to the boarding house, scanning through my phone gallery to make sure I have the picture I need.

I find it and keep it up on my screen as I toss my phone into the passenger seat and drive away from Broad Street. The shop I'm going to is almost an hour away, but now I'm getting a feeling I understand why it's the one that was chosen. While I'm driving, I pray to the gods of road safety and scan through pictures on the tablet in my lap of the night of the fire. My search changes over to Jim Calhoun's blog and I read the posts in brief snippets between watching the road. I don't have time to waste.

The drive seems to take far longer than it should, but finally, I get to the little shop with white gingerbread woodwork and a bright pink door. It's a sweet, demure exterior that belies the lace and g-strings inside.

A woman in a dress she looks incredible in but that makes me cold just looking at it approaches me when I walk in.

"Hi, there," she greets me in a warm, friendly voice. "What brings you in today? Are you looking for something for a special night with that special someone?" She glances at my hand and sees my wedding ring. "A married woman, I see. Maybe you're wanting to spice things up a bit."

"No," I say, shaking my head. "We're… spicy enough." An idea for how I'm going to navigate this comes to mind. "Actually, that's the reason I'm here. You see, my husband loves when I wear lingerie, but he can never pick the right size. Then he gets embarrassed and doesn't want to return it, so I end up with all these pieces that are too big or too small hidden around the room and it's just a mess. I'd love to return them for credit, but he also has a bad habit of cutting the tags off before he gives them to me."

"Men," she mutters with a chuckle. I think it's supposed to be in solidarity, but I'm not sure of the point.

I just nod and keep going. "He gave me a gorgeous negligee for Valentine's Day and I think he got it here, but I'm not positive. One of them actually fits me, which is fantastic, and I love it, so I would really like to get some matching pieces. And, of course, return the one that's too small. If I show you a picture of my husband, do you think you would remember what he bought?"

"Absolutely," she nods. "I am very good with faces. It helps me keep my customers happy."

"Great," I say.

I take out my phone and instead of showing her the image of the lingerie I'd pulled up, I find a picture of the sheriff that looks candid. I show it to her and she smiles.

"Oh, him! I definitely remember him. You are a lucky girl. And yes, I know exactly what you're talking about with him buying two sizes of everything. You've gotten quite a few pieces from my shop. The most recent one was this," she says, bringing me over to a display and showing me another piece of the same lingerie that I found in Genevieve's trunk. "Right?"

"That's the one," I confirm.

"Well, it is absolutely gorgeous. He bought two of them, just like you said." She laughs. "But if you want to bring back the one that doesn't fit, I'm happy to give you store credit. Now, there isn't anything that really matches that piece, but how about something like this? It would be beautiful with those blue eyes of yours."

Ten minutes later I have a bag full of satin, lace, and silk in the trunk and I'm on my way back to Cold Valley. My phone rings when I'm about halfway there.

"Dean?" I answer. "What's up?"

"I got the maps you were looking for," he says. "And I think there's something on there you'll find very interesting. Are you almost here?"

"Not close enough that I'm willing to wait," I say. "Send it to me."

I end the call and a few seconds later get a notification of an email. Deciding to be responsible this time, I pull off on the side of the road and open the attached image on my tablet. Dean has not only sent me the satellite images, he's gone in with a photo editor and drawn out different routes the car could have taken. At the back of the map, there is a large circle surrounding what looks like a home tucked away in the trees just outside of the park. I see exactly what Dean wanted me to.

I run a quick search and a wry smile comes to my lips. I pull back onto the road and call Dean.

"Change of plans," I say. "Meet me at the park."

CHAPTER FORTY-TWO

T HERE'S SOMETHING SURREAL ABOUT DRIVING DOWN HOLLYBROOK Road now that I am confident I know what happened. The first time I came here, I could see what happened. I knew where and when. I just didn't know who or why.

Those pieces have come together now. I can almost see the entire thing playing out in front of me as I drive along the curve. I go past the bike trail outlet where David Cortez died and continue around the swooping road until I get to the unpaved access path Dean outlined for me on the map.

I turn onto it and slow down. I'm not familiar with this area or what could be out in these woods, so I move gradually even though I want to get to the end. I wonder how long it's going to take before everyone gets here. I've already made all the calls I need to make. It's just a matter of time until they respond.

Maybe they'll be there before I do. At least that would show some initiative.

Rather than driving all the way down to the end of the path, I pull off on the side partway down. I don't want to advertise my approach too soon. Getting out, I make sure my gun is securely strapped to my hip and my knife is tucked in the hidden pocket in the band of my bra. As I always do, I hope I won't have to use either one of them. But I've learned in very hard ways not to go into situations like this unarmed and unprepared.

The walk down the remainder of the access road takes around ten minutes. It passes through a creek and over a rocky hill, finally exiting out of the park through a wooden gate covered with heavy chains. I step through the chains and look ahead to the gravel driveway I've been looking for.

As I walk down the driveway, I hear voices, but they hush as I get closer. By the time I step through the tree line and can see the modest house and cluttered yard, only one person is standing there. He's hunched over one of the many pieces of equipment scattered around the property. Cars, partial cars, lawnmowers, power tools, and engines sit on the grass or tarps, some on cement blocks, and others on top of each other. Out of the corner of my eye, I see larger pieces of equipment behind the house.

They are all in various stages of repair and condition, and the one the man is looking at seems as though it likely lived out its life several years ago.

He straightens as I approach.

"Can I help you?" he asks. "This here's private property, you know."

"I am very aware," I reply. "Why don't you ask your friends to come out here and have a word with me." It's not a question.

He looks around like he's trying to convince me he doesn't know what I'm talking about.

"Ain't nobody here but me," he says.

"So, I guess you get so lonely living out here by yourself you start having enough conversations with yourself that you come up with different voices to use," I counter. "I'll admit, that does make it seem more enjoyable."

I pause for a second, waiting to see if he'll call them out, but he doesn't. "Alright. Well, if it's just going to be the two of us, I guess I'll get started. You are Tyler Ennis, am I right?"

"Yeah," he says.

"Well, Tyler, I have a problem and I think you might be able to help me with it. You see, there's this big tree that's been really bothering me recently. It doesn't look like the other ones around it and I just can't stop thinking about it. It's really starting to get to me. Do you think that's something you could help me with? The thing is, there's a strange hole in the tree now. It didn't used to be there, but unfortunately, it had to be cut into, because there was something inside we needed to get out. I hear you are really good with trees," I say.

"I…" he starts.

"Don't say anything." Sheriff Boyd comes out of the house and walks toward us. "Don't say anything, Tyler."

"Sheriff Boyd," I say as if I wasn't expecting him. "What a surprise."

"She's asking about the tree," Tyler says to Boyd. "You said no one would ever know about the tree. That was the deal."

He's speaking through gritted teeth, trying to maintain composure while also seeming to already be tipping over the edge.

"It'll be fine, Tyler. She doesn't know what she's talking about."

"Don't I?" I ask. I hear a sound inside the house and I lean around to look at it behind the sheriff. "Oh, I'm not interrupting something, am I? Maybe a little afternoon rendezvous? You might as well come on out here. I think the good sheriff here has some things he needs to share with you. Like maybe about your mother."

Genevieve gives me a smug look as she comes out of the house.

"You think I don't know about her?" she asks. "About how she has been throwing herself at my man for so long. It's pathetic. He might have had a thing for her at one time, but that was before I came along. Now he has the real thing."

"And I'm sure the two of you are very happy," I say. "Tell me, do you do cute little photoshoots in your matching lingerie?"

Her face reddens and she shoots a glare in the sheriff's direction.

"You got us the same ones? You said you were done with her," she growls.

"Shut up, Genevieve," the sheriff snaps at her.

"Why?" I ask. "You don't want her finally telling the truth about what happened to her stepmother and her father?"

The sheriff scoffs and rolls his eyes. "You really need to let this go, Emma. Yes, I was having an affair with Sara, and yes, I was also sleeping with Genevieve, but that doesn't make me a murderer."

"You aren't just sleeping with me," she says with hurt, angry tears in her eyes. "You love me. We are going to be together."

"You really think that?" I ask her. "You think an adult man is going to give up everything, his career, his future, his political aspirations, all of that so that he can be with you?"

"He wouldn't have to give it up," she says. "I was helping him. He was going to have everything. We were going to have everything."

"Stop it, Genevieve," Boyd says.

"That's right," I say. "You were helping him. You knew how important it was for him to get elected and to keep reaching for that next step. So you were making it happen for him. What's more impressive than solving a tragic arson and murder case, right? Rescuing a beautiful girl from the clutches of the monster who abducted her? And for a sweet little added bonus, she got to get rid of her mother and have you all to herself."

"Genevieve?" he asks questioningly.

"She's making it up. Why would I do that to my own house? Why would I have the other girls over if it was just about creating some crime for him to solve? This is ridiculous. I already told you that Maya Cortez is the one who did it."

"See, I almost believed you. I really did. I saw how much pain that girl was suffering and the torment your friends put her through didn't help. I spoke with Olivia Bragg and found out about how she used to act in the group sessions. Nobody knew that about her. Except you, of course. You and Melanie. You were there. You would have witnessed those moments. I really thought there was a chance that she had just had too much. That the world had finally pushed her too far and she'd snapped. But then something occurred to me."

"What?" Genevieve asks.

"You. Your own words. When you were in the hospital, you said you ran from Maya and hid in that shed on the other side of the park, far away from your house, until the day you ran to the house to call for help. But then you asked about your family, and if they got out. You said Maya must have lit the house on fire."

"She did," Genevieve said with a shrug.

"But how would you know that?" Boyd asks. "If you were in that shed from before the fire, how would you know it started? The guy whose phone you used didn't even let you in the house. He wouldn't have told you. I didn't tell you. And I was standing right outside your door the whole time. None of the doctors told you, either."

"Matt..."

"The only way you would have known there was a fire at the house was if you started it yourself."

She lets out a sarcastic laugh and looks around incredulously.

"This is ridiculous. You think I burned down my own house? I shot Melanie, too? Why would I do any of that? Jeffrey would have dropped my mother soon enough anyway," she snaps, cuddling up to his side.

"No, I wouldn't have," he counters, pushing her away. "I loved her. I was trying to get her to leave Jim and marry me. I would have been your stepfather."

"Then I guess I would have had two stepdaddies who wanted to get in my pants. How many is a collection?" She's fighting tears, but her anger is winning out.

"I would have had no reason to hurt Maya or Melanie. I defended them from the guys bullying them. I hung out with them."

"It was still for him," I say, gesturing toward Boyd.

"What?" he asks. "What are you talking about? How would those girls dying benefit me at all?"

"You might not be a murderer or an arsonist, but you are sure as hell a criminal," I say. "Ten years ago a man named Shawn Reichert came to this town calling himself Michael Forbes. He pretended to be visiting, considering making his home here. But what he was actually doing was investigating. He'd uncovered a money-laundering ring that used the funeral home as its center base.

"Migrant farmworkers and other men needing work would come here with the promise of a job. Soon, there would be an accident. The worker died tragically. It was horrible, but things like that happen around big equipment and dangerous jobs. The funeral home called their home with the terrible news. Then revealed that their loved one had grown so attached to Cold Valley in even their short time here, the paperwork they had to fill out when they got the job declared they wanted to be buried here.

"Of course, to a family member who really thinks that through, it isn't going to make sense. But nothing makes sense when you're grieving. So they would go along with it. Even send money for a burial package. In return, they got a letter of condolence. A picture of their loved one's final resting place. The thing is, all of them got the same one. And according to the funeral home, every one of those men was cremated, contained within a very expensive and elegant urn, and mailed home to their families.

"It doesn't take too much imagination to figure out what was actually happening. Now, I don't know where the money being laundered is coming from other than the extortion of these families. It could be drugs. It could be weapons. It could even be good old-fashioned prostitution and human trafficking. It doesn't really matter. It won't be too hard to find out. What matters is Agent Reichert found out. He knew what was happening and he was going to blow it the hell up.

"Only, somebody got to him first. He disappeared. No one knew what happened to him. No one except the people who murdered him and the little girl who witnessed them dumping his body inside a hollow tree along the bike trail she enjoyed with her daddy.

"By now I'm sure you've seen the video where Maya describes her memories of that day. They aren't clear, to say the least. But if you pay really close attention to what she says, and what her therapist had to say about her grieving process, you'll find out some really interesting details. Like that she saw a man she knew lifting his arms up like he was praying and the dead body she saw rising up.

"Her therapist told me she would draw horrifying pictures of people hanging from trees and that she was obsessed with the sheriff, believing he could bring people back to life or send them up to Heaven. I didn't realize it at the time, but what she was drawing wasn't actually a person hanging. It was Agent Reichert being hoisted up into the tree. It would take somebody very knowledgeable about trees and how to best navigate them to do something like that, wouldn't it, Tyler?"

He shifts uncomfortably.

"He said I had to," he admits. "He had something on me."

"He'd gotten you off the hook for a burglary," I say. "When you were a teenager. You got drunk and broke into a lake house. The owner startled you and you stabbed him. He survived, but you were facing serious charges. He got you off, but you owed him."

"I didn't do any of that," Boyd says. "I didn't kill an agent. I didn't kill anyone."

"You didn't kill him, but you were there," I say. "You see, I didn't say *you* got him off. I said 'he.' This whole time I've been thinking about this the wrong way. When we first met, I mentioned that I was investigating Agent Reichert's disappearance and you told me you knew he was an FBI agent, that during the initial investigation they told you who he was."

"They did," Boyd argues.

"No, they didn't. See, I thought it made sense. They would divulge that information to the sheriff. But I didn't think that all the way through. Because you weren't sheriff at the time. Ten years ago, you were just an officer. Which means you wouldn't have gotten that information unless you were in very close contact with someone who did know.

"It also means Maya wasn't worshipping you. She didn't think you could raise people to Heaven. She saw the sheriff lift up his arms to give

Tyler the instruction to hoist up the body. And then I realized, with a little help from a friend who got a traffic ticket recently, that we're about to repeat history. Or, that's what you were hoping for."

"What do you mean?" Genevieve asks.

Boyd's jaw is tight. He knows exactly what I'm talking about.

"The sheriff becoming mayor." Her mouth drops. "That's right. Hayden is not good at keeping secrets. Good news, though, he really, really loves you."

"What is she talking about?" Boyd asks.

"You didn't tell him how you're sleeping with the mayor's son— and probably the mayor, too, but I don't have that on record—to keep the perks rolling to Jeffrey? To make sure that the mayor keeps up his endorsement?"

Boyd rolls his eyes. "Genevieve."

"It's sad, isn't it? Her thinking she had to do that when he was going to endorse you anyway. He had to. You've been holding a murder over his head for ten years. He could have turned right around and implicated you in the money-laundering scheme, but then it would just get messy. He'd rather both of you succeed and move forward. But you got greedy. Or he did. I don't know which started it, but someone started up the old game again. And now I'm here."

"She was going to destroy you. And she told Melanie everything, which meant she could have opened her mouth, too," Genevieve says. "As soon as I saw that video, I remembered you telling me about having to help a friend hide a body, but you said it was a drunk who was killed brawling over a still."

"The moonshine will get you every time," I say.

"That's enough," Genevieve snaps, reaching beside her and pulling Boyd's gun out of his holster to point it at me.

"Genevieve, stop," he shouts. "Don't be ridiculous. This isn't going to do you any good."

"She just wants to escape, don't you?" I ask. "You want to be able to leave."

Genevieve nods tearfully.

"You see, I actually believe that Maya flew into one of her rages that night. I think that she did hit you. Those injuries aren't fake. The pressure broke her as she was starting to remember what actually happened. She attacked you and left. That's when you came up with the idea of what you were going to do. She'd been tormented by the fire that night, so you would let her have her revenge. Melanie was the first to go. She went after Maya and you stopped her. Then the house went. Your mother had just gotten home and was drinking away her longing for the lover she thought she'd never get to keep, which made it just so easy to slide away in the smoke."

"Where is she, Genevieve?" Boyd asks. "What did you do with her?"

She doesn't answer and Boyd yanks her around to face him. I duck out of the way of a potential bullet, but it doesn't come. I take the opportunity to pull my own weapon and press the button on my phone that tells Dean to come.

"I wanted you to be a hero," Genevieve says, sobbing. "I wanted you to love me."

Her knees buckle and she drops into his arms. Boyd scoops her up against his chest for just a second, then steps back and lets her hit the ground.

"Emma, is everything alright?" Dean calls to me, running out of the woods.

Tyler suddenly takes off running and I point after him. "Go get him. When you catch him, have him tell you where he stashed Maya. I think she's alive."

I reach down and take the cuffs off my belt so I can put them on Genevieve.

Boyd looks at me now, an expression somewhere between heartbreak and fury glistening in them. He looks like he's about to tear himself apart.

"I hate when people get away with things," he growls. "That's why I did this. I've watched so many people never pay for what they've done and I made it my life's goal to make sure that didn't happen. The system doesn't always work. The good guys don't always win and the bad guys don't always get what's coming to them. But the world can balance things out, and that's what I wanted to do.

"You're really not all that different from me, Emma Griffin, FBI. I know the things you've done. You've made choices you didn't have to make and you made them because you thought that was the right thing. You are a vigilante, just like me."

"I am nothing like you."

He scoffs. "Yes, you are. I could have been great, you know. As Mayor. I could have really made a difference. But it always would have haunted me. It was here waiting for me. All this time. It was always going to come for me."

He reaches down to the ground to pick up his gun. I lift mine, but before I can say a word, he puts it in his mouth and pulls the trigger.

EPILOGUE

"MAYA IS GOING TO BE FINE. SHE'S SHAKEN UP, DEHYDRATED. Needs a warm bed and a few meals. And to get back into therapy. But she's alive and she's back with her mother. The sick jerk hid her in the same storage truck where he hid the car for those ten years. But he'll never hurt anyone again. None of them will."

"Good," Xavier says. He looks tiny on the phone screen Dean is holding up for me. "What about the bodies of the farmworkers?"

"They are searching the area around the funeral home for them. Most likely they were just buried on the grounds. Cheaper and easier than actually cremating them. When they find them and identify them, they will return their remains to their families."

"I'm glad. Emma?"

"Hmm?"

"Can you explain to Dean why it would ruin my street cred if he sent me a snack care package rather than just putting money on my books?"

I laugh. "I will."

"Thank you."

"You're welcome."

"What's the thing bothering you behind your eyes? I can see it there," he says.

"Just something the sheriff said to me out in the woods," I say. I let out a breath. "Xavier, am I a vigilante?"

It's something I've heard before, but somehow this time it hit me harder. Something about the circumstances made it that much more painful to hear.

"No," he says without even pausing to think. "You are many things, though, Emma."

"A phoenix constantly burning?" I ask with a mirthless laugh.

"No. You are exactly what you are meant to be. Powerful and inspiring. Tasked with guarding treasures."

"What treasures do I guard?"

"Lives, Emma. Every day you guard the lives of the people around you. And good. And justice."

"And what does that make me?" I ask.

"Majestic and sharp like an eagle. Strong and revered like a lion. It makes you a griffin."

It's good to be home. The images of what I experienced in Cold Valley will stay with me. They won't leave. But at least I'm away from them. I can curl up back in my own house and know I'm safe.

But being home brings with it the same trappings it always has. Namely, the ornament from Jonah and the mysterious clue it's supposed to represent. I'm sitting in the living room staring at it when Sam gets back from picking up dinner for us.

"Still can't figure it out?" he asks.

I shake my head. "I'm supposed to go talk to his staff again and I'm applying for a warrant to search for his fitness tracker. But I feel ridiculous even doing that."

He reaches down and picks up the ornament, turning it around in his hand.

"What song does it play?" he asks.

"What do you mean?"

"This section is a music box. What song does it play?"

I take it back from him and look at the upper portion that closes down to complete the shape when the walls are closed. I didn't notice the tiny gold piece before. I twist it, but no music plays. I try again, but it doesn't do anything. I turn it around to find another seam and a small tab. Depressing it, I remove the panel of the music box and two slips of paper fall out.

The first is a small photograph. Sam picks up the other.

"Find the Cleaners, find the Truth," he murmurs.

"Sam?"

He looks at me and I turn the picture toward him so he can see Marie smiling back.

AUTHOR'S NOTE

Dear Reader,

I hope you enjoyed *The Girl and the Last Sleepover*. Thank you for your continued support with the Emma Griffin series!

As you may know, I started a new series with FBI agent Ava. I had a great time writing it and would love for you to checkout Ava's books as well.

If you can please continue to leave your reviews for these books, I would appreciate that enormously. Your reviews allow me to get the validation I need to keep going as an indie author. Just a moment of your time is all that is needed.

My promise to you is to always do my best to bring you thrilling adventures. I can't wait for you to read the Emma & Ava books I have in store for you!

Yours,

A.J. Rivers

P.S. If for some reason you didn't like this book or found typos or other errors, please let me know personally. I do my best to read and respond to every email at mailto:aj@riversthrillers.com

ALSO BY
A.J. RIVERS

Emma Griffin FBI Mysteries by AJ Rivers

Season One
Book One—*The Girl in Cabin 13**
Book Two—*The Girl Who Vanished**
Book Three—*The Girl in the Manor**
Book Four—*The Girl Next Door**
Book Five—*The Girl and the Deadly Express**
Book Six—*The Girl and the Hunt**
Book Seven—*The Girl and the Deadly End**

Season Two
Book Eight—*The Girl in Dangerous Waters**
Book Nine—*The Girl and Secret Society**
Book Ten—*The Girl and the Field of Bones**
Book Eleven—*The Girl and the Black Christmas**
Book Twelve—*The Girl and the Cursed Lake**
Book Thirteen—*The Girl and The Unlucky 13**
Book Fourteen—*The Girl and the Dragon's Island**

Season Three
Book Fifteen—*The Girl in the Woods*
Book Sixteen —*The Girl and the Midnight Murder*
Book Seventeen— *The Girl and the Silent Night*
Book Eighteen — *The Girl and the Last Sleepover*

Other Standalone Novels
Gone Woman
* *Also available in audio*

Made in the USA
Monee, IL
02 April 2022

93935241R00143